AVENGING VICTORIO

A Novel of the Apache Insurgency in New Mexico, 1881

AVENGING VICTORIO

A Novel of the Apache Insurgency in New Mexico, 1881

by Dave DeWitt

Rio Grande Books
Los Ranchos de Albuquerque, New Mexico

Published by Rio Grande Books
© 2007 by Dave DeWitt
All rights reserved.
Printed in Canada

Book design by Paul Rhetts and Barbe Awalt
Cover design and map illustration by Lois Manno

Avenging Victorio:
A Novel of the Apache Insurgency in New Mexico, 1881

ISBN 10   1-890689-26-2
ISBN 13   978-1-890689-26-1

Library of Congress Control Number: 2007924434

Rio Grande Books
Los Ranchos de Albuquerque, New Mexico

Cover: Victorio, courtesy of the Arizona Historical Society/Tucson. AHS #19705. 1881 Springfield Carbine, 1861 Light Cavalry Sabre, and an Apache Gathering Basket, ca. 1880.

To the memory of the New Mexico Apache,
Buffalo Soldier, and the Ninth Cavalry survivors

Preface

Why would a mostly nonfiction writer who's known as the "Pope of Peppers" write an historical novel about an Apache raid in New Mexico in 1881? Because it was there and I thought it was a terrific story. I first ran across accounts of Nana's raid during research for a book about New Mexico mysteries that never was completed. The story surfaced again while I was working on a travel guide, *New Mexico*, that *was* completed and was published by *Texas Monthly Press*. I continued to read and research about the raid in between editing *Chile Pepper* magazine and later, *Fiery Foods & BBQ* magazine. I was also writing and publishing books about the many aspects of chile peppers, fiery foods, and barbecue..

Of course, I kept a physical file of every clipped article, photocopied book, and old newspaper records of the time, recovered from microfiche. The story continued to intrigue me over the years and I considered writing a documentary history of this raid. Too narrow, I concluded. And then the idea of turning the story into a novel hit me. After I decided to write the story as fiction, I realized that even more research was needed, which included understanding—as much as a White Eye can—about this particular Apache culture. It sort of became an obsession.

The amount of Apache cultural information in Southwestern university libraries is overwhelming, and I buried myself in the stacks, attempting to understand customs, traditions, and rituals. By contrast, the information on the U.S. Army side of the conflict was much easier for me to comprehend, especially considering the fact that I was brought up as a military brat and did my high school term paper research at the U.S. Army Library in the Pentagon, where my father worked for the Department of Defense.

The actual writing of the novel was easier than all the research. First, I was no stranger to novels, having majored in literature at the University of Virginia and received an M.A. in the subject at the University of Richmond. Then I taught composition and literature at Virginia Commonwealth University for three years. Second, I had written several novels before Victorio and Nana caught my attention, and one was even published: *The Mute Strategy* in 1979. Third, history had provided me a plot and a timeline, so all I had to do was fit in characterization, dialogue, and the Apache and Cavalry lore that I had learned during my research.

Thus *Avenging Victorio* is a novelization of historical events and within the context of writing fiction, I have tried to be as accurate as possible. I have also tried not to take sides in the conflict depicted here, but I must confess that I felt sympathy for the Apache as an essentially enslaved people whose way of life had been completely destroyed. Hopefully, readers will find this story to be as fascinating and moving as I have found it to be.

Dave DeWitt
Albuquerque, New Mexico, 2007

Nana's Raid, 1881

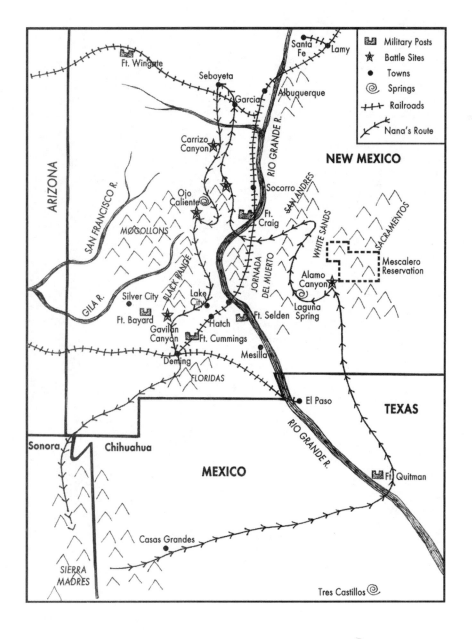

Nana

Geronimo

Victorio

Kaytennae

Edward T. Hatch

Lew Wallace

Buffalo Soldier

Birds of Death.

Prologue: Tres Castillos

At dusk, the Tarahumara scout reported back to Colonel Terrazas that Victorio's band was making camp in a rocky meadow by a small lake, which was in the shadows of the three peaks known as Tres Castillos. Speaking through a translator, he estimated that nearly two hundred of the hated Apaches were camped in the same spot. There were lookouts, he added, but his fellow Tarahumaras had located them.

Terrazas could hardly believe his good fortune. After tracking and fighting Victorio for months—and always losing—he finally had the Apache chief where he wanted him. He wondered why Victorio had camped in such an unprotected place, far east of the safety of the Sierra Madre range. He could only surmise that Victorio was leading his people back across the border into the United States and had no idea that the Mexican forces were closing in on him.

"Lieutenant," he said to his second in command, "tell the scouts to kill all the lookouts. Then divide our forces into four units and surround the Apache camp. On my signal of three shots, we'll attack the camp. Give the order to kill all the Apache men and take their scalps—with the bounty on them, they're worth a small fortune. Try to take the women and children alive so we can sell them as slaves."

"Yes sir," replied Lieutenant Padilla, who was mentally calculating his share of the scalp reward.

When heavy rifle fire riddled his camp from all sides, Victorio knew his people were trapped and that there was little he could do about it. Somehow, the Mexicans had located the Tcihene camp and surrounded it, pinning his band down with little or no cover. The lookouts had never called out a warning, and soon the Mexican soldiers had advanced, shooting anything that moved. Adding to Victorio's problems was the fact that they were nearly out of ammunition. Nana, his second in command, was off on a raid to find more bullets, but had not yet returned. Victorio was thankful that his sister and son were with Nana and not in camp to face certain death.

With two of his best warriors, Victorio took cover in the cluster of boulders closest to the lake. But the soldiers quickly located his hiding place and directed a steady fire into the rocks.

"I have only two bullets left," shouted Das-Luca. "What shall I do?"

"Shoot two Mexicans," Victorio answered grimly. His ammunition was spent, so he pulled out his knife. It was only a matter of moments before the soldiers realized they had no ammunition and charged into the rocks. Das-Luca fired his last two shots and then turned helplessly to his leader.

"Let us die with honor," Victorio told his men, "and not by the guns of the enemy." They knew what he meant. Following his lead, they pulled out their knives. "On my signal," he told them, hearing the shouts of the approaching soldiers. Then he sang a short prayer:

Ussen, giver of life to the Tcihene,
You have led us in battle, so now,
Lead us to the Underworld and peace at last.

The two warriors watched Victorio, their knives pointed at their chests. When he nodded his head, all three Tcihene warriors plunged the knives into their hearts.

Later, after scalping the dead and celebrating their victory by passing around bottles of *mescal*, the Mexican soldiers built a bonfire and burned the Apache corpses. Colonel Terrazas ordered a body count for his official report. After about a hour, Lieutenant Padilla reported back that ninety-three of the enemy had been killed, including twenty-two women and children. He added that sixty-three women and children had been captured, and that no warriors had escaped.

"Here is the scalp of Victorio," he said, passing the bloodied mass of black hair to his commander.

"Good work," Terrazas told him, taking the scalp and placing it in his saddlebag. He dismissed the lieutenant and then rode upwind to escape the stench of the bonfire.

Ninth Cavalry Troops.

1. The Adobe Palace

The telegram announcing the death of his greatest nemesis arrived just after 10 a.m. while Edward Hatch was wading through the September reports from numerous garrisons scattered throughout the territory.

"Thought you might be interested in this, General," announced Captain John Loud, who sported a broad grin on his face. He casually dropped the telegram on top of the pile of papers on Hatch's desk.

The general—his men still called him "general" despite the fact that his brevetted Civil War rank had been reduced to colonel during so-called peace times—quickly seized the cable and read:

18 OCT. 1880
COL. EDWARD T. HATCH
COMD'G, DIST. N.M.T.

SANTA FE
APACHE RENEGADE VICTORIO KILLED FRIDAY
BY FORCES OF GEN. JOAQUIN TERRAZAS AT TRES
CASTILLOS, CHIHUAHUA. DISPATCH WITH DETAILS
FOLLOWS.
LT. J.F. GUILFOLYE
COMD'G. CPY B INDIAN SCOUTS
FT. CUMMINGS

Hatch glanced up from the telegram at his second in command and made a futile attempt to suppress his sudden elation. His right hand slapped the desktop as if smashing a troublesome insect and he grinned broadly.

"Does the staff know?" he asked.

"It occurred to me that you might wish to make the announcement yourself," Loud answered. "Perhaps you could join us in the mess for lunch—I've instructed your staff officers to be present."

"Just when did this cable arrive, anyway?" Hatch asked with feigned suspicion. He realized that Loud, efficient as always, had made arrangements to assemble the staff prior to handing him the transmission from Guilfoyle.

"Oh, about a half-hour ago."

"What's for lunch, John?"

"Venison chile and beans for you, general. Pork cutlets for the men who don't eat chile."

"The sissies, you mean. Yes, I'll join you and the other officers in the mess promptly at noon."

Loud left the room and Hatch gazed out his office window at the trees turning golden in the *plaza* below. People were taking advantage of the warm and sunny autumn day to stroll across the *plaza* and chat with friends, and the scene seemed so tranquil that Hatch chuckled. In New Mexico, violence could strike at any second and could take many forms—a drunken gunfight between two former friends, a quick strike by Billy the Kid and the remnants of his Regulators eager to get even with Governor Wallace, or even an attack by a band of vengeful Mescaleros, although Hatch thought that to be extremely unlikely now.

It was possible—no, probable—that the death of Victorio meant the end of the Indian wars. With Victorio gone, there was no one left to lead the Ojo Caliente band or the Mescaleros, and the Apaches would have to be content with reservation life without raiding and warfare. Hatch, who had taken the field more than once against the Apaches, would never forget the futility of chasing Victorio through the impossibly rough mountain ranges in the territory, always one step behind the Apache.

As if the frustration of the pursuit of Victorio were not enough to endure, Hatch—because he was commander of the military district—had taken the brunt of criticism from the citizens and from the press. The Santa Fe papers had been relatively easy on him because he knew the owners personally and they understood the difficulties inherent in subduing the Apaches. But the editors of the Las Vegas *Daily Optic* had called him a "political colonel," had accused him of "utter incompetence," and had even suggested that the government should discharge him and hire Victorio to command the troops in New Mexico. "Anything for economy," they had written. The *Grant County Herald* in Silver City had described him as sitting on top of the flagpole at Ft. Craig watching for Victorio instead of chasing him.

The press had stopped their attacks only after Victorio vacated New Mexico for Old Mexico and Texas. Out of sight, out of mind, Hatch guessed. Typical frontier journalism. Not once had he ever demeaned to defend himself or to respond to the printed attacks on his character and competence—the War Department frowned upon commanders who engaged in battles with civilians.

This story would make a good lesson in military science for his staff, Hatch decided. He spent the next two hours reviewing his files and taking notes, much like a politician preparing a speech, or a professor writing a lecture.

At 11:58 a.m., Hatch left his office, walked down the narrow staircase at the end of the hall, and out the doorway into the brilliant sunshine that bathed the courtyard of the headquarters. As he strolled across the courtyard to the officer's mess, he wondered what his wife Evelyn was doing on such a beautiful day.

His small staff stood at attention as he entered the adobe building. "At ease," Hatch said casually as he took his place at the head of the long table and remained standing. "Please sit down. Before we eat, I have a brief lecture…" He waved his notes and paused for the inevitable, good-natured groans. "…On the status of the campaign against the Apaches. First, Victorio is dead."

Spirited applause replaced the groans, but Hatch realized that his officers already knew of the Apache's demise. In such a small command, it was impossible to keep important information secret.

"Second," he continued, "I have realized that the end of the campaign against Victorio represents a tremendous victory for the Ninth and Tenth Cavalries—despite the fact that the Mexicans actually finished off Victorio's forces."

His staff of nine listened intently; they too felt enormous relief at the end of the Victorio menace but regretted the fact that the Ninth had never captured or killed the chief. Some soldiers routinely called him "Victorious" and said he was like a ghost who continually returned to haunt them, appearing out of nowhere to raid and kill and then vanishing back into the wilderness.

"I'm going to take a few minutes to review our unusual campaign against Victorio because I believe there is a lesson to be learned here, a lesson that civilians will find difficult to comprehend but one which demonstrates the success of a total military campaign despite a seeming lack of success in the field."

He had their attention now, so he paced slowly back and forth, his blond head silhouetted before the window which exploded with light. "I will not bore you with a recitation of U.S. actions to control western Indian tribes. Suffice it to say that the containment policy, which holds that all Indians will live peacefully on reservations, is inadequate to deal with all the tribes which roam through this vast territory. The trouble with Victorio began after their Warm Springs land was seized by the federal government and they were ordered to move to San Carlos, a reservation they despised.

"But that was a political decision, gentlemen, and not our concern. Enforcement of peace in the territory *is* our concern, however, and the Ninth Cavalry was ordered to capture Victorio and his band and return them to San Carlos or Mescalero. Easy to order…but exceedingly difficult to carry out."

Hatch paused while Mrs. Gonzales, a shy, plump, Mexican woman about forty years old, placed mugs beside each plate on the table. She was one of several neighborhood women employed to cook and clean for the officers.

"On 4 September of last year," he continued, "Victorio ambushed Captain Hooker's Company E at Ojo Caliente. Eight troopers were killed or wounded and forty-six horses were captured by the Apaches, who then went on a rampage through western New Mexico and murdered nine civilians. I was ordered by General Pope to put every company at my command into the field.

"But as often happens in warfare, not everything went according to plan. Victorio proved to be a brilliant strategist, and Dudley failed miserably at the battle at Las Animas River. I was forced to replace him with Major Morrow. Morrow, with Negro troopers and Indian scouts, chased Victorio for hundreds of miles and engaged the enemy no fewer than three times. None of the engagements were decisive, but the important point here is that Morrow *drove the Apaches not only out of the territory, but out of the country.* Thus our first military campaign against Victorio was successful—but it was frustrating and costly in terms of men, equipment, and horses lost, not to mention the civilian toll."

Colonel Hatch took his seat at the head of the table, then shook his head sadly. "Soon after vacating the territory, Victorio attacked the Mexican town of Carrizal and brutally murdered twenty-six defenseless citizens. Finally, the Mexican government took some action and forces under General Treviño of Chihuahua drove Victorio back into New Mexico. Thanks a lot, General."

His staff chuckled and Hatch smiled. "I ordered Morrow to pick up the trail again, which he did; but Victorio eluded him again in the San Mateo and San Andres mountains, killed three of Morrow's troopers, wounded seven more, and just…disappeared. Then we learned that the Mescaleros were deserting their reservation to join Victorio, so I decided upon a two-stage plan. First, I divided up the Ninth into three battalions—under Morrow, Captain Hooker, and Captain Carroll. Indian scouts would locate Victorio's camp in the San Andres and we'd attack it from three directions: west, east and north. Second, after subduing Victorio, we would move on and disarm the Mescalero Reservation." The commander checked his notes and then looked around the table at his staff. "You gentlemen remember the Hembrillo Canyon campaign, so I won't go into all the unfortunate details. Suffice it to say that that I arrived late with Morrow's battalion because we had been delayed when a water pump broke down and we were unable to water our horses. When we did arrive at Hembrillo, Victorio had already engaged Carroll and escaped, leaving eight men wounded and twenty-five horses and mules killed. Victorio's force eluded us in the dark and we never engaged them. I moved the battalions to Mescalero, where we disarmed and dismounted all the Apaches there.

"Meanwhile, Victorio continued his rampage in the Mogollon Mountains and I personally led the battalion which chased him into Arizona. He doubled back and attempted to attack the settlement adjacent to old Fort Tularosa. Thanks to quick thinking by Sergeant George Jordan, his company of troopers reached the old fort before Victorio, built a stockade, and fought off the Apaches.

"Captain Parker then attacked Victorio's camp near the head of the Palomas River and inflicted perhaps our only clear defeat of Victorio by killing about thirty Apaches. Morrow closed in and chased Victorio back into Mexico for the second time—again the Ninth had driven Victorio out of the territory. From then on, Victorio became the problem of the Mexicans and Grierson's Tenth Cavalry in Texas.

"The Ninth had successfully executed its military strategy: to subdue Victorio and put him out of business. To accomplish that feat, we were forced to learn a new technique in the art of war. The Mexicans call it *guerilla* warfare, which means a skirmishing strategy utilizing surprise raids, quick retreats, and above all, a refusal to engage the enemy in traditional combat. To counter these *guerillas*, we have adopted some unusual methods. We have recruited and deployed Indian scouts to track down and kill their own kind. We have sent our Negro troopers, known for their incredible endurance, against the tough Apaches. We have constantly harassed them with their own *guerilla* techniques and sent them to the Mexicans. And when Grierson got ahold of them, he kept them from water, food, and their caches. Thus by using *guerilla* techniques against them, he eliminated the reasons the Apaches wanted to be in Texas and they fled back to Mexico again."

Mrs. Gonzales interrupted the general by carrying in a tray filled with bottles of Anheuser-Busch lager beer and distributing the bottles to the officers. None of the staff made any attempt to pour beer into the mugs, and Hatch ignored the presence of the beer that was set before him.

"In retrospect, the biggest problem we had was that we could not prevent the Apaches from getting arms. They were easily resupplied with guns and ammunition—in fact, the Apaches were sometimes better armed than our own men. How did they accomplish that? By trading for the arms with gold and silver they had stolen from various ranches, posts, stages, and wagon trains. Don't believe that the Apaches won't touch gold. They may not like to, but they'll do it for weapons to protect their people and to kill us. We think that Victorio had as many as a half-dozen caches in various mountain ranges in the territory and Mexico filled with gold and silver.

"Over four-hundred people died by the hand of Victorio's Apaches, but not in vain. Because of their efforts and ours, New Mexico Territory is safer than it's ever been before. And perhaps the death of Victorio will convince our territorial newspaper editors that we were using the correct strategy after all."

His staff broke into applause again. Hatch lifted his bottle of beer and inspected it. "Now what is this? You gentlemen know that alcohol is prohibited at headquarters."

"We thought that a toast was in order, General," explained Captain Loud. "And it's socially unacceptable to toast victory with coffee."

"You'll make a good politician, Loud. Carry on."

The captain rose and stood at attention. "Gentlemen, pour your beers. I propose a toast to our commander on the occasion of the fortunate demise of Victorio!"

The officers cheered and raised their mugs high in a salute to Hatch, who smiled and then drank with them. "All right, all right," he said, "here's to peace forever in the territory! Now, can we have lunch?"

During the meal, the discussion never wavered from the subject of Victorio, and Captain Loud took the opportunity to promote his idea for a celebration to commemorate the triumph over Victorio. "General, shouldn't we inform Governor Wallace about Victorio?"

"Yes. I'm going to send him a telegram at Crawfordsville this afternoon. In fact, Captain, see to it."

"Yes sir. I was thinking that perhaps the governor might enjoy hosting a reception at the Adobe Palace to celebrate the return of peace."

Hatch paused, a spoonful of red chile near his lips. "Now that's an interesting notion. But Governor Wallace won't return from Indiana until after the election in November. He won't even be here when President Hayes visits."

Major James Lee, the quartermaster of headquarters, looked up from his pork cutlet and suggested, "Why not make the reception a Christmas Ball? The wives would love that."

"Excellent idea," agreed Hatch. Aside from hostile Apaches, the most severe problem of a frontier posting was entertaining the wives of the officers, who were accustomed to considerably more civilized surroundings.

"I'll send a telegram to Governor Wallace over your name, General," said Loud. "It will announce the death of Victorio, suggest a celebration at Christmas, and congratulate him on the forthcoming publication of his book. That way we have many things to commemorate."

"Ah yes, *Ben-Hur*, the only novel ever written by a governor of a territory while on duty." Hatch was amused because he often teased Lew

Wallace about caring more for writing than governing. The governor had admitted in private the truth of Hatch's accusation.

"The governor will certainly approve of a publication party," Hatch continued. "He could sell books to half of the population of New Mexico—or rather, half of the one-fourth who can read. And while you're sending telegrams, Captain, cable all the officers still left in the territory who participated in the Victorio campaign—Guilfoyle, Morrow, Parker, Gatewood, Smith, McClellan—and order them to plan to attend. We'll notify them later as to the exact date. And have Mrs. Gonzales bring us another round. Gentlemen, by order of the commander, the remainder of this afternoon is declared a holiday."

After the long lunch, Hatch left the headquarters compound and walked under the portal of the Adobe Palace on Palace Avenue, which was extremely dusty from the lack of rain and the heavy horse and wagon traffic. Several Indians from nearby pueblos were selling pots and turquoise jewelry that was spread out on their blankets. A man and his wife, both over-dressed for the territory and looking like they just got off the stage, were prospective buyers of the handicrafts and were total strangers to Hatch. Could they possibly be tourists?

Just last week he had eaten breakfast at the Exchange Hotel, and the manager had told him of a group of rich folks from New York who traveled all over the West *just to look at it*. The notion confounded him; he could imagine himself and Evelyn touring, say, New York City or Philadelphia, but what was there to see out here?

The general turned left on Washington Avenue and strolled the short half-block to the commander's residence, which fortunately was one of the larger houses in Santa Fe and, in fact, a far more pleasant residence than the dark and gloomy Adobe Palace, home of the Wallaces. His house looked as if it had been moved to Santa Fe from St. Louis, and it contrasted greatly with the one-story adobe buildings surrounding it. It was a two-story frame structure with three gables and a porch supported by pillars that seemed puny in comparison to those Hatch had seen at plantation mansions in Alabama.

A white picket fence enclosed the yard and garden, which were Evelyn's pride and joy. The cottonwood trees shading the lot had turned golden and Hatch knew that in a few weeks he must put some of his men on leaf-raking detail. He opened the gate, expecting to spot his wife in the yard, but she was nowhere to be seen. Her handiwork was evident, though. Pink and yellow chrysanthemums in full bloom bordered the walk, grown from cuttings Evelyn had carried half-way across the country, and the windows were covered with damask and lace curtains which she had created on her sewing machine.

He knew where to find her as soon as he entered the house, for the delicious, pungent aroma that assaulted his senses could only have originated in the kitchen. She was sitting at the small kitchen table peeling the skin off a fat green chile while others, both green and red, blistered and smoked atop the wood stove.

"More chile?" He asked in his booming voice. "I had chile for lunch."

"Ed!" exclaimed a startled Evelyn Hatch, who put aside the bowl of chiles to rise and embrace her husband. "It's the last of the fresh green and red from our garden," she explained. "I'm drying the rest. What are you doing home so early?"

"I declared the rest of the day a holiday," he replied, kissing her on the cheek.

"What's the occasion?"

The general held her at arm's length and paused dramatically. "The end of Victorio," he said with a smile.

A startled look flashed through Evelyn's brown eyes as the name of the Apache triggered an avalanche of memories—all of them bad. She still had nightmares about her husband being killed and scalped by the Indians he was forever chasing.

"He's dead?" she asked bluntly.

"Quite dead. The Mexicans caught up with him and his band and killed nearly all of them."

"Thank God," sighed Evelyn, who gave him a brief hug and then released him. "Sit down and tell me all about it. I can fix something else for dinner if you're tired of chile."

"I'm never tired of chile when it's fresh." Hatch took a seat at the table while she removed the nearly black chiles from the stovetop. "There's really not much more to tell about Victorio, since I haven't received the dispatches yet. I think I told you that the Mexicans wouldn't let Grierson stay in Mexico, so General Terrazas was able claim all the glory."

"Does the glory really matter?" Evelyn asked as she sat down and resumed her task of stripping the skin from the chiles.

"Politically it does. The War Department would prefer that the U.S. Army be glorified rather than the forces of our former enemy," Hatch explained. "But in truth, no, it doesn't matter as long as Victorio is gone forever."

"I feel so relieved," Evelyn confessed. "Like a weight has been lifted from our lives."

"I've sent a telegram to Lew suggesting we celebrate with a reception."

"Celebrate Victorio's death? Isn't that a bit gruesome?"

"No, Evelyn, we're celebrating *peace*, we're celebrating the *future*, we're celebrating the publication of Lew's new book."

"I love the idea and volunteer to help in any way I can," offered his wife, who enjoyed parties. "Will Susan return with him for this big celebration?"

"I doubt it," said Hatch. "She hates it here. I think she'll stay in Crawfordsville until Lew finds himself another posting."

"Susan told me once that Santa Fe and New Mexico were not made for civilized man, and said that you agreed with her," Evelyn accused.

"I was merely trying to pacify her, Evelyn. She was distressed about her visit to Fort Stanton, where conditions are considerably less civilized than her high standards. She told me that my former commander was right: we should have another war with Old Mexico to make her take back New Mexico. Who am I to argue with General Sherman?"

"I like New Mexico—or rather, Santa Fe—where at least there is a little culture and sophistication. But I realize that we are living on the frontier, in a territory for heaven's sake. This place won't be a state for twenty years.

"Or more."

A knock on the front door interrupted them.

"Could you get that, Ed?" Evelyn asked, and Hatch left the kitchen. He opened the door to find Charles Greene, owner and editor of the Santa Fe *Daily New Mexican,* standing on the porch.

"Good afternoon, Mr. Greene," Hatch said curtly, his voice cold. He considered Greene to be the worst kind of newspaperman, a carpetbagger devoted to scandal and negative news.

"Afternoon, General," replied Greene, a thin middle-aged man with mustache and goatee who was nattily dressed in a coat, tie, and vest. "Your office said I might find you here."

"You found me. Now, what can I do for you?" Hatch declined to invite the man into his house

"I'd like to interview you, General."

"Oh? About what?"

"What else? The death of Chief Victorio."

"I received a telegram from Fort Cummings announcing his death. That's all I know."

"Well, I know considerably more than that, since I received the details from the *Rio Grande Republican* in Las Cruces. Can we sit down for a minute?"

Hatch gestured to the set of wicker chairs on the front porch and they both took a seat. "I don't have much time," he said.

Greene merely smiled. "I'm going to run a story about Victorio's death in the Sunday paper and I'd like your reaction, General."

"My reaction? I'm pleased, of course."

"But disappointed that you didn't kill him yourself?"

Hatch gave Greene a scornful look. "Not at all. We were not fighting a duel, mind you. It was a military action."

"And a frustrating one—"

"Listen, Greene, you wrote that I was incompetent, yet look at the results: my men chased him out of the territory and now he's dead. How can you get any more competent than that?"

Greene tried a more accommodating approach. "General, I apologize for that. In the first place, I was merely quoting what other territorial editors were saying, editors who were impatient and expected miracles. Now we have the chance to rectify that situation. By combining the information I have with an interview with you, perhaps we can reverse this unfortunate situation."

Although he never relaxed his stern demeanor, Hatch was pleased with Greene's attitude. Because the newspaperman had nothing negative to say about the Apache struggle now, he was fishing for a story. Hatch sensed a chance to take advantage of the situation to receive some favorable publicity for the Army.

"Let me see if I understand you, Mr. Greene. Are you saying that if I cooperate with you and give this interview you will finally tell the complete story of our strategy?"

"Of course, General," Greene promised, a sincere look painted on his face. He paused and stroked his goatee. "Why don't you tell me about the Apache strategy first—it'll be good background for the story of Victorio's death. Then I'll ask a few questions and we'll be finished."

Hatch relented and began an edited version of the same story he had told his officers a short time before. He emphasized the fact that the Army had faced—and learned—a new battle technique now called *guerilla* warfare. Then he outlined the overall strategy that kept Victorio on the run; harassed him at every step and prevented him from re-supplying. Hatch used telegraph and the railroads to coordinate troop movements. He concluded with a summary of engagements that had resulted in the Apache first being driven from New Mexico, then chased out of Texas, and finally trapped in Mexico.

After Hatch completed his account, Greene glanced over the notes he had taken, then looked up and asked: "Would you say, General, that the Apache threat to the Territory of New Mexico has ended?"

Without hesitation, Hatch uttered the single affirmative word that would soon return to haunt him—"yes."

About a month later, Hatch was beginning to think he would never escape the legacy of Victorio. General Pope had ordered him to prepare a complete report on the Apache situation so the Secretary of War could utilize it to compile his annual report to the President and Congress. Accomplishing this task had buried Hatch in paperwork to the extent that he could not even see the top of his desk. In addition to his own documents from the Ninth Cavalry, somewhere among the mountain of papers was the complete dispatch from Guilfoyle, a long report from Grierson and Buell regarding the Tenth Cavalry's excellent campaign against Victorio, plus dozens of newspaper clippings.

Although he despised the task, he had dutifully composed a draft of his report in longhand, which then would be carefully typed out on the only typewriter at headquarters by members of his general staff. In his draft, Hatch had included a summary of the territorial newspaper reports on Victorio, but had omitted mention of one article that might be misconstrued by the War Department: the story in the *Daily New Mexican* with the headline "APACHE THREAT OVER, CLAIMS HATCH."

He had good reason for this omission. On October 28, a small party of renegades attacked one of Lieutenant Grierson's patrols under Sergeant Charles Perry near Ojo Caliente in Texas, killing five soldiers and carrying off four horses and two mules. The leader of the renegades was unknown and the attack was thought to be an isolated incident in retaliation for Victorio's death, but it demonstrated that the Apaches had not been totally subdued.

Because the attack had occurred in hated Texas, the territorial press had paid little attention to it despite the death of five men. However, the newspaper editors were still uneasy, a fact easily demonstrated by a clipping from the *Grant County Herald* in Silver City which Hatch had quoted in the report: "As Victorio is killed, his band nearly destroyed, we can only look to the future and feel comparatively safe. The Indian warfare as far as Victorio's band is concerned is ended, but we must not forget one principle in evolution, the survival of the fittest. The few that are left will be more treacherous, more ugly than ever before known."

He was pondering how to end his report to Pope when the governor of the territory strolled into his office and interrupted him. "Working hard?" asked Lew Wallace, a grin peeking through his bushy beard and mustache.

"Welcome back, Lew," said Hatch, extending his hand and then gesturing for the governor to take a seat. "I'm working *too* hard. I'd rather chase rattlesnakes across the *malpais* than write reports. When did you arrive?"

"This morning. I thought I'd drop by and give you all the news."

"Presidential news, I assume?"

"Correct," agreed Wallace, who removed his spectacles and began to clean them with a hankerchief. "I have spoken at length with President-elect Garfield and even presented him with a copy of *Ben-Hur*, which he has read and loves."

"You are fishing for a new appointment, I assume."

Wallace nodded agreement. "Again correct."

"Evelyn wanted to know if Susan returned with you."

"Of course not, Ed. You know her—she's back in Crawfordsville trying to decide which country I will be ambassador to—Brazil, Belgium, or Turkey. Because of *Ben-Hur*, Garfield is leaning toward sending us to Constantinople."

"So you're definitely leaving?"

Wallace lowered his voice. "You are officially sworn to secrecy. It was inevitable. The salary of the ambassador to Turkey is four times that of the governor of New Mexico. Besides, neither Susan nor I were destined to suffocate here in the wilderness. Now I can leave the territory as a hero, with the Lincoln County War ended and the Apache threat removed—thanks to you."

"And Colonel Terrazas," Hatch added dryly. "Lew, at least you can engineer your own future. I serve at the whim of the U.S. Army."

Wallace held up a hand. "I am going to speak to the President regarding General—uh, Colonel Hatch. Ed, you know back in Washington they call the Ninth Cavalry the "colorful regiment" and, damn it all, you deserve something better than commanding niggers to fight savages. Perhaps the headquarters of the Ninth Cavalry could be moved further east—like to Kansas. From there you could request transfer to any post you desired."

Hatch didn't believe it could be that simple, but he appreciated his friend's concern. "Thank you—and good luck wherever you go. I'll certainly miss you around here. And by the way, my Negro soldiers are every bit as good as whites."

The governor waved off the notion. "Now, Ed, for the main order of business. The idea for a Christmas reception is excellent. It could be my last hurrah in the territory, a sort of going away party—although no one would officially know I was leaving. How about Saturday the eighteenth—exactly a week before Christmas?"

"Perfect," agreed Hatch.

"I think it would be appropriate to hold the reception at the Adobe Palace, but it's still in terrible condition. We've done some work since Congress rejected my funding request for a complete renovation, but progress has been slow. All we've been able to do is repair and repaint my offices and quarters. Suggestions, General?"

"We have many resources, Governor. I have hundreds of men doing next to nothing now that they're not chasing Apaches. Why don't we ask some of the local merchants to donate hardware, lumber, and paint? If they refuse, we won't invite them. The Ninth will provide the labor. All we have to do is renovate—what, two rooms?"

"Perhaps three and a hall. The House chamber, the courtroom, the library, and the main hall. But it's highly irregular, you realize. Work on territorial structures should not be done by the U.S. Army."

Hatch shrugged and held up his handwritten report. "I'm not going to report it, so who will ever know—or care? We both work for Washington."

"I appreciate it, Ed."

"*De nada*, as the locals say. Consider it done."

"And one other favor?"

"Whatever you need."

Wallace rose to leave. "Seeing that my wife has vowed never again to set foot on what she calls this God-forsaken land, do you suppose Evelyn could be persuaded to organize this reception and take Susan's place as official hostess?"

"She'd love it," Hatch assured the governor.

The night of the eighteenth of December was threatening in Santa Fe. Clouds from the north had rolled in that afternoon, and the air had turned both moist and cold, an indication of approaching snow. Also threatening were the armed soldiers patrolling the streets and alleys surrounding the *plaza*, and the sharpshooters stationed on the rooftops of nearby buildings, their faces invisible against the blackness of night.

In contrast to the seriousness of Colonel Hatch's show of force were the guests arriving at the Adobe Palace for the Christmas Reception, as it was being called. Laughing and calling out greetings to each other, the guests arrived on foot by strolling across the *plaza*, or by carriage, or simply on horseback. Nearly all of the men who arrived were dressed in three-piece suits and overcoats, while the women were decked out in the finest gowns they could buy or borrow. A few of the women even wore bustles, the latest fashion fad from the East Coast which peculiarly accented the already-broad buttocks of those who strapped on the contraptions.

One of first couples to arrive that night were Mr. and Mrs. Angus Grant, who had ridden all the way from Albuquerque for the event. Despite the fact that her bustle had made the sixty-mile trip exceedingly uncomfortable, Janice Grant was bubbling with excitement.

"Oh Angus, look at the beautiful lights," she gushed, referring to the newly-installed gas lights that illuminated the entire *plaza*. Each of the four-sided lanterns atop tall standards created its own floating island of greenish-yellow brilliance and cast an eerie glow over the bare cottonwoods on the plaza. Outlining the edges of the *plaza* were hundreds of *farolitos*, little sacks with glowing candles inside them.

Angus Grant, who was a bridge contractor for the A and P Railroad and a lighting entrepreneur on the side, was not impressed. "Gas is obsolete," he told her, "or soon will be for lighting. Edison's already developed the bulb. It won't be long before I'll be installing electric lights in Albuquerque."

"Now be nice," Janice cautioned as she stepped from the carriage with the assistance of a black orderly from military headquarters. She couldn't help but notice the soldiers stationed at either end of the Adobe Palace. "Are you expecting trouble?" she asked the orderly.

"No ma'am," he replied. "But we be ready if there is any."

"Imagine," Janice Grant chattered to her husband, "armed soldiers patrolling the Plaza. I feel so safe."

Angus Grant snorted derisively. "Welcome to the 'Land of Enchantment,' as the Bureau of Immigration now calls this useless territory."

"Be nice, Angus," she warned again as they entered the Governor's Hall of the Adobe Palace to the strains of the waltz from Strauss' *Die Fledermaus*. The music was coming from the library to the left of the hall, where the Ninth Cavalry Band, an ensemble of black soldier-musicians under direction of Professor George Spiegel, greeted the guests by valiantly playing waltzes, martial airs, and Christmas music.

Officers from district headquarters saluted the guests as they arrived and motioned them down the hall to the right, where the reception line awaited in the chamber of the House of Representatives. In line to greet the guests were Evelyn Hatch, Colonel Edward Hatch, Governor Lew Wallace, and Archbishop Jean Baptiste Lamy.

The chamber was decorated with American flags alternating with two different kinds of wreaths: some fashioned from chile pods and others from *piñon* branches. Long, draped tables were covered with food of every description, and an orderly behind a temporary bar dispensed champagne, New Mexico wine, and beer to the guests.

Hatch was yearning for a beer but had been too busy shaking hands to indulge. He thanked heaven that Evelyn had taken the lead in the reception line, because she possessed instant recall and could connect a name with every face she saw, thus saving him and Lew the embarrassment of forgotten names. Already she had re-introduced him to several people whose names he should have remembered: Eloisa Otero, considered to be the most beautiful woman in New Mexico; William Ritch, president of the historical society; and the merchant Franz Huning from Los Lunas.

Evelyn introduced him to Angus Grant and his wife, a couple he was certain he had never met before; and then came a stream of people whose names he remembered easily. Adolph Bandelier, the anthropologist who was organizing and preserving the territorial archives, as well as visiting every pueblo in the area, arrived in the company of Ben Wittick, the popular photographer of New Mexico vistas and people. In line behind them were Bradford Prince, the chief justice of the territory as well as the president of the Bureau of Immigration, who was accompanied by Henry Waldo, the territorial Attorney General and his wife. Following the judges were Jake Gold, the curio dealer, the merchant Lehman Spiegelberg, and their wives.

Hatch noted that his friend Lew was quite ebullient, greeting the men boisterously and even slapping some of them on the back. Such lack of reserve indicated that he was quite pleased that his sentence as territorial governor would soon be commuted. Hatch envied him.

At about 8:15, when a lull struck the reception line, the governor seized the opportunity and walked up to the podium accompanied by Archbishop Lamy. Wallace called out "Ladies and gentlemen!" three times before he had the attention of more than a hundred guests. "Thank you for coming this evening. With us tonight to deliver the invocation is Archbishop Lamy."

The archbishop, a gaunt man in his sixties dressed, as usual, in a long black cassock with buttons down the front and a high cummerbund, stepped up to the podium and ordered, "Let us pray."

There was complete silence in the chamber and all heads were bowed. After a long pause (which was more dramatic than his invocation) Lamy said, "A humble, fervent prayer is necessary to obtain the grace of God that permits us to practice our virtue, and to avoid sin: keep vigil and pray, find refuge in all humility, put your confidence in God, assure your salvation by your good deeds…that is the grace I ask of God for everyone.

"Lord, we are gathered here tonight to reflect on another year during which You have allowed our survival in New Mexico Territory. We also celebrate the birth of the Saviour, Jesus Christ, whose day is just a week away. Thank you, O Lord, as we recite your prayer." He then led the guests in the Lord's Prayer and, when finished, stepped aside; and Wallace regained the podium.

"Thank you, Archbishop. Ladies and gentlemen, I have a brief address to give you tonight, then General Hatch has a few words to say, and then the band will play waltzes. You may dance, wine and dine, and socialize 'til your heart's content.

He affixed his spectacles, pulled some papers from his inside coat pocket, and spread them out on the podium. "First, I would like to point out our new gas lamps around the *plaza*, ample evidence that this territory can be as advanced as any state in the Union. It won't be long before my office has a *telephone*!" Applause and a few shouts of "Statehood!" interrupted the governor, who patiently waited for the clamor to die down.

"Now, I'd like to explain about the armed soldiers around the *plaza* tonight. No, we are not expecting a band of Apaches. But there has been a threat of another kind. As you probably read in the newspaper, I have issued a reward for the capture of William Bonney—"

More applause resounded through the chamber and Wallace smiled. "Yes, it seems that Billy the Kid refuses to face justice. He wanted a blanket pardon, which was unacceptable; and after my negotiations with him broke down and he started stealing horses again, I decided to offer a $500 reward for his delivery to me. Mind you, I did *not* say "dead or alive" in the reward offer. Well, Billy took offense at the reward and bragged he was going to come to Santa Fe and put a bullet through me. Since I didn't want our reception to be disturbed by an attempt on my life, I asked General Hatch for some armed protection. Never fear, there will be no trouble tonight."

"Thank heavens!" exclaimed Eloisa Otero, who was standing near the podium with her husband, and some relieved laughter was heard from the guests.

"Now," said Wallace, "one of the reasons for this reception is to celebrate the end of the Victorio wars in the territory." Cheers and applause broke out again and Wallace was forced to wait for it to subside. He was no longer smiling when he continued. "Before we celebrate too much, I think we should have a moment of silence for the victims of Victorio's slaughter."

The guests cooperated. Wallace ended the silence after only twenty seconds and continued his speech. "The Apaches have for years preyed upon the peaceful settlers of this territory, despite all our attempts to tame them. Kindness makes no impression on them. They remain what they were when the Spaniards found them—cunning, bloodthirsty, and untamable. I recall my visit to Silver City during Victorio's rampage. When we reached the town, the people came out and greeted us with amazement; had we been newly raised from the dead, they could not have shown greater awe. We presently learned the cause. After returning their salutations, we followed them to the church. There was the explanation. Before the altar were sixteen corpses: men, women, and children, some of them shockingly mutilated."

There was a collective gasp from the audience, who definitely did not expect such words from the governor during a Christmas reception. Ever the showman, Wallace paused for the effect of his words to sink in, and then continued in a lighter tone.

"Fortunately, such butchery has ended, thanks to the good work of the men who are assembled here tonight. And we are not here to review the horrors of the past, but rather to celebrate a bright and peaceful future. Speaking personally, I should like to welcome all of you to the Palace of the Governors. Although Washington has not seen fit to honor my request for a complete renovation of this building, as you see, local volunteers have worked diligently to clean, paint, and decorate the structure to make it suitable for our reception tonight. It was in this very palace that I wrote much of my novel, *Ben-Hur, A Tale of Christ*, and I will be happy to show interested parties the very room in which this book was composed. Now I would like to present to you General Edward Hatch, Commander of the Ninth Cavalry, who has a few words to say about the demise of Victorio."

Enthusiastic applause accompanied Hatch to the podium. He stood next to Wallace and reflected that if the reception had been held six months earlier, his only greeting would have been catcalls. "First of all,"

Hatch shouted, waving a sheet of paper in the air to diminish the noise. "First of all I'd like to thank some of the people who have made this reception possible. Please hold your applause until I'm done with this list or we'll be here 'til breakfast. My wife Evelyn organized this gala affair for Governor Wallace in the absence of his wife, and she did a great job. We'd also like to thank the businessmen who donated supplies to repair and repaint this part of the Adobe Palace: Gerard Koch of Builder's Hardware and Glass and the fine folks at Irvine General Hardware Company. The beer and ice was donated by the A.L. Houck Company and the wine and spirits were courtesy of the Exchange Hotel Bar. The bread, rolls, and desserts—and oysters—were gifts of the generous Mr. Tate of City Bakery, while the meats were provided by the Eatons at the City Meat Company. Helping out with other supplies and food were Henry Kaune, Abraham Staab, and the Seligman family. We'd also like to thank all the civilian volunteers who assisted in throwing the biggest party Santa Fe has ever seen!"

After the appreciative applause for the well-known merchants had subsided, Hatch displayed a telegram to the guests. "This telegram, which arrived today, is another reason for us to celebrate tonight. As most of you know, the Ninth Cavalry in general and myself in particular have received harsh criticism from the newspapers and various politicians because we were unable to kill or capture Victorio and his men on United States soil. However, the efforts of both the Ninth and Tenth Cavalry kept the renegades constantly on the run. In fact, we chased 'em across the border so the Mexicans could grab all the glory."

Hatch paused for effect. "Now that fact bothers the politicians, but it doesn't bother me. That's because I'm a military man and what mattered was the completion of a military mission. The facts show that our co-operation with the Mexicans was successful—they finished off what we started. So be it. At least we are through with Victorio, and never again will he terrorize the citizens of this territory.

"I thought it might interest you to hear part of a telegram that General Pope sent to me on this occasion. These comments will be included in the annual report of the Secretary of War for the year 1880: 'It is my duty, as it is my pleasure, to invite the special attention of the authorities to the meritorious and gallant conduct of Colonel Edward Hatch, commanding the District of New Mexico, and the officers and soldiers under his command, in the difficult and trying campaign against the Southern Apaches. Everything that men could do they did, and it is little to say that their services in the field were marked by unusual hardships and difficulties. Their duties were performed with zeal and intelligence and they are worthy of all consideration.'"

Again the crowd broke into a spirited applause, which gave the military band the opportunity to move into the chamber and set up close to Hatch, who then proclaimed, "Now, on behalf of Governor Wallace, I propose a toast to peace in the Territory of New Mexico!" On a signal from Hatch, Professor Spiegel led the band in a spirited rendition of "Joy to the World."

The end of the speeches triggered a rush on the available food and drink. Hatch nearly made it to the bar, but was waylaid by well-wishers who wanted to bend his ear when all he cared to do was bend his elbow. Fortunately, he was rescued by Evelyn, who had invented a convenient excuse to lead him away from the group: his second-in-command needed to speak with him urgently.

The Hatchs located Captain Loud standing with some of the lieutenants from various forts in the territory. "You needed to see me?" Hatch asked Loud, who just laughed and handed him a bottle.

"Your beer, General."

"Why thank you, John. Welcome to Santa Fe, gentlemen." He then shook hands with Lieutenants John Guilfoyle, Charles Gatewood, and George Washington Smith.

"Good to be here, sir," said Smith, who at forty years was much older than the other two lieutenants. Hatch recalled that Smith was a husky man sporting both mustache and goatee, had been a colonel in the War, resigned his commission, and then re-enlisted at a much lower rank.

"Thanks for inviting me, General," said Gatewood, a tall man with a thin face which only exaggerated the size of his Roman nose.

Guilfoyle, a clean-shaven, intense man in his late twenties, edged close to Hatch and said in a low voice, "General, we need to speak with you privately sometime tonight."

Hatch was slightly surprised and tempted to tell the officer to send him a report. But Guilfoyle seemed nervous, which aroused the general's curiosity. "Oh? What about?"

"Apaches, sir."

"What else?" groaned Hatch. "All right, Lieutenant, give me a chance to taste this food and socialize for a while and then we'll talk."

As if on cue, Evelyn smiled at the officers and took Hatch's arm. Together they walked over to the food tables, which were ample evidence that Evelyn had utilized every possible Santa Fe connection to concoct the most sophisticated menu possible. Not only were there the spicy native foods of the region—*tamales, posole,* and green chile stew—there were dishes more commonly consumed on either coast. Hundreds of Baltimore oysters on the half-shell rested on beds of ice; they arrived daily on the train, as did the smoked salmon. The sliced meats included sugar-cured ham, baron of beef, roasted venison and antelope, and leg of mutton with caper sauce. Three fat turkeys had been stuffed with cornbread and chiles and roasted. Platter after platter was filled with relishes and vegetables of all descriptions, and the desserts included *flan,* Boston cream cakes, coconut jumbles, and ginger snap pyramids.

"Overwhelming," Hatch told his wife as he made his selections. "My dear, you did a wonderful job of organizing this celebration."

"I enjoyed every minute of it—" Evelyn began, but was interrupted by Mary Loud, a stout, abrasive woman who by marriage had gained a perfectly appropriate surname.

"Imagine," proclaimed Mrs. Loud sarcastically "Oysters, salmon, and fancy desserts. One might assume that civilization has finally reached the wilderness."

Evelyn, who didn't share the negative feelings the other Army wives had for the territory, responded in a bantering tone. "Now Mary, remember that this year we've seen the railroad arrive here, plus gas lighting. We must have patience and—"

"What I can't understand," interrupted Mrs. Loud, "is this. If Santa Fe is the oldest city in this country, why is it so primitive? You'd think it would be old and cultured, like Rome or Paris."

"It's not *that* old," laughed Evelyn. "Besides, Mary, Santa Fe has charm and character. There's a tradition of arts and crafts here, and I know of at least one transplanted Eastern artist who says the scenery and the light for painting is the best in the world. Maybe someday we'll even have an opera here."

Mrs. Loud could not suppress her laughter and nearly choked on an oyster. "What a sense of humor you have, Evelyn," gushed Mrs. Loud after she recovered. "New Mexico isn't even a state and there aren't twenty people here who could appreciate an opera."

During the women's debate, a bored Edward Hatch drifted away from the food tables and sought out his commander of Indian scouts from Fort Cummings, who was still in conversation with the small group of other officers. Hatch caught Guilfoyle's glance and jerked his head in the direction of the door. Together they moved out of the House chambers and into the library.

Amidst the hundreds of volumes of books and the territorial archives that were being restored and catalogued by Adolph Bandelier, Hatch and Guilfoyle found a table not covered with overcoats and sat down across from each other.

"Now, Lieutenant, what's on your mind?"

"Well, sir, I don't think we've heard the last from Victorio's band of renegades."

Hatch frowned. "How so?"

"I've learned that not all of Victorio's band were killed at Tres Castillos. Some of them, including Nana, escaped and attacked General Terrazas, who was nearly killed. And, sir, it looks like it was Nana's band that attacked Perry at Ojo Caliente in Texas."

"Nana?" scoffed Hatch. "That's ridiculous."

"But sir, my scouts insist that Nana is commanding what's left of Victorio's band, and that he's even found reinforcements."

"I am not concerned with Nana, Lieutenant. That prehistoric savage is well over eighty years old. In fact," Hatch said, counting off each infirmity on his fingers, "he is palsied, senile, decrepit, half-blind, and crippled with rheumatism. This relic ran the squaw camp of Apache hangers-on while Victorio took on my entire Ninth Cavalry. I doubt that Nana is a threat to the Territory of New Mexico. Let the Mexicans take care of him."

Guilfoyle was unfazed by his commander's bluster. "As far as we know, General, Nana is still in Mexico. But you know these Apaches. They usually move north to the Black Range in the spring."

"Thanks for the warning, Lieutenant," Hatch said dryly. "Now, shall we return to the festivities?"

The band was playing "Silent Night" in march tempo as the two cavalry officers entered the chamber. Hatch sought out Colonel Richard Parks, commander of Fort Selden and his closest friend in New Mexico. They had fought together during the War and had successfully pulled off a cavalry raid in Mississippi. After Hatch had been named commander of the Military District of New Mexico, he had selected Parks to command his most important southern fort.

"Good to see you, Ed," said Parks, a thin, slightly-balding man in his mid-forties.

"Likewise, Dick. Say, one of my men just told me he thinks that Nana and the remnants of Victorio's band might cause some trouble for us. What do you think?"

Parks laughed. "That old man? What could he possibly do against us?"

"Guilfoyle heard a rumor that Nana was the one who attacked Parker."

"Highly unlikely. I think it was some renegade Mescaleros. The Warm Springs Apaches have been wiped out."

Hatch nodded. "I agree. Now let's get back to the fun."

With Parks, he rejoined his wife, who was in conversation with Governor Wallace. Guilfoyle, who had been watching Hatch's conversation with Parks, moved over to the bar and ordered a bourbon from the bartender. Within a minute, Gatewood and Smith were at his side.

"Well," asked Gatewood in a low voice, "did he believe you?"

"Hard to say. He's still celebrating the death of Victorio and here I am predicting more trouble. He doesn't think Nana is any kind of threat at all."

"General Hatch is an optimist," Gatewood observed, placing his glass on the bar for a refill. "I have a theory that Nana was the brains behind Victorio. I was at Hembrillo, remember? The Apaches played plenty of tricks and made us look like fools. None of our men ever saw Victorio, although one of my scouts spotted Nana. He told me he didn't even think Victorio was there at Hembrillo."

Guilfoyle shook his head in disagreement. "Then where was he?"

"In Mexico."

"Do you believe that?"

Gatewood shrugged. "I don't know."

Smith, who had remained silent, finally spoke up. "I hope Nana dares to show his face again in this territory. I've got a bullet with his name on it right here." He patted his holster, which contained a Colt revolver.

His fellow lieutenants laughed at the gunfighter cliché. Smith had quite a reputation as a bold—if not reckless—soldier, but the image of him in a quick draw confrontation fight with the old Apache was ludicrous.

"I have an idea," said Gatewood in a low voice. "In a while, why don't we slip away from this reception and pay a visit to Teresa's place?"

"Good idea," Guilfoyle agreed.

"Who is Teresa?" asked Smith, who was making his first visit to Santa Fe.

Gatewood grinned. "A professional acquaintance."

"The entertainment profession," Guilfoyle added, and the three laughed again as Smith grasped the allusion.

Across the noisy chamber, near the oyster table, Lew Wallace said, "Follow me, General," to Colonel Hatch, who accompanied him to the Governor's office. He handed Hatch a large, thick volume.

"Ed, I want you to have this but I didn't dare give it to you in front of all those people. I only have a few extra copies and of course everyone would want one." He chuckled. "I'd rather they bought their own copies."

Hatch, who was flattered, opened the cover of Ben-Hur, A Tale of Christ, and read the inscription: "To my good friend and ally, Edward

Hatch. I hope this book entertains and inspires you. Lew Wallace."

"Why Lew, I don't know what to say except thank you. What a thoughtful gift for Christmas."

"Something to remember me by," Wallace said, stroking his beard. "The first edition is nearly sold out."

"I promise you that I'll read it cover to cover."

"Perhaps it will lead you out of this wilderness," joked Wallace. "It certainly did that for me."

"You must have heard from the President," guessed Hatch. "Where is your new posting?"

"Constantinople. Susan is very pleased."

"Good for you. All I can hope for is Kansas."

The band was playing "It Came Upon a Midnight Clear" when Edward and Evelyn Hatch took leave of the reception, but it was neither midnight nor clear. It was nearly one o'clock in the morning and snow had begun to fall, further diffusing the light from the gas lamps.

"How romantic," observed Evelyn, and Hatch put his arm around her for the short walk home. Once inside the house, they shared a long kiss.

"You build up the fires and I'll wait for you in bed," Evelyn suggested with a seductive look.

"And continue the celebration?" Hatch asked hopefully.

"Can you think of anything better on a snowy winter night?"

"Certainly not, my love," Hatch replied softly and then hurried outside to gather an armful of *piñon* logs.

A few blocks away, a satiated John Guilfoyle was lying in bed in one of the rooms at Teresa's while his companion, a friendly, fleshy woman named Patty, quickly opened the window to collect some snow to add to their drinks of bourbon. Looking out, she recognized the man entering the house.

"Well, well, look who's here," she said, shivering.

"Who's that?" asked Guilfoyle, who admired her naked body in the glow from the corner fireplace.

"Governor Wallace, one of Teresa's best customers," replied Patty, hurrying back to the warmth of the bed.

Guilfoyle smiled at the image of the pompous governor pounding away on top of Teresa, who outweighed him by fifty pounds at least. "A regular, huh?"

Patty handed him a drink and then joined him under the sheets and quilt. "I had him last week," she teased, "but he smells funny. I prefer soldiers—young ones, like you."

Lieutenant Guilfoyle, resting on one elbow, held up his glass to her and said, "To soldiering! Merry Christmas, darling."

Desert Vista.

2. Blue Mountains

The shaman known as The Dreamer listened carefully to the visitor who told the tale of Victorio's death. It seemed incredible to him that one of the greatest Tcihene warriors was riding the ghost trail, and even more strange that his place had been taken by this ancient man called Kaz-Tziden—or Nana, as he was called by both the Mexicans and White Eyes.

Nana was in his seventy-fourth year and was crippled from an old ankle injury, but none of his people ever mentioned his age or infirmity to his face. They knew that he was still as rugged as ever, able to ride forty miles a day without complaint or discomfort. He had been Victorio's *segundo*—second in command—during the warfare in New Mexico and now had assumed command of the remnants of the Chiricahua band that called themselves the Tcihene, or "red paint people."

After the massacre at Tres Castillos that claimed Victorio and most of their people, Nana had gathered together the seventeen survivors and moved them to a stronghold high in the Sierra Madres, or Blue Mountains as the Tcihene called the range. He had appointed Kaytennae his *segundo*, and after assuring that his people were safe, had made the long and dangerous journey to San Carlos, the hated desert reservation in Arizona where his band was supposed to be interned.

Nana's purpose in returning to San Carlos was recruitment. He needed warriors badly, but the men on the reservation were discouraged by the death of Victorio, one of the greatest war chiefs, and feared reprisals against their families if they left with Nana. However, his trip to San Carlos had not been a total failure; there, disguised as a harmless, crippled drunk, he had met a White Mountain man called The Dreamer—a shaman who said he had the Power to summon the dead.

The Dreamer was a small, thin man half Nana's age. His skin was so pale that it was almost white, which added to his mystical aura. He had attended the White Eyes' school in Santa Fe, where he had learned—but not believed in—the religion the White Eyes called Christianity. The only part of the Christian religion that had impressed him was the story of Christ's resurrection, a concept which he had adopted into his own rituals. In addition to being an influential White Mountain shaman, The Dreamer was also a warrior and had been a scout under the command of General Crook—until he was asked to track down his own people.

After Nana finished the sad tale of Victorio, the old chief proposed a plan to The Dreamer that would bring pride back to the various bands imprisoned on Arizona and New Mexico reservations and avenge the death of Victorio at the same time. In order to carry out their plan, it was necessary for The Dreamer to join Nana's band as shaman.

"I will do this thing you ask," The Dreamer replied after several minutes of silent contemplation, "but only for a short time. I must return to San Carlos and help my people here."

"Agreed," said Nana, and they began to discuss strategy. The Dreamer, who had far more experience than Nana in dealing directly with the White Eyes, made a strange proposal, one which Nana would never have considered except in such desperate times.

"I have heard that Victorio and you cached gold in a number of mountain caves," he said.

"We wanted to return the sacred metal to the ground where it belongs," Nana replied slowly.

"I have studied the White Eyes and know what they love most. It is called 'money' and the most precious money of all to them is gold. Why not give them the gold if they return your lands to you?"

"But it is forbidden to touch or possess the gold," Nana protested.

The Dreamer shrugged. "It is more forbidden to live like slaves in San Carlos or exiled in the Blue Mountains."

Nana frowned. "My people, recently defeated by the Mexicans, would not fight if they knew we were going to buy our land back as if we were buying *mescal* in some saloon."

"Then don't tell them until you have to," suggested The Dreamer. "Tell them only it is a war of vengeance."

"It might work," Nana finally agreed.

"I have another idea," The Dreamer said. "Do you know the Chiricahua the White Eyes call Chihuahua?"

"Yes," Nana replied. "He is a Blue Coat scout and therefore our enemy."

"Don't be so sure of that, Grandfather. He is here now visiting his wife and children. We should talk with him, tell him of our plan. He might help us."

"If you think so," Nana agreed reluctantly.

Two days later Nana and The Dreamer disappeared from San Carlos under the cover of darkness and, near dawn, stole two horses from a corral on a nearby ranch, taking care not disturb the White Eyes asleep in the adobe ranch house. Next, Nana led them to his cache in the Galiuro Mountains and retrieved two rifles, a small amount of ammunition, and some dried horsemeat.

By staying in the foothills of the mountain ranges and traversing the deserts only at night, three days later they crossed the border of Arizona Territory into Mexico, unnoticed and unpursued. Nana was pleased with their easy escape, but knew that he could not return to his band empty handed.

The first night after they crossed into Mexico, Nana and The Dreamer camped and took stock of their situation. It was imperative that his people be re-supplied, so as he always did when he wished to use his Power, Nana built a small fire, then sang a short prayer as he slowly turned and faced all directions:

On this earth
Where we live,
Ussen has the Power.
He gives this Power to me
For locating ammunition.
I now search for that ammunition
Which only Ussen the Great
Can give to me.

By the end of the prayer he was facing south, a certain sign that they were headed in the right direction.

"Soon, very soon," Nana promised the Dreamer, "we shall find ammunition for my people. The prayer has never failed."

The following day they skirted the small town of Fronteras and Nana spotted dust in the sky to the south. Quickly, he and The Dreamer hobbled their horses, left the foothills, and proceeded to the main trail. Each man buried himself in the loose sand within ten feet of each side of the trail. Beneath the sand, Nana said another short prayer.

Right here in the middle of this place
I become a mirage.
Let them not see me,
For I am of the sand.

They waited motionless for nearly an hour before they heard the sounds of the approaching pack train. After the horses passed by their position, Nana gave the quail-call signal and the two warriors leaped from their hiding places and began firing their Winchester carbines.

The Mexican soldiers never had a chance to defend themselves. Each was struck with a single bullet to the back or head, and those who survived the shots were dispatched with a knife thrust to the throat. Nana and The Dreamer then quickly chased down the horses and mules that had scattered at the noise of the rifles, and soon discovered that the three pack animals were loaded with ammunition that apparently was destined for the small garrison at Fronteras.

Nana grinned at The Dreamer, softly thanked Ussen for granting the Power, and then directed the clean-up procedure. They stripped the bodies of the soldiers of guns and ammunition belts, then loaded them across mules and horses and carried them a short distance to a narrow, deep arroyo. They dumped the corpses in the arroyo and then rolled heavy stones over them. Nana knew that the longer he kept their deaths secret from the garrison, the more time he would have to reach his stronghold.

After the bodies were concealed, Nana and The Dreamer used mesquite branches to obliterate the signs of the struggle. Finally, after an hour's work, he and The Dreamer recovered their horses and moved south again with the captured pack train plus the five horses recovered from the soldiers. Nana knew that the problem of fresh mounts for the remainder of the journey was solved.

"Ussen has blessed us," remarked The Dreamer, who never said much unless he was conducting a ceremony. "Let us pray for continued invisibility."

During the remainder of their journey, their prayers were granted. Despite the fact that they were mounted and leading a virtual caravan, they were not spotted by any Mexicans—or worse, by other Mexican soldiers who constantly patrolled the foothills of the Blue Mountains on the lookout for the hated enemy. At least part of the reason for their invisibility could not be credited to divine intervention, but rather to the skill of Nana, who seemingly had memorized every mountain, canyon, and stream in the enormous area the White Eyes knew as southwestern

Arizona, southern New Mexico, western Texas, and most of the Mexican regions of Sonora and Chihuahua.

Nana was also intensely aware of nature around him, for the plants and animals told him where he was and what was happening in the immediate vicinity. When he spotted a mountain lion, he knew that there were no other hunters nearby. A jaguar was a sign that he was nearing his destination, for they rarely roamed north of the Blue Mountains.

In the eighth day of their journey, he noticed green parrots with red and yellow heads eating pine cones, and knew they were getting close to the stronghold. He led the way up a narrow canyon and soon their way was blocked by a familiar stream. The Dreamer sang the Prayer to the Great River while Nana tapped a hand over his open mouth to make a haunting song. This ceremony secured safe passage across the swollen stream.

Slowly they worked their way higher and higher into the Blue Mountains. There was no trail to follow, yet Nana knew exactly where he was going. He also realized that he and The Dreamer were under observation from above and was pleased that he could not spot the lookouts. Their progress was being watched by a Tcihene boy hidden among boulders and shrub oaks who wore a bunch of grass tied to his head for camouflage.

Istee, the teenaged son of Victorio, obeyed his instructions to the letter. Once he had determined the identity of the party below him, he pulled a small piece of mirror from his pouch and flashed signals to Kawaykla, the younger lookout stationed far above him. The signals were in two sequences. The first was two quick flashes, which meant that two men were coming. That was followed by a fifteen count pause and the second sequence, a beam of light in the shape of a circle, which indicated that the men were friends.

Since only one person knew the location of their stronghold, Kaywaykla instantly understood that the mirror flashes meant the return of Nana. He left his position and ran back to the Tcihene camp at top speed.

"Grandfather is coming!" he told Kaytennae, who was on the far side of the camp playing the game of hoop-and-pole with Mangus.

"Good," acknowledged the *segundo*. "Go and tell your father's sister—and Grandfather's wife."

Kaywaykla ran off to find Lozen and Nah-des-te while Kaytennae gestured to the rest of the men to quit the game.

Meanwhile, Nana and The Dreamer were passing the position of the lookout. Istee wished to greet them but did not want to be considered a foolish child who could not maintain both his position and silence until relieved by another. Nana, who knew precisely where Istee was hiding, gave the quail call. Flattered to be treated like an adult, Istee softly returned the call.

"Here is the stronghold of my people," Nana told The Dreamer as their caravan arrived at the plateau high above the canyons. The Tcihene camp was set amidst tall pines in a flat mountain park with a spring-fed pond at the lowest edge. Nana was saddened to see so few wickiups for his band, but said nothing.

The nineteen survivors of the Tres Castillos battle all gathered to watch Nana ride into camp with his captured horses and mules—and the stranger. Kaytennae moved forward and seized the bridle of Nana's mount.

"What have you been doing, Grandfather?" Kaytennae asked in the Tcihene way of indirect greetings.

"Killing Mexicans," Nana replied, dismounting slowly. He was stiff and sore from all the days on horseback, but tried not to let his discomfort show.

Kaytennae clapped his right hand over his mouth in the Tcihene gesture that meant "What a speech!"

Nana indicated The Dreamer with a brief nod. "Here is the one from San Carlos who can bring the dead to life," he said in the oblique form that avoided the direct use of a person's name. "He will join us for a while as our shaman. Someone should construct a wickiup for him."

Nana limped over to one of the mules and opened the saddlebags to reveal the packets of rifle shells. The small crowd immediately responded with murmurs of "Um, um."

"I see you have not lost your Power," observed Kaytennae.

"Victorio and our people are gone because they ran out of ammunition," Nana said with emotion in his voice. "That is why they only killed three Mexicans while the Mexicans killed so many of us. As long as I live, the Tcihene will never lack ammunition."

Nana left the pack animals and slowly walked over to where his wife was standing. He embraced her, a gesture normally reserved for privacy, but now brought into the open because each of the survivors was so treasured.

"I am glad to see you again, husband," Nah-des-te said softly, so that no one but Nana could hear her.

Nana released her and addressed his people. "Today we shall rest, but tomorrow will be a day for feasting to welcome our guest. Also, I wish to call a council to consider a vengeance war against the Mexicans and White Eyes. In my parfleches the women will find corn we brought all the way from San Carlos. It is now sprouted and ready to make *tizwin* to go with our feast."

After his brief speech, Nana limped off to his wickiup, followed closely by Nah-des-te. But before they reached their destination, Nah-des-te ran back to the pack animals and retrieved the sprouted corn from Nana's parfleches.

"If you want *tizwin* tomorrow night," she explained with a smile, "I must start it tonight."

The following morning Kaytennae rose before sunrise. Taking care not to awaken his wife Guyan, he roused his adopted son Kaywaykla and motioned for him to leave the wickiup. Outside, he whispered instructions to round up Mangus and Istee and tell them to make preparations for an early morning hunt. Grandfather had told them of his desire for a feast, but aside from dried meat they had nothing fitting to serve him and the new shaman.

"Remember, son, do not eat anything," he reminded the boy. The Tcihene believed that they must hunt on an empty stomach, for then

Ussen would take pity on them and give them some game to shoot.

While Kaywaykla was gathering the others, Kaytennae found his rifle, ammunition, and the head and antlers of a deer he had killed several weeks earlier. A few minutes later he joined Mangus and the two boys where the horses were tethered, and together they placed bridles and buckskin saddles on the mounts they had selected for the day's hunt. Although they were not traveling very far to find the deer, Kaytennae knew it would be much quicker to carry the meat back to the camp on horseback.

Istee and Kaywaykla were excited and felt privileged to be allowed to go on the hunt. Even though they were technically under-aged, the lack of warriors in their band necessitated the quick transformation of boys into men. However, Kaytennae would not permit them to carry rifles on the hunt—they were armed with more traditional bows made from wild mulberry saplings and arrows fashioned from desert broom branches and tipped with flint points.

The first light of the sun was breaking over the tops of the easternmost Blue Mountains when the hunting party set off to the south. As they rode out of camp they could hear Nana singing the Morning Song, which was a hymn to Ussen thanking him for one of the greatest gifts he bestowed on the Tcihene, the love between man and woman. It was a familiar sound that made Kaytennae very happy because it meant their band, however small and troubled, still had purpose. He gave the quail call as they passed the position of the lookout Frank, the young warrior with the White Eyes' name.

The hunting party worked its way south through tall pine forests for nearly an hour before Kaytennae gave the order for them to dismount and tie the horses. They were on a forested ridge that overlooked a park similar to the one the Tcihene were camped in. Below, clearly visible in the early morning light, was a small herd of deer feeding on the grass in the park. He checked the slight breeze to make certain it was blowing toward their faces and then gestured for his men to take their places on stand. Mangus led the two boys away from the ridge to the right, where the park narrowed and turned into a canyon. It would be their job to pick off any deer spooked by Kaytennae.

Kaytennae placed the deer head on top of his own and tied it tight with the flaps of skin on either side. With his rifle hidden by his right leg, he moved slowing down the slope and into the park in a manner resembling a grazing deer. He carried a stick in his left hand, enabling him to stoop over periodically as if feeding on the grass.

In this way Kaytennae carefully worked his way to within fifty yards of the herd, which was ignoring him. Not wishing to push his good fortune, the hunter rose quickly and shot the largest buck, which toppled immediately. The rest of the herd, startled by the rifle shot, ran toward the end of the park, and a few seconds later Kaytennae heard the report of Mangus' rifle. He removed the deer head and followed the trail of the herd until he found the rest of his hunting party.

Soon Mangus appeared and told him that not only had he killed a doe, another buck was down at the head of the canyon, pierced by arrows from the two boys. Ussen had indeed blessed them that morning, Kaytennae thought.

Following tradition according to the way Child of the Water hunted when he was on earth, Kaytennae placed the head of his kill to the east and proceeded with the ritual of butchering the animal. He never walked in front of the deer to the east and took care not to straddle or walk across the carcass. He began at the throat, working his knife down the center of the body and along the inside of the front and back legs. Carefully he cut away the skin from the legs, then sliced through the meat, broke the ribs of the deer, and removed the entrails so the meat would not spoil. He drained as much of the blood as he could into the stomach, then tied it off so it would not leak—his wife could make his favorite meal with it. Then he turned the carcass over, skinned the other side, and carefully brushed the body with the skin in the four directions, and addressed the spirit of the animal: "When you see me again, don't be afraid. May I be lucky with you all the time."

Kaytennae completed the butchering by cutting the legs off, severing the backbone at the neck and below the ribs, and then cutting the rest of the carcass into transportable pieces. After retrieving his horse, he tied the meat to it with woven yucca thongs—including the blood-filled stomach, the intestines, and head—and then moved off to assist Mangus. He knew because of the three kills they would need the horses to carry the meat and thus would have to walk back to camp, but he didn't care. He was just happy about their great success.

Back at camp, Nah-des-te was directing the three other women of the small band in the preparations for the feast. Of course, Guyan and the others knew the routine—it was out of respect for her age and experience that they took orders from the older woman. The previous evening, Nah-des-te had ground the sprouted corn between two stones and had started the hours-long boiling process. As the hunting party left the camp she had added the boiled corn water to previously fermented *mescal* juice in several large water jars. Within an hour, the *tizwin* was bubbling as the fermentation of the corn began. With any luck at all, the *tizwin* would be ready by early evening.

Nah-des-te sent the young girl Dah-de-glash, accompanied by Sánchez for protection, down to the lower elevations to collect mesquite beans, while Guyan rode off to gather the nuts of the *piñon* tree. Even Lozen, who usually did not participate in women's work because she was a warrior, volunteered to help by finding quail's eggs and juniper berries.

While the women were gathering and preparing food, Nana constructed a small sweat lodge near the pond, using oak branches tied together at the top to make a dome-shaped structure. He sang and prayed to the sweat lodge as he built it. The Dreamer watched carefully but made no attempt to assist him—the lodge was Nana's domain and was more for health than religious purposes. After the frame was finished, Nana covered it with deerskins and brush, and fashioned a door facing east which could be sealed with a large elk hide. Then he built a fire just outside the door of the lodge and surrounded the blaze with four large rocks.

About an hour passed before he invited The Dreamer to join him. Together they used sticks to push the hot rocks into the lodge. Nana then rubbed crushed *piñon* needles over their bodies and tied wild sage branches around their heads. They stripped to loincloths and entered the lodge, carefully sealing the door so the heat would not escape. Inside, they enjoyed the heat and sang the same four songs over and over—songs about the sweat bath, the earth, the sky, and lost lands of the Tcihene and White Mountain people. When the heat became so intense they felt their skins would catch fire, they hurried out of the lodge and bathed in the pond. They repeated that cycle four times and the combination of heat and cool water soothed them, removing the aches and pains of the long ride south.

Kaytennae and the hunting party returned to camp in mid-afternoon and quietly accepted the praises of the women, who quickly distributed the meat and other parts of the deer. Kaywaykla and Istee were given instructions to find all the members of the band and tell them that food was being prepared. It was time to begin the feast.

Within a few minutes, the small group of Tcihene assembled at the main fire. After his sweat-bath, Nana had changed his clothes and was dressed as elegantly as possible under the circumstances—in a bright red cotton shirt with a buttoned corduroy waistcoat, boot-length buckskin moccasins bound above the calf, a beaded necklace, and a neckerchief tied with a silver concho. He also wore his trademark, long golden watch chains that dangled from his pierced ear lobes.

Nah-des-te, assisted by Dah-de-glash, first passed around gourd cups of the corn beer *tizwin* to everyone, and then began to grill the venison steaks, which were skewered on green branches and held over the hot coals of the fire. Guyan prepared Kaytennae's favorite dish, a sort of blood sausage, by puncturing the deer's stomach and adding mountain onions and crushed *chiltepines*—wild chile peppers—to the blood already in it. Then she placed the stomach in a circle of hot rocks on the coals to cook.

Mats of woven yucca leaves piled high with food were passed around so the people could help themselves to the other Tcihene delicacies: roasted and sun-dried *mescal* mixed with juniper and sumac berries, mesquite bean pancakes and boiled quails' eggs. When they were done, the venison steaks were eaten right off the cooking sticks. Guyan giggled as she extracted the stomach from the fire and presented it to her husband, who signaled his appreciation with a warm glance.

Although they did not use the White Eyes' term "dessert," the final dish of their feast would have qualified for that definition no matter where it was served. It was a delicious concoction of dried prickly-pear fruits with *piñon* nut and yucca pulp pudding, and Nana smacked his lips in satisfaction as he ate it with a yucca-blade spoon.

After the feast, Nana rose to his feet and addressed his people, who fell silent in respect. "It is time for those of us who are left to decide what to do. We must call a council and choose whether or not to begin a vengeance war. To help us with our choice, our guest and new shaman will perform a ceremony."

He sat down abruptly and The Dreamer rose to his feet. He wore a white cotton shirt, a two-string medicine thong strung with turquoise, shells, and beads, and a medicine hat decorated with the horns and fur of a pronghorn. His left hand was painted with the sun symbol and held a small gourd rattle. In his right hand was a medicine tray with cattail pollen, paints, and a large pile of herbs upon it.

On his knees, Nana leaned over and traced a cross of pollen on The Dreamer's moccasins, and lifted up to him the four ceremonial gifts which meant that he had been accepted as the band's shaman: downy eagle feathers, a perfectly cured buckskin, a large piece of turquoise, and an abalone shell.

The Dreamer leaned over and marked Nana's face with cattail pollen, and Nana did the same to his. The shaman then smoked a cigarette of wild tobacco, slowly puffing the smoke to the four directions: north, east, south, west. When the cigarette was gone, he mesmerized the band by slowing shaking a gourd rattle as he spoke.

"Everything in our world—the animals, the plants, the stars in the sky, lightning—has a Power behind it that makes it do the things it does. But we can see only a small part of this Power. It makes me humble when I remember that Ussen has, in His wisdom, given Power to the most innocent-appearing things which live in our world. The ordinary, sharp-spined *mescal* has the Power to feed us, to keep us alive. Recently I have discovered another such sacred plant, one previously unknown even to shamans. Here is how it happened.

"I met a Lipan man at San Carlos who told me this story. A few years ago his people had been dying off because of some disease of the White Eyes and no cure had been found. So while on a horse raid, this Lipan man decided to pray to any beautiful plant he saw, hoping that a cure-plant would reveal itself. Some time later he came upon a place where many small cactus plants were growing. The plants were covered with hundreds of beautiful pink flowers, so the Lipan man prayed to the flowers, telling them how pretty they were, and how he wished that his people were as plentiful as all the blossoms.

"Then one of the cactus plants spoke back to the Lipan man. 'Pull me,' it told him, 'and as many of me as you can. Take me home and make a wickiup with the door to the east. Then eat me, and let those others who have an interest also eat me.'

"The Lipan man hurried back to his people and told the chief what had happened. They decided to feed the cactus plants to everyone in the tribe, but were afraid that there were not enough plants to go around. Miraculously, as the people took the plants, the pile of them never diminished and there was enough for all. After they ate the plants, their sickness went away and people recovered."

The Dreamer paused and slowly gazed upon each of the faces surrounding him. Then he moved his hand over his medicine tray and retrieved some small, wrinkled buttons that resembled pieces of pronghorn sign.

"It is these small things," The Dreamer said softly, "that have such great Power. They can cure disease. They can make us so powerful that we never tire, never are hungry or thirsty, and never feel the White Eyes' bullets. By eating this plant, its Power is loaned to us for a time, and we must learn from the visions it gives to us."

The Dreamer placed four of the buttons in the outstretched hand of Nana, who passed them to Nah-des-te. Since her husband had no teeth, she would chew on the buttons until they were soft enough for Nana to swallow. Each of the other warriors, plus Lozen and Istee, received four of the wrinkled buttons. The Dreamer repeated the ceremony four times until each person had received four times four pieces of the plant.

"It is called *peyotl* and it is very bitter," said The Dreamer. "Chew them until they are soft and then swallow them. Later, some of you may vomit, but that is normal. Clear your thoughts and listen to me. It will take some time before you feel the Power of the *peyotl*. During that time, Grandfather will conduct a council meeting."

Nana rose and took the place of The Dreamer as the center of attention. "It is now the time of Many Leaves," he said slowly, looking at the attentive faces of his people, "and usually by now we would be camped in our ancestral lands at Ojo Caliente. I do not need to tell you that we must take action or our band will be *indeh*—dead and gone. I know you are looking to me for leadership, but before I tell you my thoughts, I would like to hear from you. What can we do, Tcihene?"

There was an uncomfortable silence around the fire for a few moments before Sánchez, the one who had lived for a time with the Mexicans, rose and spoke hesitantly. "We will all do as our grandfather suggests, but I think we should consider returning with our shaman to San Carlos. If we do that, maybe the White Eyes will give us back our land at Ojo Caliente as they have promised."

"I would sooner have you shoot me dead right here," Nana replied scornfully. "Don't you remember the story about the Foolish People and the soldiers? The Foolish People were camped and soon the Blue Coats camped nearby and the Foolish People thought them to be friends. One day the Blue Coats came into their camp shooting and killing. Instead of fighting, the Foolish People decided to talk about it and they asked the Blue Coats, 'Why are you shooting at us?' After the Blue Coats had killed nearly half the tribe, one of the survivors said, 'Let's get out of here,' but it was too late. They were fools, and that's why they were killed."

Sánchez hung his head and could not meet Nana's gaze. "Talking does not work with the White Eyes," the old man continued. "They would never give us Ojo Caliente back and, like Victorio, we must refuse to return to San Carlos and die like flies. It is a hateful place, a burning desert with only cactus, rattlesnakes, scorpions, rocks, and insects. White Eyes want to turn us into them—thieves and liars. We will become weak and impotent from their diseases and vices. We prefer death in battle to slavery and starvation."

Kaytennae stood up and addressed the band. He was a tall, handsome warrior wearing a Mexican's jacket with a cartridge belt and concho belt. "We know the Blue Coats have marched into Mexico and joined the Mexicans against us," he said. "Maybe we should hide for a while. I have heard that further south of here and to the west, the Nednhi people have a stronghold even better than this one, and that their *nantan* Juh welcomes people of all bands to join him. We could go there until our strength in numbers and weapons increases. I have heard that Juh's stronghold has plenty of water and game and it is safe, with only one zigzag path leading to the top of a tall, flat-topped mountain."

"Perhaps our shaman can tell us of Juh," suggested Nana.

The Dreamer remained seated but answered the question. "He is strong and stubborn, but a man of his word. I have not been to his stronghold but I have heard that it cannot be found by the Mexicans or Blue Coats—much less taken by force."

The discussion of possibilities continued for nearly an hour, with Nana listening patiently while everyone who wished had their say—including the women, who usually remained silent during council meetings. By this time everyone was beginning to feel the effects of the *peyotl* administered by The Dreamer. Nana noticed that the pain had disappeared from his ankle as waves of physical pleasure washed over his body. Young Istee was entranced by the fire—the flames seemed to have traces which extended far into the darkness, revealing strange shapes and shadows that he hoped were not ghosts. Kaytennae, who had also been steadily drinking *tizwin*, realized that colors were brighter and Grandfather's red shirt seemed to glow.

The most noticeable effect of the cactus on Lozen was slightly slurred speech. She was the last of the band to speak her mind, and she weaved slightly as she stood before them—a woman who was a warrior, dressed not in cotton blouse and skirt but rather in trousers, shirt, and vest. Her long hair was secured by a headband in the manner of men and her presence was as powerful as that of a man.

"All of this talk about hiding or returning to San Carlos is for cowards," she challenged. "Are we not the Tcihene, the feared Red Paint People who kill White Eyes and Mexicans? Have not these enemies driven us from our lands and killed our greatest *nantans*, including my brother? Are we going to run and hide forever? I call for a war of vengeance! We should return to the north and kill every enemy we can find!"

Her vehemence startled the band, some of whom involuntarily covered their mouths with their hands. Nana indicated his satisfaction with a grunt; and The Dreamer began to shake his gourd rattle as Lozen's voice pierced the night and faded away, replaced only by the crackling of the fire.

Istee stared at the fire and saw the flames divide into different colors—blue, green, red, yellow—and the tips of the flames became arrows complete with feathers shooting out into the night sky. He was so entranced by the brilliantly-colored flames that at first he barely comprehended the words chanted by The Dreamer, who held up a large, circular medallion that reflected the light from the fire. He swung the medallion back and forth on a silver chain as he spoke.

"Many years ago, I was sent to the White Eyes' stronghold which is called 'Washington.' I saw such wonders that I was certain I was in the Underworld—but I wasn't, and there is a lesson here. Tcihene, you must be brave when you think of the dead. This is not a dream but a demonstration of one shaman's Power. So stare into the fire now and remember the great *nantans* killed by the enemies who invade and steal our land. Do you remember Cochise, *nantan* of the Tsokanene Chiricahuas? Do you see that tall man, his face painted red, black hair streaked with gray, his body ravaged by the disease of the White Eyes? Now, look there, into the stars and see his body wedged into a crevice for burial, rocks sealing his spirit back to the mountain he worshipped."

"I see him," said Nana with awe in his voice as the image of the Cochise he remembered floated in the sky.

The others of the band, who had only heard of Cochise but had never met him, could not see his form—only pulsating patterns and colors in the night sky. The stars began to assume shapes and move to the rhythm of the gourd rattle.

"Do you remember the great *nantan* Mangas Coloradas?" continued The Dreamer in a hypnotic, chanting voice. His pale skin looked ghastly in the dim light. "Look into the fire and remember how the Blue Coats shot him while he was tied up. Remember how they scalped him, and then cut off his head, and then boiled it down until it was just a skull! Now look into the sky, Tcihene, and see Mangas Coloradas!"

Those who had known the Mimbreño chief—including Nana, Kaytennae, Lozen, and Nah-des-te—gasped at the horrible apparition that hovered above them. Weaving back and forth in the night sky was a giant warrior holding in his hands his own severed head.

"Father!" screamed Mangus, who was clearly terrified by the phantom hovering above them. He fell over on his side, covered his eyes with his hands and began moaning. Lozen rushed to his side and attempted to soothe him, but Mangus began to vomit uncontrollably and those close to him scurried away.

The Dreamer ignored the interruption and relentlessly continued his frightening tale. "Hear me now, Tcihene. Look into the fire and remember your own great *nantan* Victorio, how he killed himself with his own knife rather than allow the Mexicans to kill him. Imagine his face, his Power. Now, Tcihene, look to the sky and see the return of Victorio."

Since everyone around the fire had known Victorio, his image was there among the stars for all to see—proof that The Dreamer had the Power to bring the dead to life. There were gasps from the band but no screams; despite the fact that a knife protruded from his chest, the apparition of Victorio was not as frightening as that of Mangas Coloradas and the mutilated head. He floated above them, rifle in one hand, a bar of White Eyes' gold in the other. Istee, Victorio's son, stood up and opened his arms as if to embrace the specter. Lozen, Victorio's sister, called out: "Brother, tell me what to do!"

Everyone present heard the ghostly voice of Victorio clearly ring out across the Blue Mountains: "Avenge me, my people! Kill all of our enemies! Avenge me!"

"Yes! Yes!" wailed Lozen, who was joined by Istee and then the rest of the band in chanting their answer to the call of their dead chief. The sound of The Dreamer's gourd rattle was replaced by the steady thumping of Nana's drum in the familiar rhythm of a war dance. As The Dreamer began to sing, the image of Victorio quickly faded and the attention of the Tcihene people shifted from the sky back to the fire. The warriors present took up the refrain of the war dance song and The Dreamer intoned the prayers, which were half-sung and half-spoken.

"The great *nantan* has called for a war of vengeance," he chanted to the beat of the drum. Then he stood up and hurled the silver medallion into the fire. "I destroy this thing of the White Eyes! Now we will kill the White Eyes! Ussen will guide us on our mission. Who among us will join in the war dance? Who among us will avenge Victorio?"

The chant was a signal to the men, who, despite the grip of the *peyotl*, were able to find their rifles and bullets. Kaytennae, who was hallucinating intensely, rose to his feet and gestured to Mangus, Lozen, and a warrior named Suldeen. The four warriors moved away from the group, approached the fire from the east and danced around it four times abreast. Then they split apart, with Suldeen and Lozen on the north side of the fire, Kaytennae and Mangus on the south side. Facing each other in two pairs, the warriors danced in place to the rhythm of Nana's drum. Then they danced toward each other, changed sides of the fire, turned around, and changed sides again—a total of four times.

While the warriors were dancing, Nana prayed aloud to Ussen. "May we avenge Victorio and kill all our enemies," he entreated. "Will you give us the White Eyes' *nantan* named Hatch so that we may shoot him in the head? Will you let us trap the buffalo soldiers and enemy scouts and kill them all?"

Then the dancers returned to their place by the fire and were served more *tizwin* by Guyan. The Dreamer took over the prayer duties from

Nana and began calling out to the men individually—the only time the Tcihene were directly addressed by their names.

"Kaytennae, they say to you—you, you! They call you again and again!, Kaytennae, get up and go fight the enemy!"

Kaytennae leaped to his feet again, rifle in hand, and began to dance alone before the fire. "Kaytennae," yelled The Dreamer. "You are a man, a great warrior! What are you going to do when we fight the enemy?" Without missing a step, Kaytennae responded by firing his rifle into the air four times.

"Mangus, they say to you—you, you," The Dreamer continued, "You are the warrior who will avenge his father! What will you do when we fight the enemy?" Mangus, confused by the *peyotl* and still shocked by the apparition of his father, nevertheless stumbled to his feet, fired his rifle into the air and then joined Kaytennae in the fierce dancing.

The Dreamer called every man by name to the dance, plus Lozen, and all responded—thus pledging their loyalty to the war of vengeance. The last person called was Nana, who gave the drum to the shaman as his name was called. "Kas-Tziden, they say to you—you, you! You who were Victorio's *segundo*, you who now lead the Tcihene, what will you do when you meet the White Eyes?"

Nana struggled to his feet and fired his revolver four times and then joined the men in the dance. There was no trace of his limp while he danced, a fact that was later attributed to the Power of the *peyotl*.

The fierce dancing continued long into the night, fueled by the potent combination of the cactus and the corn beer. Toward dawn, the fierce dancing was replaced with social dancing and the three women of the band joined in as partners to the weary men. By that time the hallucinations had subsided, but the memories of Victorio's appearance in the night sky would never fade.

During the days that followed the fierce dancing, Nana organized his band to prepare for war and told everyone the complete plan: Except for Lozen, the women and young children would be sent to Juh's stronghold; fifteen warriors and the novice Istee would leave with him for the Mescalero Reservation. There they would get permission from the chief, Natzili, to enter and recruit reinforcements. They would pick up supplies from Victorio's cache in the San Andres mountains, trade the gold and silver for more weapons, build up their forces, kill every White Eye they could find, and regain their homeland. Nana and the war party would rejoin the women and children at Juh's stronghold, where they would hold a Dance of the Mountain Spirits. Then he would triumphantly lead them all back to Ojo Caliente. In spite of the fact that the war party had but sixteen men and they were led by an elderly, crippled chief, not one of the Tcihene questioned Nana's ability to carry out the plan.

The band responded to Nana's plan by readying their weapons. Although most of the Tcihene warriors carried revolvers or rifles, they also prepared their traditional fighting gear—bows and arrows, wrist-guards, war clubs, and stone knives. Some of the men fashioned war-caps made from buckskin and eagle feathers that were tied with strings under the chin.

Because this was to be a war of vengeance, Nana showed them how to make poison for the points of their arrows. He took a bloody, rotted deer's spleen and mixed the putrid mess with nettles, and prickly pear spines. Then Nana turned over some rotting logs, located some spiders, and crushed them with his feet. As he stepped on them he said, "Hatch killed you, spider," because he hoped that the spider clan would retaliate against someone outside the band.

He carefully added the crushed spiders to the spleen mixture and mixed it well. They would carry the poison in a little sack made from the deer's large intestine and apply it when needed to their arrows. If a poisoned arrow even scratched an enemy, he told them, it would cause terrible swelling, the wound would turn black, and the enemy would die within hours.

"If only a pregnant woman would fart in it," joked Nana, "it would really be deadly."

The Dreamer played a very important role in the war preparations. He fashioned the small sacks of pollen each warrior would carry with him for protection, and supervised the communing with the supernatural in order for each man to gain "enemies-against Power." Early one morning The Dreamer was singing and praying with a group of warriors who had consulted him when an owl flew over the camp from the south.

"Oh no," said Istee, "we are being visited by the Ghost of the Evil Dead. My father used to say that is a sign that someone is going to die."

"He was right," replied The Dreamer. "See how the owl is flying north to find the White Eyes. It is leaving our camp and visiting theirs."

Istee was the only novice in the war party, so The Dreamer fashioned a special war-cap for him that was covered with hummingbird feathers for swiftness. He also gave Istee a special drinking-tube and a scratching-stick with lightning designs painted on it.

Then he instructed Istee about the proper behavior during the war of vengeance. "Drink only from the tube and scratch only with this stick or your skin will turn soft. You may not turn around quickly—you must carefully look over your shoulder first. You can only eat cold food—never warm. Novices are never allowed to laugh, and you must always stay awake until you are given permission to sleep. And remember," The Dreamer added with a smile, "no sex with anyone while you are out with the war party."

The Dreamer taught him the eighty mystical euphemisms he was to use instead of common words: arrows were "missiles of death," the owl was "he who wanders about by night," and the heart was called "that by means of which I live." The ceremonial words would protect the boy from danger, he explained, and the warriors would refer to him as Child of the Water.

The women prepared food for the war party: dried prickly pear and mescal cakes, jerked meat, which was dried venison with juniper berries and *chiltepines* pounded into it, and a special treat of Guyan's invention which combined *piñon* nuts, yucca fruit, and honey into a sort of candy that was so sticky that each piece had to be individually wrapped in green oak leaves.

Finally, after nearly a week of preparation, the war party was ready to leave the stronghold in the Blue Mountains. The rest of the band—all five of them—assembled to watch the warriors ride off. The war party consisted of Nana, The Dreamer, thirteen warriors, and the novice Istee. All were mounted, and they led two mules and two horses as pack animals to carry ammunition, food, and water skins. Istee waved goodbye to his friend Kaywaykla.

Nana retrieved his sack of pollen from the wickiup and tied it to his medicine cord, which was draped across his body from right shoulder to left side in the manner of a Killer of Enemies bandolier. He filled his ammunition pouch with bullets for his Winchester and then mounted his horse, faced his men, and recited a prayer.

I am calling on sky and earth.
Bats will fly with me in battle.
Black sky will embrace me with protection,
And earth will do this also.

Without further ceremony, the old man urged his horse to the northeast and his war party followed. He did not wave to Nah-des-te or meet her eyes because it was unseemly to show emotion at that time, and because he had said farewell to her the previous evening. He knew she would be waiting for him at Juh's stronghold.

As soon as they were out of sight of the camp, Nana gestured to Kaytennae and Lozen. The two warriors knew what to do without Nana having to speak a word. They would scout far ahead of the main party and report back at sunset—or earlier if they spotted the enemy. Nana chose Kaytennae because of his extensive raiding experience and Lozen because of her Power to locate enemies. Then he gestured to Sánchez and Mangus to scout their rear flanks, a task that would become more important after they left the safety of the high peaks of the Blue Mountains.

Because he did not wish to antagonize the Mexican villagers who lived close to the stronghold, in the foothills to the east of the Blue Mountains, Nana avoided the settlements for two days.

He was tempted to raid a ranch near Casas Grandes, but since they were well supplied, he decided to wait until they were closer to the Rio Grande. It was standard Tcihene practice to raid in Mexico and escape to the United States; or raid in Arizona, New Mexico or Texas and then flee to Mexico. Nana knew that usually each country's soldiers were required to stay on their own side of the border.

On the morning of the third day, Nana requested that Lozen use her Power to find the enemy. She agreed, left the camp, and climbed to the top of a nearby rock formation. With her eyes closed, Lozen stretched her arms wide, palms up and hands cupped, and slowly turned around to address each of the four directions. As she revolved, she sang a prayer.

Ussen has Power
Over everything in this world.
Sometimes he shares it
With those of us here.
He has loaned me his Power
For the benefit of my people.
This Power is good
As He is good.
I use this Power
For the good of my people.

Lozen stopped turning when she faced east. "My palms are tingling now, very strong," she called to Nana. "The enemy is there, to the east. White Eyes."

"White Eyes?" Nana questioned. "But we are in Mexico."

"White Eyes," insisted Lozen.

Nana, who respected her Power, did not question her again. Instead, he turned to Kaytennae and said, "Locate the White Eyes and return so that we can plan our attack."

Kaytennae left and later rejoined the war party. He told Nana that the enemy force consisted of four White Eyes and one Mexican—and that none of them seemed to be armed.

"What are they doing?"

"One of them looks through a far-sight mounted on some sticks," replied Kaytennae, who had no idea what the enemy was doing. "The others are pounding sticks into the ground."

"That is what they do before they build a road or railroad tracks," said Nana. "Tell me what the land looks like where they are going."

After Kaytennae described the landscape, Nana divided the war party into two groups. Kaytennae would take seven warriors, skirt ahead of the enemy, and hide in some small hills close to the road. Nana and the rest of the Tchihene would chase the enemy into the ambush.

They rode hard to reach the enemy quickly. Instead of stalking the White Eyes and then surprising them, Nana began shooting from quite a distance away, which gave the four White Eyes and the Mexican teamster time to climb into the wagon and drive off in panic. Nana laughed as the loaded wagon lumbered away and then gave the signal for pursuit. They chased the wagon right into Kaytennae's ambush. The warriors leaped from their hiding place and quickly shot the lead mules, which caused the rest of the team to stumble over them. The wagon left the road and turned over, killing the teamster instantly. The White Eyes managed to leap off the wagon, but they didn't get far. Lozen shot two of them in the back, and the other two were quickly dispatched by Kaytennae and Mangus.

Nana arrived and quickly surveyed the battle scene. "Make certain they are dead," he ordered, and Lozen calmly fired one bullet into the back of the head of each White Eye. Then the Tcihene looted the corpses and the wrecked wagon for anything they might need. Nana found another gold watch chain, which he immediately looped through his right ear lobe.

"This is the road the stagecoach takes between Chihuahua and Paso del Norte," Kaytennae reminded Nana.

"Then maybe we should look for a stagecoach," said the old man, who led the war party south.

A half-day's ride south of the wagon wreck, the Tcihene spotted dust in the sky, which usually indicated a stage, a wagon, or at least several horses. This time Nana did not split up his band, but rather stationed all of them on one side of the road, hidden among the rocks. If a stage came by, they would attack. But if the dust was caused by heavily-armed Mexican soldiers, they could let them pass by or attack, depending upon the size of the patrol. While they waited, they ate dried *mescal* cakes and some of Guyan's *piñon*-honey candy.

Thirty minutes later, Mangus, who was the lookout stationed in the rocks high above, called to Nana that the dust was caused by a stagecoach. Nana told his warriors to shoot the horses first and then the men driving the stage. When the stagecoach passed by the rocks, a volley of rifle shots felled the lead horses and the driver, causing the stage to veer into a large rock and crush its right front wheel. Nana's men lost no time in shooting the conductor and one of the male passengers who had pulled out a revolver.

Another male passenger and two women in the stage were not harmed during the initial attack but they were obviously terrified. Hesitant to kill the unarmed women, Kaytennae gave the order to stop fighting until Nana decided what to do. The Mexican man in the stagecoach pleaded in Spanish, "Don't kill us, please. We mean you no harm."

Sánchez, who had lived with Mexicans for a few years and knew the language, translated the plea for Nana, who seemed to find it amusing. "Kill him," he ordered, "but let the women live to tell the story of the vengeance of the Tcihene." Sánchez then shot the passenger between the eyes. The warriors ransacked the stagecoach and searched the bodies of the dead, but found little of value except two axes, which they took. They freed the one uninjured horse from its traces, joined it to their pack train, and rode off to the south.

That night they camped along the upper Rio del Carmen, and in case the Mexican soldiers had picked up their trail, Nana posted three lookouts at all times and would not allow a fire to be built. For entertainment and inspiration, Nana and The Dreamer told the war party the best stories of the exploits of the three war chiefs who had returned from the dead.

Early the next day, after he sang his morning song, Nana told his warriors, "I have always wanted to kill a train. Let us find one."

They broke camp and headed back toward the railroad tracks that paralleled the stagecoach road. Nana sent Mangus and Istee south to locate an appropriate lookout spot and gave instructions for them to flash the mirror four times when they spotted a train heading north. He and Kaytennae would then lead the ambush. After the scouting party left, Nana lost no time in selecting the location for the battle. He found a short wooden trestle crossing a shallow arroyo, then directed his warriors to chop down the support posts with the axes they had found in the stagecoach. It was a long and tedious job because there were as many posts as the fingers on four hands, but they worked steadily in shifts until the trestle no longer had any supports.

They waited patiently until sunset, but no signal came. Nana sent for Mangus and Istee, and the Tcihene camped beside the tracks that night. The following day, Nana posted his lookouts again. The rest of the war party waited until the sun was high in the sky before the flashing signal from the south alerted them that a train was approaching. Nana ordered Sánchez to take the pack train and horses out of gunshot range, and then stationed his men high in the rocks, warning them not to leave cover unless he gave the signal. He said he was cautious because sometimes Mexican soldiers were aboard the trains.

The locomotive pulling eight freight cars rounded the curve and approached the trestle. When the locomotive crossed it, the tracks collapsed and the locomotive smashed through to the ground below. The rest of the cars were jammed up and thrown off the tracks in a huge, thunderous crash. Nana and Kaytennae exchanged appreciative glances at the destruction. In a few moments, when some of the railroad men left the train to inspect the damage, Nana gave the signal to fire.

From their excellent position, the Tcihene rained down a withering hailstorm of bullets that immediately felled five of the Mexicans. The remaining men took cover and returned the fire, but were unable to spot the well-concealed Tcihene warriors among the rocks. Then a group of about twenty Mexican soldiers emerged from the last wrecked freight car, spread out, and began to work their way up the rocks. They were heavily armed and Nana knew that if the battle went on much longer, the soldiers and the remaining railroad men could circle their position and pin them down. In the Tcihene manner of striking quickly and then retreating to avoid losses, he gave the signal and his band withdrew from the rocks and joined Sánchez with the pack train and their horses.

During the retreat, Lozen took up the rear position and managed to wound two of the soldiers; and Nana praised her courage. They joined up with Mangus and Istee and rode hard toward the northeast in order to put as much distance as they could between themselves and the soldiers.

That night they camped high in the small, desolate mountain range the Mexicans called Sierra Borracho, which overlooked the green Rio Grande valley. Nana was in great spirits; in the last few days they had killed at least twelve of the enemy without even one of the Tcihene being wounded. He even permitted a small fire to be built to roast the jackrabbits that Istee had shot with arrows.

"Now that I have killed my train," he told his war party, "it is time to go to Mescalero. The Mexican soldiers will soon be on our trail, but we will cross the river before they get close."

The following day, The Dreamer sang the Prayer to the Great River and then the Tcihene war party waded across the shallow Rio Grande near Fort Quitman, Texas. For Nana's band, the time of the year was now known as Large Leaves. According to the calendar of the White Eyes, the date was July 13, 1881.

Dunes of Gypsum.

3. White Sands

"Interesting reading, General?" asked Captain Loud. He and Hatch were drinking coffee and breakfasting on *huevos rancheros* in the dining room of the Exchange Hotel while the general perused the *Daily New Mexican*, which was his morning ritual. Loud's question had been prompted by a serious look on the face of his commanding officer.

Hatch was dressed in the dark blue suit that many officers wore instead of a uniform when they were stationed at a peaceful garrison such as Santa Fe. Only the shoulder straps gave any indication whatsoever that he was in the Army. He rubbed his mustache and frowned.

"The surgeons had to open another hole in the President's back to release what they call 'laudable pus,'" reported the general. Ever since an assassin had shot President Garfield on July second, newspapers had been publishing daily reports on his condition, which seemed to be worsening.

"I don't think he's going to make it," said Loud.

"There are a couple of humorous stories here too, Captain. The first concerns our old friend Billy. Surely you remember his threat to come up here and shoot Lew Wallace—"

"How could I forget posting guards all around the Plaza? And waiting—hell, praying—for him to show up?"

"Well, Captain, Lew doesn't have to worry about the Kid finding him in Constantinople. That trigger-happy sheriff Pat Garrett finally tracked Billy down at Fort Sumner and killed him—in bed—that's the funny part. But listen to this obituary: 'No sooner had the floor caught his descending form that had a pistol in one hand and a knife in the other, than there was a strong odor of brimstone in the air, and a dark figure with wings of a dragon, claws like a tiger, eyes like balls of fire, and horns like a bison, hovered over the corpse for a moment, and with a fiendish laugh said, "Ha, ha! This is my meat!" and then sailed off through the window. He did not leave his card, but he is a gentleman well known to us by reputation, and thereby hangs a "tail."' Now, Captain, what do you make of that?"

Loud chuckled and shook his head. "Sounds like a bunch of bullshit to me."

"The imagination of journalists never ceases to amaze me. Here's the other humorous item, an editorial about how peaceful New Mexico has been since the death of Victorio. Greene writes, 'It is not very probable that there are any Apache in this territory to disturb the citizens.' Imagine that."

"Ah," agreed Loud, "the eternal optimist. Undoubtedly you inspired him with your speech last Christmas."

"Things change," Hatch observed dryly. "Any word from the south?"

"Just confirmations of the first reports. A small band of Apaches attacked and killed the Upham survey crew in Chihuahua, then ambushed a stagecoach, and then had the gall to derail a passenger train. Ten killed, three wounded. Apache casualties apparently zero. Terrazas' men couldn't catch 'em this time."

"Was it Nana?" Hatch's question sounded innocent enough, but Loud knew he was seething inside.

"Not confirmed as yet, but the Mexicans think so. One of the women who survived the stagecoach attack described the Apache leader as being very old and wearing a watch chain from his ear lobe."

"That's got to be him," said Hatch. "Damn it all, Guilfoyle was right. Who could believe that senile savage is on the warpath again? How many men did he have with him?"

"About fifteen, sir, according to the witnesses."

"He's got to be on his way to Mescalero for reinforcements. Have you heard from Guilfoyle?"

"Not since he left Fort Cummings days ago with Frank Bennett and his scouts. He should be getting close to the Mescalero agency by now."

"Well, I certainly hope they catch the old fart before he does any damage in the territory. We'd never hear the end of it."

"Bennett's scouts are excellent, General," Loud assured him. "Apaches can always find other Apaches."

"Too bad Garrett killed Billy the Kid," mused Hatch. "We might have recruited him to go after Nana. Governor Sheldon could have offered to pardon Billy if he captured or killed the old chief."

Despite the fact he had known him for three years, Loud could not tell if the general was serious or not.

Two hundred miles due south of Santa Fe, Lieutenant John Guilfoyle estimated that by noon the temperature had reached at least one hundred degrees in the shade—and that was a big problem, the lack of shade to escape the sun. Although his troop of Indian scouts rarely used tents while on the trail, he had ordered sheets of canvas strung between several tall yuccas to create some shade for his men. All eight of his Apache scouts of Company B were sprawled beneath one awning, waiting for his orders. A short distance away, his black troopers were resting under a second canvas. Guilfoyle and chief-of-scouts Frank Bennett were resting under a third awning nearby.

Under orders from Colonel Hatch, they had ridden from Fort Cummings in the direction of Mescalero, with instructions to track down and intercept renegade Apaches believed to have attacked a stagecoach and train in Chihuahua. Along the way, Bennett, a sarcastic but experienced chief-of-scouts, had taken several of the scouts, left the main group, and checked some old Apache camps in the West Potrillo and Organ Mountains, but had found nothing. It had been Bennett's suggestion to search Dog Canyon, which was the reason they were camped near its mouth in the searing heat.

"Have you heard the stories about Dog Canyon, Lieutenant?" asked Bennett, who was perspiring profusely, his soiled blue shirt soaked through.

"Can't say I have," answered Guilfoyle.

Bennett reached into his boot and retrieved a long plug of chewing tobacco and bit off a piece. "That's not surprisin', seeing as you're new to these parts. It's what you call a box canyon," Bennett explained as he chewed furiously. "Not supposed to be any way out of it. It's been a Mescalero stronghold for ages, and they used it as headquarters for raids on ranches in the Tularosa Valley. Finally things got so bad about twenty years ago that Colonel Kit Carson was called in—he was over at the Bosque Redondo at the time. He actually beat the Mescaleros and cleaned out Dog Canyon—for a while."

"But how did it get that name?"

"Well, a few years after Carson left, the raids started again and a bunch of these damned ranchers decided to try their hand at soldierin'. They formed up a vigilante force and chased a band of Mescaleros into that canyon right over there. They figured that since it was a box canyon, the Apaches must be trapped in there."

"Makes sense," said Guilfoyle.

"Not really, if you know Apaches," countered Bennett. "When the ranchers rode into the canyon, guess what they found."

"A dog?"

"You easterners are right smart. Yep, just a dog. The Mescaleros had disappeared. They knew all the secret trails."

Guilfoyle took a long drink out of his canteen. "So you think that the renegades might be camped there?"

Bennett shrugged. "Might be. Worth a look-see, Lieutenant."

"How much time do you need? We should contact the agency at Mescalero."

"A day anyway. Let me take the Apaches and search the canyon. Send the wagon and two of the troopers to Mescalero for food and to find out if there's any new orders from Santa Fe. You stay here with the rest of the men and we'll be back by sunset." Bennett spat a long stream of tobacco juice at a nearby horse-crippler cactus.

Guilfoyle wondered if Bennett was deliberately trying to protect him, but decided that the plan was a good one. After all, Bennett had seen extensive action against the Apaches and he had not. Besides, there was no real hurry to get to Mescalero, and if Dog Canyon was a former stronghold, it needed to be searched. "I'll give the orders," he told Bennett.

The search of Dog Canyon proved fruitless; and when Bennett returned, he told Guilfoyle that not even a dog had been found this time. After spending another day searching the area for signs of the renegades, they broke camp and moved north toward Sierra Blanca and the Mescalero agency.

They had just passed by the tiny town of Tularosa when one of the packers, a black soldier named Carter Smith, approached them from the east, riding a mule as fast as it would go. When he was within earshot, he shouted, "Sir, sir, those damned Apaches done attacked us and gone and shot Packer Burgess," which sounded to Guilfoyle like, "Sah, sah, dose damn 'Paches done tacks us an' gone an' shot Packah Buhgiss."

Guilfoyle immediately ordered his troop to ride hard toward Alamo Canyon, where the attack had occurred. Along the way, Smith told him what had happened. They were on their way back to the camp at Dog Canyon with fresh vegetables and beef when the Apaches, hidden among the rocks, had opened fire on the small pack train. One mule and Burgess had been shot immediately; Smith had managed to find cover and return the fire. The Apaches apparently were not determined to fight for very long, because they disappeared after capturing three of the loaded mules. Bennett believed they were looking for ammunition.

At Alamo Canyon they found Packer Burgess still alive, though seriously wounded by a bullet in his thigh. He insisted he had killed two Apaches, but a thorough search of the area by Bennett's scouts turned up no evidence of any Apache casualties. They loaded Burgess aboard the wagon and took him to the Mescalero agency, which was only a few miles north.

As they rode into the beautiful valley of the Tularosa, Guilfoyle was amazed by the single spot of civilization in the vast wilderness. The agency headquarters at Blazer's Mill looked as if it should have been back east somewhere. The ten or so buildings had pitched roofs—a far cry from the usual adobe structures in the territory. The agency grounds were neatly groomed and surrounded by white picket fences, and it was difficult to imagine that it was in the middle of an Indian reservation.

Guilfoyle led his men to the agency clinic, where an orderly began to dress the packer's wound, which he termed "very serious." At the agency office, William Llewellen, the Indian agent in charge at Mescalero, was clearly irritated by the presence of Guilfoyle's troop in his domain. He complained to Guilfoyle that everything had been peaceful until his scouts had arrived.

"I'm under orders from General Hatch to track down renegades," protested Guilfoyle.

"This reservation is a sanctuary, Lieutenant," snapped Llewellen, who was dressed—incredibly—in a suit and tie. "So-called renegades surrender here for protection, but they won't if the U.S. Army is hounding them all the time."

"Those 'so-called' renegades just shot one of my men and you're going to help him, by God. Now, where's that telegraph?"

Grudgingly, Llewellen wired General Hatch in Santa Fe about the attack on Guilfoyle's pack train. While he was waiting for a reply, Bennett entered the agency office and told Guilfoyle he had to talk to him privately. They went outside and spoke near the corral.

"The leader of the renegades is Nana," Bennett told him.

"How do you know that?"

"Some of these Mescaleros told my chief scout, Chihuahua. They said Nana was leading a band of Victorio's men—survivors of the Tres

Castillos battle."

"Oh, shit."

"It's worse than shit," insisted Bennett. "It seems that about twenty-five Mescaleros have deserted the agency here and are riding with Nana."

"Where did they go after the Alamo Canyon attack?"

Bennett shrugged. "¿Quien sabe?"

Guilfoyle and Bennett entered the agency office and the lieutenant requested that Llewellen send the news to Hatch. The agent said, "See what I mean? Look at the trouble you're causing. I order you to leave this reservation."

"I remind you, sir," Guilfoyle said stiffly, "that you are no longer a major in the Army but rather a civilian."

Llewellen turned as if to leave the office but his way was blocked by Bennett, who drew his knife out of its sheath and snarled, "Look here, Mr. Agent, if I hear one more word out of you, I'm going to stick this up your ass. Now send that goddamn telegram."

"Calm down, Bennett," Guilfoyle ordered, but he was pleased to note that Llewellen's face had turned white with fear. He moved away from the door and over to the telegraph table, where he tapped out the message Guilfoyle dictated.

The reply from Hatch arrived fifteen minutes later and directed Guilfoyle to take twenty troopers from Company L, which was stationed at the agency, and pursue Nana. "The renegade is probably headed to Hembrillo Canyon in the San Andres," said the wire. "Victorio had a cache of supplies there."

At the agency barracks, Guilfoyle showed the telegram to Sergeant Moses Williams, the commander of the small, peace-keeping contingent. Williams, a tall, broad-shouldered black man with graying hair, seemed pleased by the break in routine. "When do we leave, sah?" he asked with a grin. "It shore can git borin' 'round here."

"Immediately. Saddle up your men, Sergeant," ordered Guilfoyle. "The renegades already have a head start."

"Immediately" proved to be nearly two hours later because rations, trail gear, and ammunition had to be located and packed. During the delay, Guilfoyle located Llewellen and apologized for Bennett's knife display, but the Indian agent was still uncooperative.

"I don't like to be threatened, Lieutenant," he said. "I'm reporting this incident to Washington."

Guilfoyle had neither the time nor patience to deal with the man. "Say hello to President Garfield for me."

Llewellen eyed Guilfoyle with malice. "You realize that Nana was probably on his way here to surrender and your forces scared him away."

"That's nonsense," Guilfoyle snapped, finally losing his patience with the agent. "That old man's band just killed ten people down in Mexico— quite a start at surrendering, wouldn't you say? Now your orderly told me you don't have surgical facilities here to remove the bullet from Burgess, so I expect you to transport him to Fort Stanton to receive medical attention."

Llewellen made a dismissive gesture. "I'll wire them and they can send a wagon for him."

"Forget it," snapped Guilfoyle, who left the agency office to find Sergeant Williams.

The sergeant was in the corral directing the saddling of the horses and the loading of the mules. There would be no supply wagon on this pursuit. Guilfoyle directed him to detach two men from his garrison to transport Burgess to Fort Stanton. Finally, his force—although undoubtedly outnumbered by Nana's war party—was ready to take up the chase.

In Alamo Canyon, the scout Chihuahua was able to pick up the trail of the renegades, and soon Guilfoyle found himself retracing their path of earlier that morning. In fact, to his amazement, the trail led them back to Dog Canyon, where Bennett's scouts soon discovered the remnants of the renegades' camp. It was hidden in an arroyo, but was just two miles from their own camp at the spring near the mouth of the canyon.

"Tell me, Bennett, how come your scouts can find this camp now but they couldn't locate it yesterday?"

The chief-of-scouts looked embarrassed and asked the same question of Chihuahua. The stone-faced Apache replied in his dialect and some broken English that Nana's trail had led them to the camp; before, they had been unable to cross any sign of the renegades.

"He also says that Nana's men made no fire," explained Bennett, but Guilfoyle was not convinced.

"Let's move out," he ordered sharply, and his troop galloped off to the south, following the road to Las Cruces. Nana's band had made no effort at all to disguise their trail and seemed to be riding hard in the direction of the San Andres range, as Hatch had predicted.

Guilfoyle's troop rode hard in the extreme heat of the late afternoon for about ten miles and then spotted the tiny settlement of Laguna Springs on the edge of the dunes known as the White Sands. Suddenly, they heard gunshots ahead, and hoping to save anyone still alive there by scaring off the Apaches, Guilfoyle ordered his men to commence firing.

At a fast gallop the scouts and buffalo soldiers stormed into the compound, which consisted of two run-down adobe houses and a corral. There were no Apaches in sight, but they had left gruesome evidence of their recent visit.

Two Mexican men lay dead in the corral—apparently they had tried to prevent Nana's warriors from stealing their horses. Both men had not only been shot, but also their bodies had been mutilated. To Guilfoyle, whose stomach was queasy, it was obvious that the renegades had worked over the bodies with knives, for their clothes were in tatters and there were deep gashes all over their torsos and legs. Although they had not been scalped, the victims had been castrated.

"My god," Guilfoyle said to Bennett, "I always heard that Apaches never did this sort of thing."

"They do now," Bennett replied dryly.

"Ask Chihuahua what's going on," ordered Guilfoyle, and Bennett called the scout over to the bodies.

Chihuahua glanced at the mutilated corpses and said just two words: "Mangas Coloradas."

"What does he mean?" asked Guilfoyle. "Mangas has been dead for years."

"That's the point, sir," Bennett replied. "After our troopers killed

Mangas in Arizona, they cut off his head and boiled it down to just a skull. I heard some doctor wanted to study it. This mutilation is the Apaches' revenge for Mangas."

They were interrupted by a call from Sergeant Williams, who was inspecting one of the houses. They left the corral and entered the small adobe structure, only to discover another horrible sight. Sprawled on the dirt floor was the body of a young Mexican woman. Her throat had been cut and her breasts had been sliced off.

Guilfoyle nearly vomited but managed to control his stomach. "Those bastards can't be far away. Let's go."

"What about buryin' these folks?" asked Sergeant Williams.

"That's what the Apaches expect us to do—while they get away. Give the order to move out."

"Yes, sah."

They left the house and were hailed by one of the scouts, who had climbed the windmill on Bennett's order. From his vantage point, he had spotted Nana's band in the white dunes.

Guilfoyle's quickly mounted and gave chase east through the gypsum sand. Guilfoyle, Bennett, and the Apache scouts took the lead, with Williams and the pack mules following as quickly as possible. Although it didn't seem possible to Guilfoyle that the horses could move through the dunes that towered as high as forty feet, the path of the renegades weaved among them on relatively stable terrain. Above the dunes towered the San Andres range, where purple clouds indicated a fierce thunderstorm was raging. The force of the storm was already being felt in the dunes as the wind whipped the tops of the dunes.

"Do any of your scouts know this area?" he shouted at Bennett. When Bennett nodded yes, Guilfoyle gestured in a sweeping motion of his arm for a flanking movement and his chief-of-scouts detached Chihuahua and five others to angle southeast in an attempt to cut off Nana's band. The tactic probably saved the lives of some of his men, because it disrupted an ambush.

About half of Nana's warriors were hidden in the dunes along the faint trail when Chihuahua's men literally stumbled across them—just moments before Guilfoyle's force arrived at the trap. Confused, the Tcihene and Mescalero fighters fired a few wild shots at the scouts and then broke from cover, mounted their horses and rode west toward the mountains. The scouts rejoined Guilfoyle's main force and, sensing victory, pushed their mounts to the limit and gained on the renegades.

Several volleys of shots were exchanged between the combatants, but none found their marks. Guilfoyle cursed aloud in frustration at their inability to catch the renegades, who would be in their sights one minute and obscured by the dunes the next. He was also worried about three factors completely beyond his control: the increasing wind of a thunderstorm, the approaching sunset, and the fact that their horses were giving out.

Suddenly they came across eight of the renegades' horses milling about in confusion, and for a moment Guilfoyle feared another ambush. But when no shots came, he halted his force and captured the horses, knowing he would need them soon. At that moment very high winds struck the dunes and raised a sandstorm that reduced visibility to only a few feet, forcing the pursuers to cover their eyes and noses.

Guilfoyle knew the immediate chase was over and was already planning his strategy of tracking the renegades when the downpour began. Although the intense rain settled the sandstorm, he knew that any tracks left by Nana's band would be obliterated. Bennett rode up to him, a disgusted look on his face. "Looks like Nana and nature outfoxed us this time," he said. "Orders, sir?"

"We'll wait here for Williams and the rest of the men," Guilfoyle directed as the rain dripped off the brim of his cap. "Call Sergeant Chihuahua over here."

Bennett gestured to his scout and the drenched Apache approached. "Ask him if he knows the location of Hembrillo Canyon."

As Bennett asked the question both in English and broken Apache dialect, the expression never changed on Chihuahua's face. He merely shook his head negatively. "I don't think he places the name with the location, Lieutenant. The Apaches don't use the same names for places that we do."

"It's the canyon where Victorio escaped from Hatch," Guilfoyle persisted, and was rewarded by a faint smile on Chihuahua's face.

"I know it," said the scout. "Victorio fool the White Eyes there."

"Don't say that," Bennett warned Chihuahua. "I don't allow them to use that insultin' term," he explained to Guilfoyle, who noticed that Chihuahua's eyes were gray, almost blue.

"Let's head to Hembrillo," ordered Guilfoyle. Within a half-hour Sergeant Williams and the rest of the troopers with the pack train had caught up, and Chihuahua led the soaked Army units out of the white dunes and into the foothills of the San Andres.

Up in Santa Fe, conditions were much more comfortable. The sky was clear and the temperature was in the low eighties at 5:30 when Edward Hatch walked the two blocks between his office and his house. As usual, he found Evelyn in the kitchen. She was attempting to construct a salad, but her efforts were hindered by the two kittens she had rescued from a coyote. The two tabby littermates were having a wrestling match between Evelyn's feet.

"Got some help there, I see," he said as he kissed her on the cheek.

"They're into *everything*," Evelyn replied with mock outrage.

"Have you named them yet?" he asked as he poured himself a shot of Jack Daniels. He removed his jacket and took a seat at the kitchen table.

"Because they're both so pushy, I decided to call them Grant and Sherman."

Hatch laughed. "My former commanders would be honored, I'm sure."

"How was your day?"

"Let's see. I reviewed the troops."

"And they're still there."

"They're still there. Look just the same as always. Then I had a meeting with Governor Sheldon."

"Oh?" Evelyn raised her eyebrows because she knew that her husband did not particularly like the new governor.

"It was uneventful," the general explained. "I told him about renegade activity down south but he didn't seem very interested. All he wanted to talk about was statehood. Six weeks in office and already he's tired of being governor of a mere territory."

"He's a nice man and you should give him the benefit of the doubt," Evelyn advised.

"Oh, I received a letter from Lew Wallace today."

"You did?" asked a surprised Evelyn. "Where is it? Why are you keeping it from me?"

"All right, all right," he said, pulling an envelope out of his jacket pocket. "All the way from Constantinople. Here, I'll read it to you.

"Dear Edward and Evelyn, I am getting along pretty well here. As you know, every American is supposed to be equal to any office, or rather the requirements of every position; but to me diplomacy was a new business to be learned *ab initio*. I do not believe men are born to anything; art, poetry, oratory, the counting of money—mastery comes only by long study and practice. And I have acted on my belief in this matter and have tried to profit by the mistakes of others.

"The Sultan Abdul Hamid is very friendly. He sent, a few days ago, to inquire if I was fond of riding, and to ask if I would accept the present of an Arabian stallion. Of course, I had to refuse because of the law prohibiting ambassadors from the acceptance of valuable gifts.

"Then, while I was off touring the Blue Mosque, the sultan sent over a beautiful golden-haired slave girl—and a note, which Mrs. Wallace opened, thinking that the slave was intended for her use. The note said, 'I am sending this lovely creature with my compliments. I trust she will be a welcome assistance in your daily toilette. She will gladly assist you in your bath.' Needless to say, Mrs. Wallace promptly returned the gift to the sultan."

Evelyn laughed so hard that tears came to her eyes. She could just picture stuffy Susan Wallace being confronted by a harem girl. "Sorry, Edward," she apologized after she recovered from the attack of giggles.

Her husband continued reading. "My dear Edward, before I left Washington, I spoke with President Garfield regarding a new posting for you, and he seemed to be amenable. He told me that as long as the Apache situation remained calm in New Mexico Territory, he was inclined to bring you back east. I trust this situation will occur. Mrs. Wallace sends her dearest regards to Evelyn and sends the message that the shopping in the bazaar is wonderful. Have you finished *Ben-Hur* yet? If so, do write and tell me what you thought of it."

"You haven't read a chapter yet," Evelyn accused.

"Wrong. I've read three chapters."

"And how many pages is that?"

"Thirteen."

"But the book is over five hundred pages long," teased Evelyn, who had finished the book months earlier.

Hatch shook his head. "I truly respect Lew Wallace both as friend and author, but his novel is boring."

"That's because you wish it began with a battle. Just give it a chance."

The general retreated from his position and regrouped. "You're right, dear. I should finish it and write a letter back to Lew. I shall confront this task in an orderly manner and read exactly fifty pages per day. No more, no less. Then I shall be done in less than two weeks."

"That's the spirit, Edward. Attack the novel as if it were an enemy position."

"Precisely," agreed the general in his best military voice.

"It was nice of Lew to speak to President Garfield," Evelyn said.

"But since he's been shot, all bets are off."

"Maybe he'll recover."

"My wife, the eternal optimist," Hatch said, kissing her on the forehead.

Later that night, Hatch was short of his reading goal by twenty-six pages when he fell asleep in his favorite chair in the living room. The novel *Ben-Hur* was open on his chest and Hatch's finger rested on the line where Joseph says to the Rabbi, "I am a carpenter and Nazareth is a village."

Guilfoyle's troop was camped beside a small stream only a few miles from the white sands. The climb had been rough, and darkness had overtaken them long before they could reach their goal of Hembrillo Canyon. Rather than risk the steep trail at night, Guilfoyle had decided to regroup, rest, and catch up with Nana the following day.

Private Jefferson Woods, the black orderly assigned as cook, had served up the usual dinner of salt pork, hard bread, boiled beans with dried chiles, and black, bitter coffee. The Apache scouts refused to touch the food, preferring *mescal* cakes and the tough, sun-dried beef they had acquired at the Mescalero agency.

After the meal, the camp split up into its three factions. The scouts built their own fire away from the black troopers, but Guilfoyle was amused by the fact that both groups were playing the same card game, coon-kan, using coffee beans and cartridges for chips and wagering tobacco and silver coins.

Guilfoyle and Bennett comprised the third faction, and their number that night was increased by one: Sergeant Moses Williams, who had gained their respect with his efficient handling of the pack train. The three officers sat around a third fire discussing possible strategies for outmaneuvering Nana and agreed that the old Apache chief was totally unpredictable.

"I'll drink to that," Bennett said, pulling a flask from his pocket and taking a quick sip. Then he passed it to Guilfoyle, who did likewise and then passed it surreptitiously to Williams. Although drinking while on patrol was against Hatch's specific regulations, none of the officers said a word about it. So long as the scouts and the enlisted men did not get their hands on whiskey, no one would ever know. Guilfoyle wondered where Bennett had bought the liquor—its sale had been forbidden on military property since February.

"As long as we're chasing him, we have to react to what he does," reasoned Guilfoyle. "Unless we can out-guess him and anticipate his movements."

"At least we outnumber them," Bennett said. "It wasn't that way the first time I fought Indians."

"What happened, sah?" asked Williams.

"Well, after the war I was posted to Colorado, where I led scouts against the Cheyenne. Major George Forsyth was in command, and we had about fifty local volunteers. We were patrolling along the Arikaree River when we were ambushed by a huge force of Cheyenne—maybe six hundred or more. We retreated to a sand bar some joker had named Beecher's Island and held them off with concentrated fire. They kept chargin' across the water hopin' to overrun us, but we kept pickin' 'em off one by one. Those bastards kept us pinned down for a week on that goddamn sand bar, but they never took us. We lost eight killed and six wounded before the Cheyenne decided to move on."

"At least they came out in the open and did battle," Guilfoyle said. "Something the Apaches never do."

"That's the truth. Even the Sioux fight like a real army rather than sneaking around like these Apaches."

"Where did you fight the Sioux?"

"Around the Red Cloud agency. I fought under General Crook, and then Colonel Wesley Merritt. Once I even served under Custer."

"Oh?" Guilfoyle knew that most of the men who had served under Custer had died.

"I was reassigned to Merritt's command a few weeks before the Battle of Little Big Horn," the chief of scouts explained. "I got lucky. Then I was transferred to Fort Apache, where I first ran into Chihuahua." He nodded in the direction of the Apache scouts and took another sip from his flask.

Guilfoyle rolled a cigarette and lit it. "I've been meaning to ask you about him. What's his story?"

"He's a Chiricahua, about fifty years old as far as I can tell. Like most of these Apache scouts, he signed on as a scout because he was bored on the reservation and workin' for the Army gave him somethin' to do. He could leave his wife and kid, knowin' that they were safe back on the San Carlos reservation."

"But why do Apaches scout—or fight—against their own kind?"

Bennett grunted in disgust and passed the flask. "When Apache scouts were first recruited, they were used against the Navajos, their enemies, or against other Apache bands. Until now we never used them against their own relatives, but now they're under orders and have no choice. I'm pretty sure that Chihuahua knows Nana. For a while they were both at San Carlos."

"Hell, whose side is he on, anyway?"

"Lieutenant, sometimes I wonder. His enlistment ends the last day of August and I'm bettin' that brave is long gone."

Sergeant Williams smiled in the flickering firelight. "Don't worry 'bout that. Let the Apaches do the scoutin' and my men'll do the fightin'."

"Sounds like you've done quite a bit of that," Guilfoyle said. "What's your story?"

"I was born a free man in Carroll County, Pennsylvania. When I was seventeen I enlisted in the 116th regiment of colored infantry and fought under General Grant in Virginia. I was there at Appomattox when Lee surrendered to him."

"How the hell did you get way out here?"

Before the sergeant could answer, Bennett laughed and said, "He might ask the same question of you, Lieutenant."

"And I'd tell him that the Army sent me here straight from West Point—to punish me. Go ahead, Sergeant."

"After the war was over I got discharged. But Army life was all I had. So I done enlisted in the Ninth Cavalry and was stationed at forts all over the west—Concho, Stockton, Bliss, Quitman, Stanton. I fought the Apaches at Eagle Springs and the Comanches on the Staked Plains. And you know, sah, I ain't ever been wounded, not once."

"And what's your secret to surviving?"

"Don't ride into no ambushes. The Apaches got this trick where they act like they're scared as hell and ride off all in a panic. This happened at Eagle Springs after we drove 'em off the first time. It shore was temptin' to chase 'em, especially since they had jest killed one of my men. But I reckoned that they were leadin' us into an ambush in Buss Canyon. So I foxed 'em by headin' south and made them come to me."

"How did you manage that?" asked Bennett.

Williams grinned. "I guessed them Apaches was raidin', not runnin' away. Near the Rio Grande we met a mule train loaded with Army supplies on the way to Fort Bliss. I told the driver to corral the wagons and use them as bait. When the Apaches attacked the wagons, my men surprised them from the rear and drove 'em all the way into Mexico. Killed six of 'em and only one of my men got wounded."

"Let's hope we get that lucky," said Guilfoyle, accepting the flask once again.

Bennett shook his head and stroked his handlebar mustache. "Williams' fight happened years ago when the Apaches were much stronger. Our problem here is findin' Nana and pinnin' him down. He's on a raid, all right, but he's too smart to stand and fight. He knows we're tailing him, so I don't think he'll turn around and attack us and risk an ambush like the Sergeant was talkin' about. He'll keep his warriors on the run and attack what's *ahead* of 'em, not what's *behind* 'em."

Guilfoyle knew that since he lacked experience in fighting the Apaches, he must depend on the advice of his men. "Sounds too simple to me, but you've been in this position before and I haven't. If you're right, Bennett, I'll buy the drinks at the first bar we happen upon."

"But if I'm wrong?"

"Then the drinks and the girls are on you, providing…."

"Providing we're still alive to enjoy it?" Bennett offered.

"Correct," said the lieutenant.

"It's a wager. You're on, Lieutenant."

"Now let's turn in. We have a hard day tomorrow."

At first light, Private Woods awoke the troop by whistling his version of "Reville" and then began brewing coffee. Refreshed—and with an air of expectancy—the troopers quickly began to break camp, pausing only to wolf down a breakfast of hard bread and cold beans. Lieutenant Guilfoyle, feeling a bit guilty about drinking and fraternizing with his men, adopted his most military manner and gave orders quite formally, almost as if General Hatch were watching his every move.

"Mr. Bennett, kindly inquire of Scout Chihuahua how long it will take to reach Hembrillo Canyon. Sergeant Williams, prepare your men to move out."

Bennett spoke quickly to Chihuahua in a bizarre patois of Spanish, English, and Apache dialect; and then reported back to Guilfoyle. "He says if we ride hard and don't wait for the pack train, maybe four hours. Maybe twice that long if we march at the pace of the mules."

Guilfoyle decided not to risk dividing his force. The pack train would be easy prey for just a few of Nana's warriors, who apparently knew this mountain range very well. If the pack train were captured, his men would be without food and extra ammunition.

"Have Chihuahua take two scouts and ride ahead to locate Nana's camp," the lieutenant ordered. "We'll follow as fast as we can. Tell him as soon as he finds Nana's camp to report back."

"Yes, sir," said the chief-of-scouts, but not before giving Guilfoyle a skeptical look.

After receiving Bennett's orders, Chihuahua nodded to two of his men and they rode off quickly. Guilfoyle made a brief inspection of the camp and when he was satisfied that nothing had been left behind, he shouted, "Mount up!"

Bennett took the lead with the remainder of the Apache scouts, followed by Guilfoyle and most of the buffalo soldiers. The packtrain, guarded by Sergeant Williams and three of his men, completed the cavalcade that began to trot briskly up the trail. Guilfoyle checked his watch and discovered it was only seven o'clock. With any luck at all, he thought, they'd be able to catch up to Nana by early afternoon.

But good fortune was not with them that morning. After just a half-hour on the trail, the mules were spooked by a rattlesnake. The western diamondback—nearly seven feet long—slithered harmlessly across the trail, but the lead jack mule bolted, jerking the lead from the fingers of the packer, and proceeded to scramble down the side of a steep arroyo. Only quick thinking and firm hands by the other packers prevented the rest of the mules from following. Since the lead mule carried most of the spare ammunition, he could not be left behind. Sergeant Williams dispatched five of his men to track down the maverick, who was moving through the chamisa and junipers faster than anyone thought possible.

The soldiers finally caught up with the mule, but not before the animal had managed to shake loose his packs by scraping them against the sharp boulders, breaking the girth in the process. Guilfoyle considered giving the order to shoot the deserter between the eyes, but realized that he needed every available mount. By the time repairs were made, the packs located, and the mule reloaded, they had lost nearly an hour of travel time during the coolest part of the day. Guilfoyle cursed the delay and ever-increasing heat, but there was nothing he could do except push ahead.

When his force finally regained its pace on the trail, Guilfoyle realized that West Point had not prepared him for incidents like that. In fact, although he had taken many classes in military science, not one of them had ever covered the procedures involved in chasing renegade Indians through some the roughest terrain in the country.

But at least he was out in the field doing something rather than being mired for weeks on end in the tedious routine of Fort Cummings. He believed that such boredom was easily as dangerous as chasing Apaches, and he had proof of that conviction. His fellow officer and good friend Bill Taylor was in the brig at Fort Bayard for being drunk on duty, and his former classmate David Ayers had gone mad after discovering a particularly brutal Apache mutilation of a mother and her daughter. Mike Cockey, the assistant surgeon at Fort Cummings, had told him Ayers was hospitalized at St. Elizabeth's sanitarium in Washington with little hope of recovery.

Guilfoyle knew that the danger of battling the Apaches was better than boredom, but it still was not his idea of an ideal military career. He recalled his Christmas visit to Santa Fe, and envied General Hatch for his comparatively luxurious posting and the fact he had his wife by his side and in his bed. That was the worst of it, he decided as he sweated profusely under the fierce New Mexico sun—there were few women around frontier forts. He longed for his fiancee Cathleen, who was a nurse at Johns Hopkins Hospital in his home town, Baltimore. Hell, he thought, he was so lonesome for female companionship he even missed Patty, his girlfriend for a night in Santa Fe.

His reverie was shattered by the voice of Bennett. "Lieutenant! Look over there!"

The chief-of-scouts was pointing to the circling forms of turkey vultures that glided in and out of sight beyond the next ridge. "Take two men and have a look-see," ordered Guilfoyle, who then gave the order to halt and dismount. He knew better than to take any chances with an Apache trick. It would be just like Nana to kill a deer to lure the buzzards, and then attack from the rear while the soldiers were distracted.

Bennett rode up in a few minutes with a grim look on his face. "I think you'd better see this, sir."

"Mount up!" ordered Guilfoyle, and he took the lead of the patrol as it moved up the steep slope. After he cleared the top of the ridge, he could see what appeared to be a mining operation. In a clearing surrounded by junipers was a small shack, a timber-lined opening to a mine shaft, and a run-down adobe furnace. As he moved closer, he spotted what had attracted the buzzards: the blood-smeared, eyeless body of a white man strung upside-down from the headframe of the mine. It was difficult to tell if its wounds were from Apache mutilation or from the sharp beaks of the vultures.

"Apaches hate miners worse than anyone else," Bennett observed as they approached the body.

"And why is that, Mr. Bennett?" asked Guilfoyle, who again felt like vomiting but tried not to show it.

"They believe that gold is a part of their sun god, and that the miners are stealin' it from Mother Earth."

"How ignorant. Sergeant Williams, have your men bury that poor soul. And search that shack too. We'll stop here for lunch—if anyone feels hungry, that is."

Fifteen minutes later, Sergeant Williams reported back to Guilfoyle, who was sprawled in the shade of a juniper. "Sah, his name was Henry Coleman—I found it wrote in his Bible. My men dug up dis here gold—"

"Let me see that," ordered the lieutenant, and Williams handed him three small buckskin bags tied at the top with rawhide. They were half-filled with a mixture of gold dust and small nuggets. "Property of the U.S. Army now," Guilfoyle said ruefully.

"I know, sah," Moses agreed with broad grin on his face. "Spoils of war."

Guilfoyle studied his sergeant's black, sweaty face for a moment. The man continued to surprise him—he was intelligent, efficient, and had a good sense of humor. He could even read, a feat that few of the troopers had mastered. "Is the late Mr. Coleman buried yet? We've got to move out."

"I'll check and see," said Williams. As he turned to leave, Bennett passed him and sat down next to Guilfoyle. The lieutenant passed him the bags of gold.

"It doesn't make much sense," Bennett said after a few moments.

"What do you mean?"

"Well, Lieutenant, I'm trained to read sign; and the signs 'round here just don't add up. That poor soul's name is Coleman, but there's another name carved into the timbers just inside the mine. That name reads 'Fr. La Rue.' The minin' equipment here doesn't fit with Coleman—it's Spanish and at least a hundred years old. I found two old *vassos*—adobe furnaces—some bull-hide bellows, and ingot molds, so somebody had a smeltin' operation. But this gold here is placer gold and hasn't been smelted."

"So maybe Coleman stumbled across this old Spanish mine and decided to work it, and then Nana's men got him?"

Bennett shrugged his shoulders. "Maybe. But where's the gold ingots that were smelted here?"

Guilfoyle rose to his feet. "I don't know the answer to that, and we don't have time to look for any gold right now. I'll file a report with General Hatch after we catch Nana. How did a scout like you learn so much about mining, anyway?"

"I've camped with prospectors on the trail dozens of times, and lots of 'em used to wander into Fort Apache," said Bennett. "They'd bend my ear for hours with their treasure stories. Some got rich. Some went crazy."

"And some were killed by Apaches," added Guilfoyle.

"Hundreds of them. Renegades have raided every minin' town I can think of—Silver City, Lake Valley, Mogollon, all of them."

"Well, Mr. Bennett, have the men mount up and we'll see if we can't extract a measure of revenge for Mr. Coleman here. God rest his soul. Now then, where the hell is Chihuahua, anyway?"

His rhetorical question would not be answered for nearly six hours, when Guilfoyle's Apache scouts led the party through a narrow passage in the towering rocks and into a small, secluded canyon. Waiting for them beside an inviting spring was Chihuahua and the two other scouts.

"It's about damned time," snapped Guilfoyle, and without waiting for orders, Bennett urged his horse forward into a trot. After he reached his three men, the chief-of-scouts began questioning them in a loud voice. By the time Guilfoyle pulled up, Bennett had all the answers.

"Chihuahua says he's been waiting here two hours for us. I told him about the dead prospector holdin' us up. Nana's whole band is camped at Hembrillo Canyon, about an hour's ride from here. It's too late today to mount an attack—it'd be after dark by the time we got there and all the men are tired. It's best to wait until morning and surround their camp."

"Well, shit," said a disappointed Guilfoyle. "I had hoped we could end this chase today."

"Don't get too anxious, Lieutenant," Bennett warned. "Remember that Nana's force is strong with those deserters. It's better to plan this out—"

"At ease, Bennett."

The chief-of-scouts grinned. "Sorry, sir. Here's my idea. We make camp here and send Chihuahua to watch Nana's camp and make sure they don't attack tonight."

"A night raid?" asked the lieutenant doubtfully. "I've never heard of Apaches doing that."

The chief scout paused and spat tobacco juice on the ground. "With our luck, Lieutenant, tonight would be the first time."

Guilfoyle considered his options. Everything Bennett said was true: it was getting late, the men were exhausted from the day's ride in the heat, and Nana seemed perfectly positioned for a daybreak cavalry charge. But he just didn't trust Chihuahua. The Army practice of using Apaches to find Apaches was good in theory, but where did Chihuahua's loyalties really lie? Was the scout deliberately stalling them so Nana could escape? He decided that some further reconnaissance was necessary.

"Sergeant Williams!"

"Yes, sah."

"Dismount the men and make camp. Post at least three sentries."

"Yes, sah," said the sergeant.

"Mr. Bennett, inform Chihuahua that he will guide you and me back to Nana's camp. I want to see this for myself." He paused and smiled at the chief-of-scouts. "That way I can do my best planning, as you suggested."

Bennett frowned. "Very dangerous, Lieutenant. We could be caught or killed."

"I'm counting on the abilities of your scouts to keep us out of harm's way. Now, let's move out before it gets any later. Sergeant, you're in command here."

"Yes, sah. You take care now, you hear?"

"We will run rather than fight," joked the lieutenant, but he was serious. At the first hint of enemy resistance, he and Bennett would retreat immediately back to camp.

It was nearly sunset when they left for the reconnaissance of Nana's camp. Chihuahua led the way, riding as fast as the terrain and his horse would allow. Guilfoyle and Bennett followed in single file, with another Apache scout taking the rear position. After they had ridden for about fifteen minutes, Bennett pulled his mount abreast of Guilfoyle's.

"There's no need to file a report on that prospector's gold," he told Guilfoyle in a low voice.

"Oh, why not?"

"Because no one will ever know you have it, otherwise."

Guilfoyle studied Bennett for a moment. "What are you suggesting?"

"I just don't think the U.S. Army needs any gold, Lieutenant. But us poor, underpaid soldiers really do need it."

"How much money are we talking about here, Mr. Bennett?"

"A couple of hundred dollars, I guess. Enough to buy us both a few weeks of booze and whores in Santa Fe."

"So," Guilfoyle summed up, "you are proposing we steal gold belonging to the Army and spend it on our own pleasures."

"Right."

"Why should I split it with you?"

Bennett grinned at him. "Because if the subject ever comes up, I'll back up your story about the lost saddlebag."

"The lost saddlebag containing the little bags of gold."

"That's the one."

"I think your idea is excellent, Mr. Bennett. We'll discuss this further when we're alone."

By Guilfoyle's watch, the trip to Hembrillo Canyon took forty-seven minutes. The four of them worked their way on foot to the crest of the ridge overlooking the canyon with the small peak within it. There was still faint light in the western sky and Guilfoyle could discern Nana's campfire at the foot of the peak and what seemed to be a team of warriors removing things from the summit and carrying them down to the camp.

"What are they doing?" he whispered to Bennett. The chief scout asked the same question of Chihuahua but received only a shrug in response.

"He doesn't know," Bennett reported, "but I have a pretty good idea. It's one of Victorio's old caches. He had dozens of 'em scattered all over the mountains of New Mexico and Arizona."

"You mean for food, ammunition?"

"Yeah. And sometimes more. If Nana's men are takin' stuff out of there, they must be gettin' ready to move out."

"Not before we get a shot at them, I hope."

"We'll see, Lieutenant. I think Chihuahua better stay here and keep an eye on Nana. We can get our men up here before daybreak, meet Chihuahua, and either attack or trail Nana."

Guilfoyle agreed, and as Bennett whispered instructions to the scout, a large owl glided silently a few feet over their heads. Chihuahua's eyes went wide and Guilfoyle was certain he saw fear there. This Apache could face death without changing expression, but was spooked by an owl. Some primitive superstition, he supposed.

Bennett led them away from the ridge and retraced their route, which he had marked by slashing junipers with his knife. As they slowly worked their way back to camp, they were aided by the soft illumination of a three-quarter moon. It took them twice as long to return as it did to find

Nana's camp, and when they arrived, Guilfoyle immediately wished he had never left. The first indication that something was very wrong came from the sentry they encountered on their way into camp. The man was at his post, but instead of standing, he was writhing on the ground, moaning and clutching his stomach.

"Private, what's wrong with you?" asked Guilfoyle as he dismounted to inspect the ailing soldier.

"Sorry, sah," gasped the man. "I've got de shits. Cramps and shits."

Guilfoyle was at a loss about how to help the man. What was wrong with him? He had heard of diseases like dysentery immobilizing entire regiments. As he considered the location of the nearest doctor—Las Cruces—a sinking feeling in his own stomach caused him to abandon the sick soldier where he lay. "Bennett, let's get into camp, now."

His worst fears were soon realized. The entire troop of soldiers was sprawled around the campfire, each man enduring his own degree of agony. He looked around for a minute until he spotted Sergeant Williams, who was kneeling in the shadows, retching. Guilfoyle tactfully waited until Williams was finished and then said gently, "Report, Sergeant?"

Williams looked up and managed a weak grin. "Don't drink the water from the spring, sah. It's poisoned or somethin'. All my men are shittin' their brains out. We're in no condition to fight."

Furious, Guilfoyle turned on his chief-of-scouts. "Goddamn it, Bennett, we've been set up. Chihuahua did this to us. He was waiting right here at this poisoned spring, yet he didn't warn us not to drink the water."

"Well, Lieutenant, he didn't *tell* us to camp here—we chose the spot. Maybe he didn't know. I'll go speak to the other scouts."

"You do that. Sergeant, can you stand up?"

"I think so." He staggered to his feet with Guilfoyle's assistance and the two of them moved slowly over to the fire and sat down. The pitiful sounds of moans, flatulence, and retching surrounded them, and Guilfoyle thought briefly that under different circumstances their predicament would be humorous. If the men stationed at Fort Cummings ever heard about it, he'd never live it down. He took a moment to inspect some of the horses and decided that, although some were sick, most were in better condition than his men.

Bennett returned shaking his head. "We're in serious trouble, Lieutenant. All the scouts are gone."

"Gone? You mean deserted?"

"Looks that way. I guess we'll know for sure in the mornin.'"

"Sit down. We need to think this out. Got any more of that whiskey?"

Bennett passed him the flask, which was nearly empty. Guilfoyle took a swallow, then passed it back. Sergeant Williams appeared even more distressed at the very thought of drinking whiskey. "Bennett, pretend you're an Apache and you know about our situation. What do you do?"

"Well, I'd attack at first light. First I'd surround the camp and station my men up in the rocks. Then I'd order them to shoot the horses and all the sleeping men. Finally, I'd send a mounted raiding party through the camp to finish off any survivors."

"Then that's what we must defend against. And there's only one way to do that."

"How, sah?" asked Williams.

"We'll seize the superior position—be above 'em when they get here. We're going to have to get all the men up onto that slope somehow. Sergeant, Bennett, round up all the men, no matter how sick they are. Get 'em over here so I can give the orders. We're movin' out—or *up*, I should say."

It took the three of them nearly ten minutes to gather the men, some of whom had to be dragged up to the fire. Sergeant Williams indicated the men he thought had mostly recovered. Guilfoyle wasted no time or sentiment in his speech.

"Here's the situation, men. We've been tricked. Our scouts have deserted and Nana's renegades may attack at any time. If we stay like this, we'll be perfect targets. I know you're all sick, but it's better to be sick than dead. We've got to move out of this camp and high up into the rocks. You can lie here in your own shit and die, or you can do what I tell you and at least stand a chance. Now, take your weapons and ammunition but leave your bedrolls and extra clothes where they are. Follow Sergeant Williams as best you can. Mr. Bennett and I will be along shortly and help any of you who need it. Privates Walley and Rogers, remain with me. Company, dismissed."

Williams gathered some inner strength and began to yell at his men to help each other. Guilfoyle checked his watch and discovered it was nearly eleven—which meant he had only six hours to get his men into position. But before he began carrying sick men up the eastern slopes, he had to make certain that their camp looked normal when Nana's men rode up to it before daybreak. He ordered the two privates and Bennett to stuff the bedrolls with the extra clothing so they would appear to be sleeping men.

Unfortunately, Guilfoyle was in a quandary about the horses and mules. He knew if he moved them away from the camp to safety, their absence would alert Nana instantly. But certainly the Apaches would shoot the horses first to leave the soldiers on foot. Which was more important, the element of surprise or having horses to ride? He wondered if Nana or Chihuahua would take the trouble to count the horses at the camp.

Finally, he decided to take a chance and divide the herd. With Bennett's help, he separated the horses and mules into two groups and left the ones in poor condition hobbled at the camp. When the privates had completed the task of simulating a company of sleeping troopers, Guilfoyle ordered them to move the good mounts to a small canyon about a mile east of the camp.

"Stay with the horses," he told them, "and whatever happens, don't try to save us. Protect the horses and make sure the Apaches don't capture them—shoot 'em if you have to. If the shooting stops and one of us doesn't contact you by noon, take the horses and ride like hell to Las Cruces. You follow our trail back to the white sands, find the main road and turn south. Send a telegram to General Hatch and explain what's happened. Then wait for orders from him. And good luck.."

"Same to you, sah," said Private Walley. The two men saluted and moved off with two groups of horses

Guilfoyle then checked his watch; it read ten minutes after two. He inspected the progress of his soldiers and discovered that although most of them had managed to climb into position, a few needed to be carried or dragged further up the slopes. He called to Bennett for assistance and when his chief scout arrived panting with exertion, Guilfoyle said, "It wasn't your fault, Bennett. Here's a little token of my appreciation."

He passed Bennett one of the small sacks of gold nuggets and dust and received a rueful smile in return. "Hope we both live to spend it," Guilfoyle said. "Now, let's get these men in position."

An hour later the two officers were exhausted, but Guilfoyle knew there would be no sleep that night. On a hunch, he decided to post sentries at the very top of the eastern ridge, just in case Nana sent men that way. He found three relatively healthy soldiers and gave them orders to conceal themselves and keep watch by looking away from the camp. Since Nana's camp was west of his, he expected that the attack would come from that direction, but of course there was no way to be certain.

Finally, he decided he had done all he could. He gave the order for the men to rest and save strength until the morning action, and then flopped down next to Bennett and Sergeant Williams, who looked like he was feeling better.

"Lieutenant, I think I know what done poisoned us," said the sergeant.

"Oh yeah?"

"I recall that medicine taste, or somethin' like it. Epsom salts, my mama calls it. She used to feed it to us kids to clean out our innards."

"A damned laxative," moaned Guilfoyle. "Just what we need in the middle of an Indian war."

Bennett suddenly laughed. "I've heard of being scared shitless, but this is ridiculous."

"Just before daybreak," Guilfoyle suggested, "let's remind all the men just how stupid the Apaches made 'em look and how bad they made 'em feel."

"Don't worry, sah," said Williams. "My men got pride. They'll take their revenge all right."

Guilfoyle certainly hoped so—it was their only chance for survival. But at the moment things were looking up—the sounds of gagging, retching, and moaning had been replaced by acapella music. His troopers were softly singing the refrain, "swing low, sweet chariot."

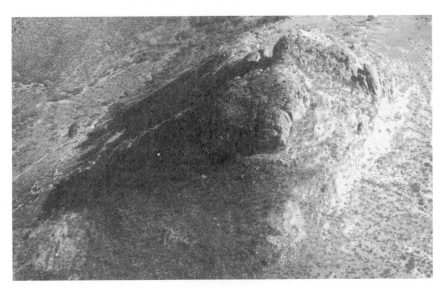

Treasure Trove.

4. Victorio's Peak

The novice warrior Istee was one of six Tcihene and Mescalero sentries stationed in a rough circle around the camp at the foot of the small mountain. He was apprehensive for the first time on the raid because he was in possession of a rifle. Usually, novices were permitted only bows, knives, and lances tipped with bayonet points. But Grandfather had personally given him his own rifle along with strict orders: if he spotted approaching Blue Coats, he was to fire twice in the air and instantly run back to camp. "Do not try to fight them yourself," Nana had told him, "but rather lead them to us."

Istee was nervous but his senses missed nothing that was happening in the darkness surrounding him. He noticed the bats cutting through the night sky, smelled the smoke from the distant juniper-wood fire, and heard the faint breathing of Sánchez, the sentry to his left. He knew that at some time in the past his father had stood on this very ground, and he felt a sudden chill as he recalled the shimmering image that had appeared in the smoke of the fire in the Blue Mountains. The Dreamer had used strong magic to call his father back from the Underworld, and Istee believed the spirit of the great warrior was now here with them. Although he had not seen her image, he believed that his mother—also killed by the Mexicans—was at his father's side. Perhaps their spirits were in the sky above him now, watching over the camp, ready to send a signal if the Blue Coats came near.

Suddenly he was startled to hear a soft quail call close by. It could not be from one of their band because Kaytennae had given orders to use the dove call. As he raised his rifle, a stranger appeared from the rocks in front of him. Despite the darkness, Istee recognized the man was of their people, but that fact did not allow him to relax.

"Stop and speak," he ordered, pointing his rifle at the stranger's head.

The stranger smiled. "I am the one the White Eyes call Chihuahua," he said. "I wish to speak to *nantan* Nana."

Istee was suspicious. "Grandfather said you were a scout for the Blue Coats. How do I know you are not a spy for them?"

"I will explain everything to Nana. Are you the son of Victorio?"

Istee was startled by the question. "Yes. How did you know?"

"You look like him. Will you let me pass?"

"No," Istee answered firmly. He then imitated the sound of the dove and instantly Sánchez was at his side. The warrior recognized Chihuahua, who repeated his request to speak with Nana.

"We consider you an enemy," Sánchez said.

"I have the Blue Coats trapped," Chihuahua told them. "Let me tell Nana about it so he can decide what to do."

"Only if you give us your weapons," ordered Sánchez.

Without protest, Chihuahua removed his knife sheath, placed it carefully on the ground along with his rifle, and then showed his open palms in the signal of the unarmed man.

"Do you have warriors with you?" Sánchez asked.

"Beyond the ridge behind me," Chihuahua replied. "They will stay where they are until I return."

Sánchez was satisfied with the arrangement. "Take him to Nana," he told Istee, "and ask him to send some of our warriors to me."

Istee motioned for Chihuahua to follow and moved quickly through the rocks toward the camp, which Nana had made no attempt to hide. Unlike other camps they had made on this raid, this one was in plain sight and Grandfather had even permitted a large fire. When he had asked the reason for *not* concealing it, Nana had laughed. "I *want* the Blue Coats to know where we are," he had answered mysteriously. Istee had a feeling that Chihuahua might be the reason for such a strategy.

Except for the rather large bonfire, the encampment was actually difficult to detect. There were no wickiups or rough sleeping lodges; blankets spread among the large boulders were the only signs of the presence of warriors. Istee knew that Nana would be holding court at fireside, and that is where he led the stranger. There were murmurs of surprise from the warriors as they approached.

"Grandfather, we have a visitor," Istee announced.

The old chief, who was in conversation with Lozen, turned and spotted Chihuahua. A flicker of a smile crossed his face but his voice was casual.

"Well, where have you been?" asked Nana in the oblique Tcihene way of greeting.

"Tricking the Blue Coats, *nantan*—as you requested."

"Sit and take some food. Where are your warriors?"

Chihuahua made a sweeping gesture to the east. "Out there, beyond the first ridge."

"Sánchez is on guard—" began Istee, but was waved to silence by Nana, who turned to Kaytennae.

"Bring them here and offer them our hospitality," he requested. "Even more reinforcements have arrived." Then he turned back to Chihuahua, who was already chewing on a *mescal* cake. "What has happened?"

Chihuahua finished his cake, wiped his lips, and said in a loud voice so all would hear, "After we spoke at San Carlos, I remembered what you asked and led the Blue Coats to the medicine water spring. They camped there, but the lieutenant wanted to see your camp, so I led him and the chief-of-scouts to that ridge over there. While we were there, the buffalo soldiers and their horses drank the medicine water and became very sick. My warriors then crept away from camp but were not able to steal any horses because they were well guarded. The lieutenant and the chief-of-scouts returned to their camp while my warriors were coming here. That is all I know for certain, but I think we should attack them at first light."

Nana grinned broadly and there were shouts of pleasure and encouragement from some of the assembled warriors. "You have done well," praised Nana. "Tell me of this White Eye lieutenant."

"He is called Guilfoyle and his men respect him."

"Is he a warrior?'

"He appears to be. His men follow him without question and they are not cowards. Even sick they will fight to the death."

Nana nodded agreement. "Even though we hate them, we must respect our enemy."

"When we met at San Carlos," Chihuahua said, "I was going to quit being a scout for the Blue Coats. It was good that you told me your plan, because now we have them trapped."

Nana nodded in agreement. "We will take care of them in the morning. But first, you must help me with the Mescaleros."

"What is wrong?"

Nana rose to his feet and picked up a torch made of rags soaked in pine pitch. "I will show you. Victorio's son should see this also." He lit the torch from the fire and then limped up the slope in the direction of the top of the small mountain. Chihuahua and Istee followed.

"For many years Victorio, Cochise, Mangas Coloradas, and I raided wagons, mail trains, and ranches from San Carlos to the land of the Comanches, and south to the Blue Mountains," the old chief explained. "Very often we found gold and silver that the White Eyes had taken from the earth in defiance of Ussen. Victorio did not want to touch it, but also he did not want to leave it for the White Eyes to find and use as money. So we cached it here."

Soon they came to a small opening in the steep face of rocks and Nana stepped through it, immediately disappearing from sight. All that was left of the chief was a faint glow from the torch, and then Chihuahua vanished as well. Istee felt apprehensive as he followed their lead. He had heard talk from the other warriors about the cache, knew what he would see, but still dreaded the moment.

He kept his hands on the rocks as he followed the glow along a passageway for a short distance. Then the shaft widened into a small cave with a shaft in it that plunged down into the center of the mountain. Nana and Chihuahua stood beside a stack of gold and silver bars. Nearby were several cloth sacks and a chest filled with coins and brightly-colored stones that sparkled in the weak light from the torch.

Chihuahua felt dread at seeing the gold. It was the color of the sun—of Ussen himself—and should never be seen by one of the people, much less touched. "There is so much of it," he said in awe to Nana.

The old chief laughed and pointed to the shaft that disappeared down into the darkness. "What you see here is a very small part of what is down below. We have taken only a small portion of it."

"Grandfather," Istee began, trying to keep fear from voice, "Please explain to me what all of this is."

Nana opened one of the sacks and displayed the gold nuggets inside. "These are stones of gold that are found in streams. A White Eye named Adams and some others found these in Sno-Ta-Hay canyon on our ancestral lands near Ojo Caliente. I took the gold stones after we killed most of the White Eyes."

He moved the torch close to the pile of bars. "When gold stones are melted by fire, they are poured into forms to make bars. These came from a mine very close to here that was operated by Mexicans many, many years ago. Most of the bars of gold were already here when Victorio began to use this mountain as his cache, but we captured more from White Eye miners in the Black Mountains. We never touched the gold ourselves but used captives to carry it. Victorio said we were returning it to the earth where it came from."

Nana then pointed to the chest. "This box was taken from Mexicans who were traveling east. They have made coins from the gold. They also treasure these colored stones, which their priests and women wear as ornaments."

"What are you going to do with all this gold?" Chihuahua asked solemnly.

"You recall the White Mountain man known as The Dreamer," Nana said. "He is here with us and we have a plan to use this gold to regain our land at Ojo Caliente, but the Mescaleros object to removing it from this cache. They will not touch it."

"None of our people would either," Chihuahua pointed out.

Nana shook his head slowly. "Not in normal times. Things are desperate now. The Mescaleros have been on the reservation too long and are so hungry for freedom that they do not think clearly. They joined us of their own will, but now they believe it is *their* raid. But they have no plan. We need them, but we do not need a divided people."

"What do you want me to do, Grandfather?" protested Chihuahua. "I have no influence over the Mescaleros."

"We are having a council with them. Listen to the arguments and consider our plan. Support me and the rest of the Tcihene."

"I will listen," Chihuahua agreed, "but I cannot promise that I will ride with you and the gold."

They returned to the camp's fire in silence and found that both the Tcihene and the Mescaleros were already assembled around it. Comescu, the leader of the Mescalero warriors, rose to his feet and respectfully nodded to Nana, acknowledging his age and leadership. But the old chief refused to accept the invitation to speak first.

"You called this council," he told Comescu, "so you begin it."

The Mescalero, a tall man who looked much older than his twenty-five years, hesitated at first and stared at the ground as if collecting his thoughts. After a few moments, he began to speak, but his initial concerns did not involve the gold in the cave.

"My warriors wish to help the Tcihene in the fight against the White Eyes, but they believe it is bad luck to ride with a woman warrior." With than terse statement, Comescu sat down and silence descended over the assembled people.

His statement further convinced Nana that the Mescaleros had been on the reservation too long. They were forgetting the ways of raiding and warfare, forgetting the legacy of many women warriors such as Lozen who had ridden as equals with men. He slowly rose to his feet and then made a calming gesture to Lozen, whose expression told him she was ready to cut Comescu's throat at any moment.

Standing now, Nana began to laugh softly and one by one the Tcihene followed his lead until all except Lozen were chuckling. The Mescaleros were caught off guard, unsure of whether or not they were being insulted. Before they could decide, Nana gestured for silence and faced Comescu.

"We are laughing because it is obvious you have never been on a raid with Victorio's sister. Let me tell you about her. When she was very young she was not interested in women's work but in the ways of warriors. She learned to ride horses, to shoot arrows with great accuracy, to track enemies and to kill them. One day she was riding in the mountains alone and she met the Gray Ghost."

That comment brought a gasp from the Mescaleros, who believed—as did the Tcihene—that whoever saw that Gray Ghost was being sent a direct message from Ussen.

"Even though the Gray Ghost left our land and moved west," Nana continued, "she had seen him and afterward no other man interested her. She refused offers of marriage and chose to ride as a warrior beside her brother. And this woman became one of our best warriors. She is an expert roper and shooter, good at dressing wounds, and once killed a longhorn steer with just a knife.

"In addition, she has the Power to locate the enemy. She stands with arms outstretched, palms up, and prays to Ussen. Then she turns slowly toward the sun, continues, and feels the location and distance of the enemy in the palms of her hands. If she had been with Victorio at Tres Castillos, her brother never would have fallen into the trap set by the Mexican Terrazas.

"You will accept her as a warrior," Nana concluded, "or you may return to Mescalero with my regrets, but not my hatred."

After his speech, Nana sat down and Comescu stood up again. "We did not know all these things you tell us. We accept Victorio's sister as an honored warrior. But there is another matter that bothers us, and that is the gold in the cave. As you know, *nantan*, we hate the White Eyes' lust for gold, and we hate the miners who have taken our land to grub it out of the ground. They lie, steal, cheat, and kill for it. They incur the wrath of the Mountain Spirits by taking it from the mountains. It is the essence of the Sun, of Ussen himself, and thus is forbidden to our people. Leave the gold where Victorio hid it."

As Comescu was sitting down, Nana gestured to The Dreamer, who pulled his thin frame erect and faced the Mescaleros. "They call me The Dreamer, the one who summons the dead, and I speak to you as shaman of the Tcihene. Twice I have been to the cities of the White Eyes, where I learned about their peculiar ways. The first time I went to Washington, which is more than a moon's ride to the east. Then I was sent to the White Eyes' Indian school in Santa Fe, where I was taught their religion."

The Dreamer paused and looked up to the sky as if silently requesting divine guidance. "You must believe me when I tell you that the White Eyes worship a thing called 'money.' Unlike us, who trade items for what we need, the White Eyes pay for things they want with coins such as these." He held a silver dollar high for all to see and then, as if by magic, it was replaced with a piece of colored paper. "This paper also is money, and can buy food or weapons—or even land. Gold is not really gold to the White Eyes–it is money. They only want it because it can buy them what they want."

The Dreamer moved beside Nana and Kaytennae. "These men will tell you that Victorio came back from the dead and visited us in the Blue Mountains. What was he holding, *nantan*?"

"A rifle in one hand and a bar of gold in the other," replied Nana.

"And what did he tell us?"

Kaytennae took the cue. "He said, 'Avenge me! Regain our lands!'"

"Now," said The Dreamer, his voice rising in pitch, "when I was still in San Carlos, I called Victorio back from the dead and he spoke to me in a vision. Again he was holding the gold and I asked *nantan* what this meant. *Nantan* told me that Victorio had a plan when he cached all the gold in that cave up there."

Nana interrupted, "Victorio believed that some day the White Eyes would lust for it so much they would give us anything we wanted."

The Dreamer closed his eyes but continued to speak. "We must ask ourselves what Ussen would wish for us. For this gold, which has already been stolen from the earth and cast into bars and coins to stay in the cave forever, or for it to help us regain the land which is rightfully ours."

"What is your plan?" asked Comescu.

Nana took the lead. "We have fought for our land for years and have been defeated by the White Eyes' superior numbers and better weapons. Since all else has failed, I say we regain our land in a manner the White Eyes will understand—we *buy* it from them.

"As in the White Eyes' way of paying for things?"

"Yes, a trade. All the gold for all our land. Remember that we have often traded silver to the Mexicans for guns. The survival of our people depends upon using the White Eyes' gold and silver against them. This was what Victorio believed; that's why he hid the gold and silver in that cave. He returned it to the earth, where it would be hidden until needed. Victorio always said, 'I do nothing for fame. I seek only the preservation of my people.' Ussen has sent us a message through Victorio: we are permitted to use His gold to accomplish this."

Silence descended over the camp as the warriors considered the heretical plan. Nana was pleased that none of the Mescaleros had protested as strongly as he had expected.

The Dreamer suddenly interjected, "When Victorio appeared to us holding a bar of gold and telling us to avenge him and regain the ancestral lands, *nantan* and I believed him and came up with a plan. There will be many uprisings all over our land—much like the revolt of the Pueblo people against the Spanish in the far distant past. We will continue this raid all over the land, terrifying the White Eyes and burning their ranches and towns. I will return to San Carlos and lead a revolt there. Perhaps some of you can persuade the rest of the Mescaleros to join us. We will kill as many White Eyes as we can, and then we shall sue for peace. Our terms will be the return of our ancestral lands and removal of all the gold from our sacred shrines. We will take a small portion of this gold as a sample, and tell the White Eye leaders that there is so much more. Only when the Congress–the government of the White Eyes—issues deeds to this land do we reveal every one of Victorio's caches of gold."

The arguments concluded, all attention was now focused upon Comescu, who stood up once again. "The plan might work, and I will ride with you. But I will not touch the gold. My warriors can decide for themselves and anyone who does not wish to join the raid with the Tcihene can return to Mescalero without fear of disgrace. Agreed?"

Nana agreed with a nod, smiled, and the warriors relaxed for the first time since the Mescaleros had joined the war party. "We will attack the Blue Coats at the spring of medicine water at first light," the old chief directed.

Kaytennae waited respectfully until Nana had spoken and then said, "I believe that Victorio wants us use the gold. I saw him in the sky myself. I will carry the gold if you wish me to."

"I will tell you the plan in the morning," Nana replied, and it was obvious to Kaytennae that the old chief did not want the Mescaleros to know where the gold would be.

"Grandfather?" asked Istee hesitantly during a lull in the council meeting.

"Yes, son of Victorio?"

"You promised you would tell us Coyote stories."

The warriors showed their agreement with Istee's suggestion by clapping their hands and whistling—a command performance for Nana, who was considered to the best storyteller of them all. Nana knew that telling Coyote stories would divert attention from further consideration of the gold in the cave, so he waved them to silence and without introduction began to tell them of the wily Coyote who was a reflection of all of them.

"I will tell of Coyote, and then we will play the moccasin gambling game. Man does everything just like Coyote did," he said. "Ever since Coyote did these things, our people do the same no matter how bad they are. Since we are here without our women—except Victorio's sister, who is not spoken for—it is a good time to tell of Coyote's trickery with women.

"At first Coyote learned that women were very dangerous, and here is how it happened. Coyote found a very pretty woman and tried to have sex with her. He was just about to put his penis into her when he looked down and saw teeth in her vagina. He thought about what those teeth could do to his penis and he was afraid. So he grabbed a stick and a long, thin rock.

"Instead of putting his penis inside her, he put the stick in it and her vagina chewed the stick up into little pieces. Then he put the rock in there and all the teeth were knocked out and her vagina became like all women's are now. Then he had sex with her safely."

Despite the fact that the warriors had heard the story dozens, if not hundreds of times, everyone laughed and cheered Nana on. Again he waved them to silence.

"The woman said, 'Now I shall be worth a lot and men will give me many horses and gifts to marry me.' And that is why we men give horses and gifts when we marry women today.

"But Coyote was not content to have just one woman; he wanted all women, even those forbidden to him by Ussen. Once when he was a married man he was camped near his mother-in-law, but of course never looked at her. One day Coyote told his wife he was going hunting and he left the camp. Not far from the camp he saw a rabbit and chased it, but it ran into a hollow log. Coyote did everything he could to get that rabbit, but he could not reach it.

"Coyote returned to camp and told his wife to ask her mother to try to get the rabbit, saying that maybe her arm was longer than his. Coyote's wife showed her mother the log and then returned home. Coyote made excuses about leaving camp and pointed to a nearby mountain. 'I'm going to hunt in that direction,' he told his wife.

"But Coyote circled back and returned to the log just as his mother-in-law was crawling into the log. She was about halfway inside, reaching for the rabbit when Coyote ran up to her as fast as he could. While she was stuck in the hollow log, he stuck his penis into her from behind and she didn't know who did it!"

Nana was again interrupted by laughter and he waited patiently until it subsided.

"Coyote's mother-in-law was angry and she looked around for tracks to see who had tricked her. When she found them she measured them with a stick and took the stick back to her wickiup. Then she called for her daughter and told her the story. She gave the stick to her daughter and told her to measure her husband's feet.

"Coyote was stretched out on his bed, singing and pretending to be innocent. Soon his wife came in and without saying a word began to measure his feet. He looked up and said, 'What are you doing? What is the matter with you?'

"'While my mother was trying to catch that rabbit, someone played a trick on her and had sex with her! She thinks it was you!'

"Coyote thought quickly and then said, 'You are talking like a witch. Your mother is lying. Leave me alone and don't bother me with witch talk.' And so Coyote got away with having sex with his mother-in-law."

There were murmurs of appreciation from the assembled warriors, who had no intention of allowing Nana to stop the storytelling so soon. "Tell us more, Grandfather," pleaded Istee. Nana had no objection; the storytelling was one of his great pleasures in life and he could tell Coyote stories all night long. He took some time to smoke a cigarette of wild tobacco and then spoke again.

"There was another Coyote, one that hated the White Eyes." His opening line produced a gasp of admiration. "Coyote went to the ranch of a White Eye who was herding sheep. This man had two pretty daughters helping him herd them.

"'What pretty sheep you have,' Coyote said to the White Eye. 'May I herd them for you?'

"The White Eye said, 'No, I know that you are a very bad fellow. I like my sheep and don't want you taking them.'

"But Coyote was clever and begged. 'Mister, please let me herd them for you. I promise I won't hurt them.' After pleading like this for a while, Coyote made the White Eye change his mind.

"'You can herd them,' he told Coyote, 'but don't let the sheep go in that mud puddle over there. Herd them around it.'

"Then the White Eye and his daughters went back to his house. Coyote chased those sheep around and killed most of them. First he bit off their heads and tails and stuck them into the mud hole, then he ate all of the sheep himself and hid their bones.

"When the White Eye returned he asked Coyote where his sheep were. 'They fell in the mud and got stuck,' Coyote told him, pointing to the heads and tails. 'We need a shovel to get them out.'

"The White Eye agreed with him. 'You go to the house and tell my daughters to give you the shovel,' he said.

"Coyote went to the White Eye's house, but he was looking for something better than a shovel. 'Your father sent me over here to have sex with you,' he told the daughters.

"'You're lying,' said the oldest daughter. 'Our father loves us so much he would never make us do that!'" Nana's high-pitched imitation of a girl's voice brought a good laugh from the crowd.

"Clever Coyote said, 'If you don't believe me, step outside and I'll call to him and ask him.' Coyote then yelled at the White Eye, 'These daughters of yours won't do what you ordered.'

"The White Eye called back, 'Do what he tells you to do.'

"'You heard him,' Coyote said. 'Take your clothes off.'

"The White Eye girls obeyed and Coyote had sex with the oldest daughter face-to-face, in the style of the White Eyes. Then he had sex with the youngest daughter, climbing on top of her Coyote-style. Still not satisfied, he had sex with the oldest daughter again, but this time in the manner of Mexicans, sticking his penis up her rear end!"

Nana was interrupted by the noise of the near-hysterical laughter. He could see that Lozen was giggling so much she was nearly in tears, and that the Mescaleros had finally relaxed and joined in the fun.

"But this story is not over," Nana said. "Coyote got away after having his way with the daughters and soon the White Eye came back to his house. 'Where is that Coyote? I sent him over to get the shovel.'

"His oldest daughter answered, 'You sent him over here to have sex with us, and that's what he did.'

"The White Eye father was very angry. 'Get ready. We're going to track him down.' And they left on a long journey to find Coyote. But Coyote had circled back and met them on the trail. He said, 'What are you people looking for?'

"White Eye said, 'We are looking for a fellow just like you.'

"Coyote said, 'Well, I've been coming in this direction and I didn't see anyone. But all coyotes look alike, so you'll need some strong medicine to find him. I'll make some for you.'

"The White Eye agreed and Coyote went and gathered some red mountain laurel berries. He pounded them up and then mixed them in some water. Those people drank it and became sick—just like the Blue Coats at the medicine water spring! While the White Eye and his daughters were crazy and crawling on the ground, Coyote cut their hair in patches so they would remember him when they got sober."

Nana waited until the laughter ended and said, "That is all. Now it is time for the moccasin game." All of the Apache bands loved to gamble, and although the moccasin game was usually played in the winter, Nana made an exception because he wanted the Mescaleros to bond with his people. He chose five warriors for each side of the fire, and they donated four moccasins each. The moccasins were buried to nearly the tops of their open side, with the open sides facing away from the opponents. A bone was placed in one of the four moccasins and the opponents guessed which moccasin the bone was in. If they guessed wrong, they were forced to give up a number of specially carved yucca pieces. If they guessed right by striking the correct moccasin with a stick, the bone passed to them. There were many side bets taken on each stroke of the stick. The game and wagering ended when all of the yucca pieces were in possession of one side.

Nana allowed various teams to play the moccasin game for nearly two hours and then called a halt. "We should rest now and gain strength so we will be at our best when we kill the Blue Coats tomorrow."

The group of Tcihene and Mescaleros quietly dispersed, each warrior moving away from the fire to find a place to sleep. Nana chose a spot that was a natural depression at the base of a large boulder and there he spread grass and leaves and then some blankets on top of the pile. He lowered himself carefully and rested upon his rough bed, lying on his back and staring at the brilliant array of stars.

Before allowing himself to fall asleep, he thought of Nah-des-te, the best wife of all the wives he had taken. He imagined her in the Blue Mountains, working and waiting for him, and he was grateful to Ussen for the fact that she was safe. Would she be awake at this moment, he wondered, and would she be able to receive a message from his mind? *I am well and will see you soon,* he composed, concentrating intensely. *Tomorrow we kill more White Eyes. Pray for our victory, my wife.*

Before he attempted to sleep, Nana remembered a trick first used by Geronimo. During one battle, he did not want first light to come before his warriors could surround the Blue Coats, so Geronimo had prayed for Ussen to make the night longer. The next morning was delayed and Geromino's warriors had time to take the best positions against the Blue Coats. Since he couldn't remember the exact words of Geronimo's song, Nana improvised.

> Ussen who controls night and day,
> Hear my song.
> Grant me the Power to lengthen the night
> And shorten the day.
> In that way we can surprise our enemies
> And victory will belong to the Tcihene.

Istee was unable to sleep that night, his mind filled with thoughts of the upcoming revenge against the White Eyes. It would be the greatest battle he had ever fought in and he was nervous with anticipation. Would he be allowed to keep his rifle and actually fire it? Usually, he knew, novices were not allowed to fight until the fifth raid, but this battle was different—the Tcihene were fighting to avoid becoming *indeh*, a dead people.

He lay on his back on his rough bed and watched the stars, waiting for the ones that formed the dipper to turn upside down, a sure sign of morning. But the stars were slow and time dragged on. Only a falling star broke the tedium as it dropped to the east, pointing the way toward the enemy. He wondered who was on lookout duty and then remembered that Kaytennae had volunteered. He too would be without sleep the night before the big fight.

The soft sound of moccasins on a rocky trail close by alerted Istee, and he silently rose from the ground, picked up his rifle and concealed himself between two rocks.

"It is only me, son of Victorio," came the whispered voice of Nana. Istee emerged from the rocks and quickly spotted Grandfather on the trail, his face paint glowing in the moonlight. "Come," he ordered, "and bring your things." Istee silently obeyed and followed the limping old chief.

Soon they came to the place where the horses and mules were tethered, and waiting there was Kaytennae and two other Tcihene warriors, Gordo and Cadete. The mules were packed and the horses were ready to ride. Istee saw the disappointed look on Kaytennae's face and knew what was coming next—he would certainly miss the battle.

"It is time to divide our forces," Nana told them. He paused, stared directly at Kaytennae and continued: "There will be many chances to kill the White Eyes on this raid, but it is important to move the gold and our supplies out of their reach. You will lead the mules and the spare horses in the direction of the Black Mountains, and soon we shall catch up to you. Ride fast and send scouts ahead to watch for other war parties of Blue Coats. Remember that you must be like the geese, who gain their power from heaven, not earth. They have speed, endurance, and discipline. Once a flock of geese started flying from north to south. Each of them had twelve pieces of bread. They traveled for exactly twelve days without stopping and had just enough food to arrive safely. Be like the geese, my people."

Nana watched them ride away without a word and knew they were disappointed to miss the battle. But he was proud of them for not protesting his orders. He turned back to the camp and quickly roused the rest of his warriors. A few minutes later the entire war party was mounted and ready to move out.

With Nana at the lead and Chihuahua riding beside him, the Tcihene and Mescalero warriors rode as quickly as possible along the rock-strewn trail. Ussen had blessed them with strong moonlight, Nana thought. He was making it easier for them to attack the Blue Coats.

By the time they arrived near the medicine water spring, the first faint light from the east was glowing on the horizon. Nana gestured for his men to stop and then sent Sánchez and Mangus to scout around. He and Chihuahua rode to the highest point off the trail and looked down on the enemy camp, but it was still too dark to see any of the soldiers.

"There is no campfire," said Chihuahua.

"They know we are coming for them," Nana replied.

The scouts returned shortly and reported to Nana that the Blue Coats all seemed to be asleep.

"How many lookouts?" asked Nana.

"We saw no lookouts," Mangus answered.

"Something is wrong," Chihuahua warned. "Guilfoyle always posts sentries."

"I think it's a trap," mused Nana. "How many horses and mules did you count?"

Sánchez flashed the fingers of both hands and Chihuahua snorted with derision. "Not enough," said the former scout. "They have many more horses than that."

"Scout around again," ordered Nana. "This time, find our enemies."

"Maybe they ran away," Sánchez suggested.

Chihuahua disagreed. "No, that is not Guilfoyle's way. They are here somewhere."

"We shall find them," Mangus said and then rode off with Sánchez.

As the morning light increased, Nana could see what appeared to be men sleeping in bedrolls around a dead campfire, but he did not believe that even Blue Coats would be so careless. He would not waste bullets by firing into the camp. He gestured for the warriors to dismount and then waited patiently for his scouts to return. He knew that time was on his side. The sun was just rising over the ridges when Sánchez and Mangus rode up again.

"We found them," said Sánchez, squinting into the sun and pointing to steep slopes just east of the spring. "They are up there in the rocks, waiting for us to raid the camp."

"We caught sign of the other horses," added Mangus. "They have been moved back along the trail toward the white sands."

Nana considered this intelligence and quickly formulated a plan. He nodded to Chihuahua. "You take two of your warriors and follow that trail to the rest of the horses. Capture the best ones and kill the rest. Watch out for the Blue Coats guarding the horses."

The old chief pointed to the north slope flanking the soldier's position, then to Lozen and five other Tcihene warriors who were the best shots in his band. "Climb the rocks over there and get above the Blue Coats. Flash me a signal when you are in position, but don't fire until you hear us shooting. Then kill as many as you can and try to drive them out of the rocks. Go now."

To Sánchez and Mangus he said, "Sneak down to the camp on foot and take those horses. Keep them between you and the Blue Coats in the rocks. If the enemy shoots, they will hit the horses, not you. Bring them back here and guard them." The two scouts dismounted, tied up their horses, and quickly trotted downhill in the direction of the camp.

Finally, Nana turned to Comescu and his band of Mescaleros. "All the rest of us will leave our horses here, spread out, and sneak up into those rocks where the Blue Coats wait."

"But the White Eyes will see us," protested Comescu.

"Yes," agreed Nana, "but they are weak and sick and their aim will be bad. And as soon as they start shooting, Victorio's sister and the rest of her warriors will see where they are and be able to pick them off. And besides, we will have protection from Ussen because our shaman will first perform the Gun Ceremony."

He signaled to The Dreamer, who dismounted and gestured for the rest of the warriors to do the same. When they were gathered around him, The Dreamer began the ceremony by spitting in the palm of his left hand. "Do as I do," he directed the warriors, and they imitated him. He dipped the index finger of his right hand into the saliva and made a cross on his left foot. "Black Thunder," he said. He continued with crosses on his left thigh, forearm, and cheek, reciting "Blue Thunder, Yellow Thunder, White Thunder" as he made the crosses.

The Dreamer looked to the heavens and sang:

Ussen, grant us your protection.

Black flint is over my body four times

Take this black rifle to the center of the sky.

Let the enemy weapons disappear from the earth.

The war party recited the prayer four times, changing the color of the flint each time, and then imitated The Dreamer by rubbing their index fingers against their lips four times. Then The Dreamer showed them how to hold the rifle against the chest and first pointing it down to the left, then up to the right while facing the eastern light. He placed the rifle on his right shoulder, moved it across his back, and then down into his left hand. The warriors imitated his every action. To end the ceremony, The Dreamer placed the barrel of the rifle briefly in his mouth to extract its "juice," which he spit into his left hand. The crosses were made again, the prayer repeated, and The Dreamer abruptly ended the ceremony by stating, "Now that you are protected from the White Eyes' bullets, go climb that hill and kill them."

Nana took over from The Dreamer, directing the warriors to fan out along the base of the slope. "Start moving slowly but don't shoot unless you see a Blue Coat in the open." The warriors moved off quickly, darting between the rocks and taking cover where they could. Nana waited until he saw the flash of light from Lozen's mirror that indicated the sharpshooters were in position and then limped off into the rocks himself. Although he had not seen exactly where the Blue Coats had made their stand, he suspected they were hidden among the tallest rocks about half-way up the slope.

Slowly he and his warriors worked their way up the steep grade but no shots came from the Blue Coats. Nana knew why—the Blue Coat lieutenant was smart. He had the position, knew the enemy must come to him, and he would not allow his men to waste bullets on bad shots. He would wait until the Tcihene came close and then open up with heavy fire. When he judged that his warriors were close enough to hit their targets, he flashed a signal to Lozen. Immediately, she and her snipers opened fire on the Blue Coat position and Nana was pleased to hear a scream of agony from one of the soldiers.

Scattered return fire from the buffalo soldiers gave Nana's approaching warriors a better idea of where to concentrate their attention, so they shot a few rounds into the tall boulders in an attempt to flush them out for Lozen. But the soldiers held their position and directed a withering series of volleys against Nana's forces, causing the warriors to take cover and temporarily abandon their advance.

The battle was not going the way Nana had planned it, but he was not about to quit. He gave a crow call that attracted Comescu's attention, then signaled for the Mescalero to flank the Blue Coats from the south. Comescu immediately located six of his men and moved away from the large rocks, but still climbed higher on the slopes. Soon the Blue Coats would be surrounded in three of the four directions.

Meanwhile, Kaytennae had led the pack train out of the San Andres and into the low, sweltering valley the Mexicans called *Jornada del Muerto*, or Journey of the Dead. It made him nervous to be in the open, away from the shelter of the mountains, but their trip across the valley would only take a few hours and then they would be safe again in the Caballo range. Once they were well in the desert, Kaytennae sent the two warriors to scout around and kept Istee with him to help with the mules and horses.

Istee had recovered from his disappointment of missing the battle and was excited to be on the move again. He now understood why Nana had sent Kaytennae and him away with the gold—they had been closest to Victorio and had seen his image in the sky carrying the gold bar. But he was bothered by the fact Chihuahua had joined up with Nana and the war party, and decided to question Kaytennae about it.

"Why do our people become scouts for the Blue Coats?" he asked.

"Hiring scouts is a White Eye trick," Kaytennae replied. "It is difficult to understand for someone like yourself, who has never lived on a reservation. Our warriors are penned up like goats, with nothing to do. They are not allowed to hunt or to raid. Then a Blue Coat officer will come to them and say, 'we will make you a scout, pay you money, give you a rifle, and allow you to leave the reservation. All you have to do is help us track down some Navajos or Comanches, your old enemies.' The warriors say yes, and then they are trapped—they must do everything the Blue Coats order them to do or they will be called deserters or traitors and will be shot or hanged. So then the Blue Coats send these scouts against their own people."

"But how can Chihuahua be our enemy one moment and our friend the next?"

Kaytennae chuckled. "He was never our enemy—he just pretended to be. We never worry about Tcihene or Mescalero scouts, only Navajos and Jicarillas."

Their conversation was interrupted by the return of Gordo, the Tcihene scout sent north, who reported that a wagon was moving down the north-south trail and it was not protected by Mexicans, Blue Coats, or other White Eyes. Kaytennae was pleased with the news and turned to Istee. "Are you ready to kill the enemy, young novice?"

"But novices don't get to fight until their fifth raid," Istee said, shocked.

"This is not a raid. This is war."

"I am ready," replied Victorio's son, nervous but not afraid. "Tell me what to do."

"Grandfather taught me this trick. First, we leave the horses and mules here with the others. Just you and I will take positions by the trail. But first we must make you ready. Take off your clothes."

Istee obeyed, stripping to just his loin cloth. Kaytennae pulled some White Eye clothes from a mule's pack and helped Istee dress in it, taking care to fold his long hair under a floppy hat. With water from a rawhide canteen, he removed the war paint from Istee's face. Then Kaytennae did something that Istee thought very strange. He took out his knife, sliced a vein in the shoulder of a mule, and caught the spurting blood in a gourd dipper. When the dipper was full, he threw the blood over Istee. Satisfied with the appearance of the novice, Kaytennae made a mudpack and placed it over the small cut in the mule to stop the bleeding.

"Now you look like a Mexican who has been knifed and shot by the Tcihene on the warpath," laughed Kaytennae. "Here, put this under your shirt." He handed Istee a revolver and the novice was thankful he had practiced shooting one in the Blue Mountains.

"Am I going to be the bait?" Istee asked.

"You are going to be the bait and the snare. Can you now tell the difference between a Mexican and a White Eye?"

"Yes."

"Now you must learn two enemy words. If you see a Mexican in the wagon, you say 'ayuda'; if it is a White Eye, you say 'help.' Say these words several times out loud. We leave now."

Istee obeyed as he mounted his horse. "Ayuda, help. Ayuda, help," he repeated.

They left the pack train with Gordo and Cadete, and Kaytennae told them to follow after they heard gunshots. When Istee and Kaytennae reached the trail, they could see the wagon's dust to the north. Kaytennae chose the spot for the ambush with care, ordering Istee to lie in the shade of a large growth of mesquite bushes to the left of the trail. He backed up the novice by hiding deep within the vegetation. So set, they waited patiently for the wagon.

"If it's a Mexican, what do you say?" whispered Kaytennae.

"Ayuda."

"If a White Eye?"

"Help."

"Good. Then what do you do?"

"I know what to do," insisted Istee, and Kaytennae fell silent.

Istee thought about his father as he waited for the wagon and wondered if Victorio had ever used this trick. *This is for you, Father,* he promised, cocking the revolver. *You are riding the Ghost Pony but I am avenging you.*

The wagon moved into sight but it was too far away for Istee to see the driver. Playing the role, he began to moan and gasp as if in great pain.

"What is wrong?" whispered Kaytennae.

"I've been shot and stabbed, remember? Now be quiet."

Istee could see that the wagon was covered with a white tent, was pulled by four mules, and that there were two White Eyes riding up front, a man and a young girl.

"Help, help," he said between moans.

The girl said, "Look, Daddy, someone's hurt," but Istee had no idea what the words meant. The man stopped the wagon directly in front of Istee, who immediately leaped to his feet and pulled the revolver out of his shirt. The man reached down to pick something up and Istee shot him three times. The girl began to scream as her father's body tumbled out of the wagon and onto the dusty trail. She jumped down from the wagon and threw her arms around the body, sobbing hysterically.

Kaytennae emerged from the mesquite and nodded his head in praise. "Why didn't you shoot her too?" he asked.

Embarrassed, Istee looked away. "I don't know. Are warriors supposed to kill little girls?"

Kaytennae laughed. "I do only if they are shooting at me. But Nana would have killed her."

"Then you shoot her," suggested Istee.

"First let's see what's in the wagon," Kaytennae replied. "It is a trader's wagon and could have some things we need. But first get out of those clothes."

Istee ripped off the bloodied clothing and they began to search the wagon. The little girl was still crying loudly. "This is what the White Eye was reaching for," said Kaytennae, lifting a rifle from beneath the front seat. "He would have killed you." Istee climbed into the back of the wagon and stared in amazement at all the strange things. There were metal tools of every shape, brightly colored cloth wrapped over and over upon itself, dozens of boots and shoes, belts with silver shells on them, and many mysterious objects. There were boxes of sticks with red ends, and he took a box. Istee also snatched several other things that he could not identify. He found some round pieces of metal that made clicking sounds, but since they looked like they were made of gold, he did not touch them. Istee gathered his treasures and put them in a small cloth sack. Then he found a box of bullets and proudly showed them to Kaytennae, who had discovered where the trader kept his provisions.

"White Eye food," Kaytennae said with disgust, but Istee noticed that he took several loaves of bread. They were interrupted by the arrival of the pack train, and Gordo and Cadete joined in the ransacking of the wagon.

"Shall we set the wagon on fire?" asked Istee when they were done.

"No," said Kaytennae. "If there are Blue Coats around, the fire would lead them to us. We will take what we want and leave the rest."

"And the girl?"

Kaytennae stared at the shivering form sprawled atop her father's body. "We'll take her too. If we leave her here, she will certainly die."

Istee felt enormous relief that he did not have to shoot the girl. He would have killed her if so ordered, but in his heart he felt that his battle was with the Blue Coats, not helpless White Eye females.

Nana was frustrated. The sun was now directly overhead, which meant they had been fighting the Blue Coats for nearly half a day. Yet they had not been able to dislodge the enemy from the tall rocks. A few of the buffalo soldiers had fallen to Lozen and her sharpshooters, but his main force had not been able to gain an advantage. Every advance of his warriors up the slope had been met with very strong return fire, and his attempt to flank them to the south had not worked because Comescu's men had little cover and were nearly out of rifle range. He knew it was not a Tcihene battle plan, but he was reluctant to leave when he had the Blue Coats pinned down.

Sánchez and Mangus, having completed their task of securing the Blue Coats' horses, returned to Nana for instructions. They were surprised to see that the old chief was holding a bow and selecting the straightest arrow from a quiver. He picked one with a flint point rather than the steel points now used by the young men when they ran out of bullets for their rifles.

"Sometimes the old ways are best," Nana said. "Bring me some pitch."

Sánchez opened his parfleche and removed a gummy piece of pine pitch wrapped in an old cloth. He used it to help start fires when the wood was damp.

Nana stuck the pitch on the end of the arrow, wrapped some sinew string around it, and tied it tight. "Make a small fire," he told Sánchez, who promptly pulled out his fire drill, collected some dried grass, and soon had a small blaze going.

Nana gestured for Mangus to join him, and when he did, pointed to the tall rocks. "What do you see at the bottom of the rocks?"

"Brush," Mangus answered.

"Yes, it is dried brush which has been blown there and trapped by the rocks. Shoot this arrow into it and the Blue Coats will have fire and smoke all around them. We will see if they can fight the fire and us at the same time."

Mangus grinned at the idea and took the bow from Nana. He lit the pitch-tipped arrow on fire, drew back the bowstring in one fluid motion and released the arrow. His aim was slightly high—the flaming arrow struck one of the boulders and then dropped into the brush below. Soon dark grey smoke began to rise and Nana knew the fire had caught. He flashed Lozen and Comescu twice with the mirror—"get ready."

The sound of coughing and shouting came from the rocks, followed by several of the buffalo soldiers breaking from cover and moving up the slope. One of them had his trousers on fire and Nana laughed out loud. A withering cross-fire from Lozen and Comescu downed two of the soldiers, but the others made it to a smaller group of rocks unharmed. Nana gave the signal for his men to advance; but despite the fire and smoke, the Blue Coats kept the Tcihene warriors pinned down. One of his men, Janos, was shot through the left shoulder but continued firing.

After a while both the smoke and the shooting diminished. Nana realized that there was not enough brush in the rocks to drive the Blue Coats out. He would have to think of another way.

"What do we do now?" asked Sánchez. "This is not the way we usually fight."

"We have food and water," Nana replied. "Do they? And they are trapped and we are not. We have killed six of them and have lost none of our own warriors. What do we do? We wait. Soon they will die of either bullets or thirst."

When Chihuahua and his two fellow scouts located the main herd of Blue Coat horses and mules, it appeared that animals were unguarded. They were squeezed into a narrow box canyon with ropes stretched across the small canyon opening to make a rough gate. The herd was foraging near a small, spring-fed pool in the rocks and Chihuahua could see that the mules still had their packs on and the horses were saddled—as if the soldiers were ready to leave immediately. But Chihuahua was suspicious because no sentries were posted, and it was unlike the Blue Coats to change their standard procedures. So, knowing that they could kill the horses any time they wanted, the three scouts dismounted, tethered their horses, and took a position in the rocks above the canyon.

They remained on watch for quite a long time. Slowly the sun moved above them and they could hear the sporadic gunfire from Nana's battle. Finally, Chihuahua was satisfied and gave the hand signal for his men to move down the slope and take the horses while he cut the rope gate. What a victory it would be to kill all the Blue Coats and capture their horses and supplies, he thought. What revenge for being made their slaves!

He crept silently down to the mouth of the canyon, taking cover behind rocks and mesquite bushes as he went. When he reached the crude gate, he set down his rifle, pulled out his knife and began to cut the ropes. Then, out of the corner of his eye he saw a flash of blue and suddenly a grinning black face of a buffalo soldier materialized from behind some rocks outside the mouth of canyon. Chihuahua felt an enormous blow to his right side, heard a gunshot, and then lost consciousness.

He never heard the other gunshot, but the two scouts did. They had almost reached the pool when the shots rang out through the rocks, causing them to take cover. One of the scouts, Black Knife, gave a quick quail call, but there was no answer from Chihuahua. Fearing the worst, they quickly moved back up the slope to reconnoiter the situation.

Black Knife led the way along the ridge to a position overlooking the mouth of the small canyon. No Blue Coats were visible but they could see Chihuahua, bound and gagged, lying in the bloodied dust near the rope gate. There was no way for them to tell how many Blue Coats were down there, so Black Knife gave the signal and the two of them quickly left the canyon to return to the battle. Nana would know what to do next.

The old chief was conducting a ceremony to send rattlesnakes into the tall rocks when Black Knife appeared and told him what had happened to Chihuahua. He realized that the White Eye lieutenant had planned well, for there was no way to tell how many Blue Coats were in the tall rocks and how many were at the box canyon. In order to handle both troops of soldiers he would have to divide his forces again, and if reinforcements came from one of the forts, the Tcihene warriors would be both outnumbered and outmaneuvered. It was time to move on while they still had the advantage.

"Bring Victorio's sister to me," he told Mangus. To Sánchez he said, "Go up there and tell Comescu I need to speak with him. Keep the Blue Coats pinned down in the rocks, but don't waste bullets."

In a few minutes Lozen and Comescu joined Nana and he held an impromptu battle council with them and Mangus and Sánchez.

"Chihuahua has been captured," he told them, "and the Blue Coats have divided their forces. We would have to stay here for days to drive this group out of the rocks and to track down the other group. I say we should move on to other battles."

"I agree," said Comescu. "We are too close to Mescalero and Fort Stanton."

"Let's catch up with Kaytennae and join forces," suggested Sánchez. "Raiding is better than fighting this kind of White Eye battle."

Nana nodded his head in agreement. "We have won this battle, but not by much. The Blue Coats will be slow to follow us because we already have half of their horses and mules. Here is the plan: Victorio's sister will stay here alone and keep the Blue Coats pinned down in those rocks for as long as she can. Then she will vanish and the soldiers will think she has left with us. When the Blue Coats move from this place, they will probably go to a fort and resupply. She will track them and free Chihuahua—if he is still alive. If he is dead, she will rejoin us."

He looked at Lozen to see her reaction to his plan. As usual, the woman was a good warrior. "I will do as you say, Grandfather—and I will bring Chihuahua back to you."

"I know you will," Nana agreed with a smile. "We will be raiding all around but heading in the direction of Ojo Caliente."

"I will find you," Lozen assured him, turning away to climb back to her position in the rocks.

"Let's go home," Nana said to the rest of them.

Frontier Fort.

5. Fort Craig

How times have changed, Hatch was thinking as he left his house for the short walk to the Adobe Palace. An hour before, one of the sycophants who surrounded Sheldon had appeared in the general's office and demanded—yes, demanded—that Hatch appear before the governor *immediately.* Lew Wallace would never have pulled that trick; he simply would have dropped by the office for a chat.

Hatch's response to the summons had been brusque at best. He had told the man that he would see the governor when he had the time, and then ordered him out of the building. He knew he could not refuse Sheldon's demand, but he certainly was not going to drop everything and run over there. Instead, he leisurely returned to his house and changed his clothes, choosing a field commander's uniform to replace his usual informal suit.

Hatch assumed that the word was out on the Apache massacre at

Laguna Springs. Undoubtedly, Sheldon would be questioning him about the situation and what action he was taking to protect the citizens. He wished he had some encouraging news for the governor, but Guilfoyle had not yet reported. In this case, no news was definitely not good news.

He prepared mentally for what was to come by reminding himself that he was the most powerful man in New Mexico. The interloper Sheldon was merely some political appointee from back east who had no idea what was going on in the territory.

When he arrived at the Adobe Palace, Hatch was immediately recognized and escorted into the governor's office by a somber male secretary, someone obviously brought to Santa Fe from Washington. Sheldon was sitting behind his desk studying documents, and he waved for Hatch to take a seat on the settee directly opposite. He was a thin man, slightly balding, dressed in a suit jacket that was buttoned right up to the knot in his string tie. He sported a thick mustache but was beardless, and appeared somewhat scholarly because of the narrow, wire-rimmed reading glasses that were perched on the end of his nose.

"Good morning, Governor," said Hatch.

"Not too much good about it, Colonel," Sheldon replied sardonically.

Silence descended over the room and Hatch quickly analyzed the situation. It was a typical politician's ploy—get someone on your territory, try to exert authority, make the other one nervous. Two could play this game, he decided.

"I imagine there must be a reason you've interrupted my morning and requested my presence here," Hatch said in a neutral tone.

Hatch's feint startled Sheldon, and his eyes widened momentarily. But he quickly recovered his aplomb, straightened up in his chair and stared at Hatch. "Indeed there is. I had a visitor this morning, a newspaperman by the name of Mr. Greene. He brought me this."

Sheldon placed a newspaper clipping on the edge of his desk and Hatch picked it up and scanned it. "Apaches Kill Three; Bodies Mutilated," read the headline from *The Rio Grande Republican*.

"What I want to know, Colonel, is why I had to learn this bad news from a Las Cruces newspaper rather than from the Army headquarters less than a block from my office."

Hatch remained calm. "I am waiting for Lieutenant Guilfoyle, who is chasing the Apaches, to report in. After I had all the facts, I intended to send you a full report."

Sheldon raised his voice. "But I seem to be the last person to know these things!"

"And if you had been the first to know, what would you have done about it?"

Hatch's logic frustrated Sheldon, who held up a fistful of telegrams. "I'm being deluged with reports of Indian atrocities."

"I am too," Hatch replied.

"Here's one that says the entire Mescalero tribe has escaped the reservation."

Hatch shook his head. "Not true. I had a telegram from Agent Llewellyn yesterday, and he said that only about twenty or twenty-five Mescaleros had joined Nana." Hatch deliberately neglected to mention the agent's harsh criticism of Guilfolyle and Bennett.

Sheldon scanned another sheet of paper. "What about this report that says two towns near Fort Selden were sacked and twenty-seven of twenty-nine inhabitants killed?"

"No verification as yet. I wired Colonel Parker and he reported that there were no raids near his fort. Just rumors, I'd say. As far as we know, Nana's band has killed four soldiers and about six civilians. We've heard tales that sixty Apaches were seen at Acoma, that another bunch shot up Socorro and killed six people, but I don't have enough troops to check them all out. Every little town in the territory is screaming for protection, but the Army's job is to catch Nana."

Sheldon fell silent again and stared at the ceiling as if considering his options. After a minute or so, he took a breath, stared at Hatch, and spoke in a low voice. "I suppose you know that I'm well acquainted with Mr. Robert Lincoln, the Secretary of War. Of course, I wouldn't want to bother him with a minor issue such as this. But if these raids continue, I'm afraid I must."

Hatch smiled to deflate the threat. "Go ahead—maybe he'll send me some badly-needed reinforcements. Mr. Governor, let me explain the situation. Nana's band is small and it moves very fast. I have my best Indian scouts, Companies A and B, chasing Nana this very moment—"

"Remember, Colonel Hatch," interrupted Sheldon, "I was a brigadier general in the Union Army and have extensive military experience. How difficult can it be to find this Nana? And how many more innocent citizens will this merciless renegade murder and torture before your men catch up to him, Colonel?"

A typical politician's question, Hatch thought. *This interloper thinks rhetoric will catch Indians.* He very nearly lost his temper, fighting the urge to pull the little man across the desk and pummel him with his fists. But he controlled himself and settled for staring Sheldon down while stating, coldly, "I assume those are rhetorical questions, Governor. Don't forget that the Territory of New Mexico is nearly three times the size of your home state of New York—and much less civilized."

Sheldon's facade finally broke and the governor managed a weak smile. "No need to remind me, Colonel—how well I know. Back in Washington New Mexico is called 'a large, underfed tick on the backside of America.' And now I'm the tick's leader." He lifted the telegrams and letters off his desk and let them fall among the clutter. "Just help me get rid of all these complaints."

Hatch sensed victory and decided to take pity on Sheldon. "It's my top priority. I'm mobilizing all my troops at this very moment and we're setting a trap for the hostiles. The Ninth Regiment of Cavalry and the Fifteen and Sixteenth Regiments of Infantry will soon be in the field and it's only a matter of time until we kill Nana and his men or drive them back to Mexico."

Sheldon relaxed visibly. "Thank you, Colonel. Sorry I interrupted your work. Just, please, keep me informed."

"I'll assign Captain Loud the responsibility of giving you a daily report," Hatch promised as he left the office, adding mentally, "*you pompous ass.*"

In fact, Hatch was indeed mobilizing his troops. He could not risk a repeat of the Victorio situation or a complaint to the Secretary of War.

When he returned to headquarters, he called Loud into his office and demanded a status report. But the captain had no news at all.

"Where the hell is Guilfoyle?" Hatch demanded.

Loud shrugged. "He hasn't reported in yet, sir."

"And where is Nana, for Christ's sake?"

Loud made a sweeping gesture with his right arm as if to encompass every square mile to the south of Santa Fe. "Somewhere out there in the wilderness, General."

When the shooting stopped, Guilfoyle assumed Nana was pulling another one of his tricks. He gave Bennett a questioning glance, but the chief-of-scouts merely shrugged his shoulders, a silent rendition of "beats the hell out of me." So Guilfoyle waited a half-hour before taking any action at all. Then he ordered Williams to take a few shots at the Apache positions. When their was no return fire, he sent Williams down the slope to investigate. The sergeant returned a few minutes later, unharmed and with a wide grin across his face.

"Have we got a su'prise for you, sah!"

"What's going on?"

"My men have done brought you a present."

Guilfoyle gave the order to move out and his troops carefully worked their way to lower ground. Waiting for them on the valley floor were Privates Walley and Jackson. With them were the horses and the deserter Chihuahua, wounded and tied up.

"Good work, men—" Guilfoyle began, but was interrupted by a shout from Bennett.

"You fucking deserter!" he screamed, and before anyone could stop him, kicked the Apache in the groin.

"Stop it, Bennett!" ordered Guilfoyle, but the chief scout ignored him. "Separate those two, Sergeant!"

Even though he sided with Bennett, Williams moved quickly to restrain him, but not before the scout had twirled Chihuahua around and pushed him face-first into a patch of prickly pear cactus.

"You'll hang for this, you asshole heathen," panted Bennett.

"Enough!" Guilfoyle shouted, his face inches away from Bennett's. "The Apache will be punished for what he did."

The chief-of-scouts stared at Guilfoyle and snarled, "Let's just shoot the fucker right now and be done with it. Who'll ever know?"

Guilfoyle grabbed Bennett's arm, dragged him away from the men, and spoke in low, urgent tones. "I'd like nothing better, but you know it's against regulations. If just one of our men says a word, it'll be you and me tried for murder."

Bennett finally seemed to calm down. "Okay, okay, I just lost my temper. Sorry, sir."

Guilfoyle grinned at Bennett. "I understand. Just control yourself and let's get the hell out of here."

Williams and Walley had pulled Chihuahua out of the cactus and were busy plucking the sharp spines from his face and neck. Despite the obvious pain, the Apache never flinched nor made a sound.

"How badly is the prisoner wounded, Private?"

"I done shot him twice, sah," Walley replied proudly. "But nothin' too serious."

Guilfoyle looked around at his men. "All right, listen up. We need reinforcements and supplies, but we also need to find Nana. We're going to head to Fort Craig *and* also follow the Apaches' trail so long as it's in the same general direction. Sergeant, give the orders to mount up. Bennett, check the maps for the location of the nearest safe spring."

They spent an hour burying the one soldier who had been killed by a sniper's bullet and bandaging the other four wounded men. Bennett located a spring with good water near the spot where the Apaches had camped, and Guilfoyle ordered his company to move out.

"Looks like I'm going to have to find some new scouts," Bennett observed once they were under way. He had calmed down considerably since his attack on Chihuahua.

"I suggest you select the next ones more carefully," teased Guilfoyle. "Scouts who don't poison the springs, desert our troops, and then shoot at us."

"No Chiricahuas?" Bennett asked with mock innocence.

"Try some Cherokees or Seminoles," Guilfoyle joked. He was so relieved over their narrow escape that he was almost giddy.

"What we need are some Navajos," Bennett suggested, "traditional enemies of the Apache."

"That's a good idea," said Guilfoyle, suddenly serious. "When we get to Fort Craig I'll send a telegram to General Hatch and ask him to get us some from Fort Wingate."

As expected, the spring was a short distance from the Apache camp in Hembrillo canyon, at the base of the small mountain. Once there, they filled canteens and refreshed the horses. Then Guilfoyle gave new orders that surprised Bennett.

"Take the men and continue tracking Nana's band," he said. "I'm going to stay here for a while and look around. I'll catch up later."

"But Lieutenant, the Apaches could be setting another trap," Bennett protested.

"I don't think so. They're on the run now. Anyway, don't worry about me. I'll keep Private Walley with me."

Bennett eyed him suspiciously. "What are you looking for?"

"You're the one who brought up the story about Victorio's cache being here," Guilfoyle reminded the chief-of-scouts. "Besides the spring, there must be a reason they camped right here in the open. Maybe they have guns and ammunition hidden somewhere. If I find such a cache, I want to destroy it. Now move out."

After his men had ridden away, Guilfoyle and Walley searched the remains of the Apache camp but found nothing of value. Then Guilfoyle remembered that he had seen the Apaches near the summit of the small mountain, which was labeled "Soledad" on Bennett's map. *Soledad, a fitting name*, thought Guilfoyle as he walked up the narrow, barely distinguishable path to the top. *Nothing but solitude up here.*

The top of the peak consisted of a series of vertical stone formations similar to the ones they had used as cover from the Apache gunfire. The tall rocks concealed deep crevices between them, and Guilfoyle suspected that if there was a cave containing Victorio's cache, one of the crevices would lead to it. They explored the rocks at the peak for nearly two hours in the hot sun before Walley spotted a particularly dark crevice tucked away under a large rock ledge.

Guilfoyle squeezed his body between the rocks and found himself in a shallow cave. It had obviously been inhabited at some time because he found remains of a campfire. In the dim light he could also see a wall painting that consisted of designs similar to those he had seen carved into rocks—animal figures, suns, moons, and stick figures representing people. In the center of the cave floor was a round, flat rock about three feet in diameter. Guilfoyle wondered if it were an altar of some sort, but when he walked over it, he detected an unusual, hollow sound.

Curious, he knelt down and brushed the dirt away from the edges of the rock and then attempted to move it. The rock yielded slightly and Guilfoyle used all his strength to dislodge it. The rock covered a shaft that fell away into total darkness. A damp, musty odor assailed Guilfoye's nostrils as he poked his head into the shaft. He could see nothing, but as he probed with his right hand, he encountered a thick rope that was tied to a sharp outcropping and dropped into the shaft. He could not tell how long the rope was. He dropped a stone down the shaft and counted the seconds until he heard it hit. Three seconds. How deep was it? A hundred feet? Anyway, certainly deep enough to kill him if he fell.

Guilfoyle left the cave, squeezed through the crevice, and found Walley sitting in the shade of the rocks. "Private, I need to make some torches."

"Torches, sah?" asked Walley.

"I found a dark cave. Use your knife and cut me some branches from those bushes. We'll see which ones burn the best."

A few minutes later, they discovered that the dried branches of several of the desert plants burned very well but produced lots of smoke. They collected a large bundle of them and hauled them up to the crevice. Guilfoyle re-entered the cave and Walley passed him the branches, which Guilfoyle promptly dropped down the shaft. At least he would have some light down there, he thought.

"This may take some time," he called to Walley. "Stay on watch until I come back."

"Yes, sah," came the reply.

Guilfoyle lowered himself feet first into the shaft and grabbed the rope with both hands. It was not as difficult as he thought it would be to lower himself into it because the shaft was so narrow he could brace his feet and knees against it the sides as he went down.

The descent took about ten minutes. Guilfoyle wiggled free from the shaft, lit a match, and discovered he was in a narrow cavern perhaps seven feet high that descended even further into the heart of the mountain. He gathered up his branches, lit one afire, and followed the cavern.

He traveled perhaps a quarter-mile and then crossed an underground stream—undoubtedly the source of the spring at the base of the peak; and then a short distance further on, the narrow cavern opened up into a large room with a very high ceiling. He noticed that the smoke from his torch was drawn straight up. Needing additional light, Guilfoyle set several of the oily branches on fire. He was stunned by what he saw.

On the ground to his left was a human skeleton with the bones of the hands tied behind the back with a rotting rope. Nearby were Wells Fargo chests, trunks, and other wooden boxes. Across the room were dozens of other skeletons chained to wooden posts. Guilfoyle was not superstitious, but the unexpected graveyard caused shivers down his spine. He shook off the feeling and made a quick search of the room.

He discovered Spanish swords and daggers, rusted old rifles and pistols, and two saddles. Near the first skeleton was what appeared to be a religious altar of some sort. He opened one of the chests and found gold and silver coins, and some loose jewels that appeared in the dim light to be rubies and emeralds. He took a few coins and jewels for samples and put them in his pocket. One of the trunks contained old clothing that was falling apart, some bibles written in Spanish, and some statues of religious figures.

One of Guilfoyle's most curious finds was what appeared to be a smelter. In the center of the large room there was a crude adobe furnace, ingot molds, a stack of firewood, and two bellows made from hide. To the right of the room entrance, on the far back wall, Guilfoyle discovered a long stack of metal bars covered with buffalo hides. The bars, coated with soot and dirt, were stacked like cordwood in a pile about four paces long and chest-high. It looked like pig iron to Guilfoyle, and he was about to disregard the metal when he changed his mind and retrieved a single bar measuring about six inches long and two inches thick, and placed it in his pocket with the coins and jewels.

He realized that a complete search of the large room would take hours and recovery of the chests and trunks might take days. He decided he'd better return to the business at hand—chasing Apaches—and leave the treasure hunting for another time. After lighting some of the sticks of firewood by the adobe furnace, Guilfoyle slowly made his way back through the narrow cavern.

He was completely baffled by what he had found. Besides being a cache, was the cavern a dungeon for prisoners? An underground smelting operation? A hideout of some sort? He had found a strange group of objects, but no evidence that Apaches had used the place to hide guns and ammunition. Yet he had seen them at the summit. Maybe they had been praying, or making an offering to whatever god they believed in.

Guilfoyle found the vertical shaft without difficulty, extinguished his crude torch, and began the tedious and uncomfortable job of pulling himself up the rope. It was dirty work because the rope kept dislodging dirt and stones, which fell on his head and shoulders. After a few minutes, though, he learned the trick of using his feet to brace himself against the shaft to rest, and then pushing forward while pulling on the rope. In that manner, he reached the top of the shaft in about twenty minutes. At the top, Private Walley was waiting and literally pulled him out.

"I was about to go lookin' for you, sah," he said.

"No need," said Guilfoyle.

"Find anythin'?"

"Nothing of interest," Guilfoyle lied. "If the Apaches ever used this place, they took everything with them. Let's get out of here."

While Walley went to fetch the tethered horses, Guilfoyle stepped into the sunlight and pulled the bar out of his pocket. He spit on it and rubbed some of the dirt and soot off it and could barely make out some letters inscribed on it. They spelled "LaRue," the same name they had found at the old mine. Using his knife, Guilfoyle scraped through the remaining dirt and into the soft metal below, which glimmered brilliantly in the sunlight. He realized that the bar was solid gold.

Guilfoyle and Walley caught up to Bennett and the troopers in the flat, arid plain known as the *Jornada del Muerto*—a name that was particularly appropriate because it was obvious that his men had just finished filling in a grave.

"What's this?" demanded the lieutenant.

"More of Nana's work," Bennett replied. "A trader, by the looks of the wagon. Shot in the chest but not mutilated. The Apaches ransacked the wagon. You find anything?"

"Nope. A waste of time." Guilfoyle turned to Sergeant Williams. "Have the men mount up and move out."

Bennett pointed due north. "The Apaches are headed that way… toward Fort Craig."

After they set off in pursuit, Guilfoyle first wondered if Nana's Apaches would dare to attack the fort. Then his mind wandered back to the cache of gold. For the first time since he had joined the Army, he thought seriously about resigning his commission. He had planned a lifetime Army career, as would any West Point graduate; but finding a multi-million-dollar treasure certainly changed everything. Right now, he was risking his life for twenty-five dollars a month, while eating terrible food and risking dysentery on a daily basis. And at the current rate of promotion in the Army, it would take him twenty-three years to make the rank of major.

He imagined how he might play the game. He would tell no one about his find and patiently wait out his fifth and last year as an Army lieutenant. Then he would resign his commission, buy a wagon and team of mules, and recover the gold from the Soledad Peak cave. Rich beyond his wildest dreams, he could return in triumph to Baltimore and claim his bride-to-be, Cathleen.

Bennett rode up beside him and shattered his reverie. "What about that gold?" he whispered.

Guilfoyle was startled. Had Bennett somehow seen him enter the cave? "W-what about what gold?"

Bennett grinned at him. "You know, Lieutenant, the gold nuggets we found at the old Spanish mine. You still goin' to turn 'em in to the Army paymaster?"

Relieved, Guilfoyle chuckled as if he had been joking all along. He reached into his saddlebag and felt the two remaining sacks of nuggets. In a low voice, he told Bennett, "One sack for me, one for you, and one for Uncle Sam. Does that sound fair?"

"'Specially if you tell that paymaster that you combined all the sacks into one for safekeepin.'"

"Good idea."

They followed the Apache's trail north from the *Jornada del Muerto* through the western foothills of the San Andres range, but Guilfoyle's troop did not make much progress that day. Soon darkness overtook them and the lieutenant called a halt. They pitched camp on a bluff overlooking a wide arroyo called Cottonwood Draw and ate their usual meal of beef jerky, stale bread, and boiled beans. Their Apache prisoner refused to eat but no one knew if his hunger strike was the result of pride or the fact that his lips and throat were so swollen from the cactus spines that he could barely swallow. However, he did deign to drink some water offered by his guard, Private Walley, who finished his beans and fetched a short piece of rope from the saddle that also served as his pillow. He looped it through the tied wrists of Chihuahua, and dragged the Apache to a mesquite thicket, and tied him to the thickest trunk.

"Don't you be hurtin' dat 'Pache," joked Sergeant Williams, who was relaxing nearby.

"No, sah, I won't. I'se makin' shore he don't run nowhere."

"Mebee tomorrow dat brave have hisself a bad acc'dent," the sergeant speculated, his voice loud enough for Chihuahua to hear. "Fall clean off 'is horse, hit 'is head on a rock an' split his skull wide open."

Walley was silent for a moment and then looked at the sergeant defiantly. "He deserves a fair trial."

Williams was flabbergasted. "He *deserves* shit! He's a fuckin' traitor."

"But sarge, de army made 'im a slave! Made 'im fight 'gainst his own people."

"You mind youh tongue, boy," Williams warned. "This be a white man's army and youh just a no-count niggah."

"Well, anyways I'se a free niggah," Walley retorted. "Dat 'Pache dere, he still be a slave."

"Shut youh mouth, Private. Dat's an ordah!"

Walley fell silent as Guilfoyle walked up to them. "Any trouble, Sergeant?"

"No sah," Williams. "We was jist talkin' 'bout de prisonah. Private Walley heah volunteer to stay up all night an' watch 'im."

"That's the spirit," praised Guilfoyle. "All right, Private, you take first watch. Wake Private Woods at 2 a.m."

"Yes sah," said Walley while giving his sergeant a dirty look.

For the next three days, Guilfoyle's buffalo troopers tracked the elusive Apaches but never got close enough to see them, much less to engage them in battle. The trail turned northwest near the Chalk Hills and crossed the *Jornada del Muerto*. Guilfoyle suspected Nana knew the soldiers were following, because once they entered the Fra Cristobal range, the trail no longer went north but wandered wildly through what seemed to be every canyon in those mountains. Finally, after determining that the Apaches had reversed direction and were headed due south, Guilfoyle gave up the pursuit in frustration and decided to push on north to Fort Craig, about twenty-five miles away.

When they finally approached the sanctuary of the fort, the men were half-starved and their horses half-dead. Fort Craig was built on a mesa on the west bank of the Rio Grande, so it was necessary for the troop to ford the shallow river at the tiny town of Paraje and approach the fort from the south. Bennett took the lead and followed the trail to the left side of the fort.

As they crossed a wooden bridge over the wide ditch that encircled the fort, Guilfoyle noticed that unlike Fort Cummings, which was constructed entirely of adobe bricks, the ten-foot-high wall around Fort

Craig was built with upright tree trunks chinked with mud. There were large gaps in the wall where the mud had fallen out, an indication that the fort was in dire need of repair. He guessed they had been spotted by lookouts and identified by their Ninth Cavalry flag, so he did not waste the energy to hail the fort.

They entered Fort Craig through the gate on the west side, and were immediately greeted by the post commander and his staff. Guilfoyle and Bennett immediately saluted. "Second Lieutenant John Guilfoyle and Chief-of-Scouts Frank Bennett reporting, sir."

The commander, a middle-aged man who was surprisingly overweight, greeted them with a jovial smile. "Well, Lieutenant, good to see you. I'm Captain John Bean. Everyone seems to think you and all your men are dead."

"Close to it, sir. We have a prisoner who needs immediate medical attention and my men need food."

Captain Bean ordered his men to assist Guilfoyle's troop. The soldiers were taken to the barracks on the south wall of the fort, where they were served a hot meal and allowed to rest. Their horses were unsaddled and released in the corrals and fed hay for the first time in weeks.

Chihuahua was carried to the post hospital by three burly soldiers who handled him as if he were not unconscious but might—at any moment— rip free from his bonds and leap over the wall to freedom. At the hospital, his wounds were cleaned by assistant surgeon James Collins, who also found in his face about twenty small cactus spines overlooked by Sergeant Williams. After treatment, Chihuahua was taken to the dungeon beneath the guard room on the northwest corner of the fort and placed in a cell measuring four feet on a side. He was left there on the dirt floor, alive but still unconscious, with a single cup of water and a piece of hard bread beside him.

Meanwhile, Guilfoyle and Bennett were having lunch with Captain Bean in the officers' mess. The meal, served by a pleasant Mexican woman named Maria, consisted of chicken and dumplings with a bowl of green chile on the side.

"Here's a telegram from General Hatch," Bean said as he passed it to

Guilfoyle. It requested a status report on Nana as soon as the lieutenant arrived at Fort Craig. "You can wire him after lunch," Bean added.

"This place seems busier than usual," Bennett observed.

Bean beamed. "At last, it's a real fort again. Reinforcements arrive daily on the train from Fort Wingate and soon we'll be at full strength. You probably don't realize it, Lieutenant, but Fort Craig was nearly abandoned three years ago. Believe it or not, then this fort had only one officer and seven enlisted men. But Victorio's raid changed all that and Company H of the 15th Infantry was transferred from Fort Stanton. Now we have enough strength to run all the renegades—"

He was interrupted by the appearance of a tall, thin man with a handlebar mustache and long, curly locks that flowed from beneath a wide-brimmed hat. "Beggin' the Captain's pardon," he said.

Bean was annoyed by the intrusion. "What is it, Crawford?"

"With the Captain's permission, Maria and I would like to organize a little celebration tonight for these noble fighters against the heathen Apache."

"Sure, sure, fine with me. Lieutenant Guilfoyle, do you think your men would enjoy some entertainment?"

"Yes sir," he replied, amused.

"Make it so, Captain Jack," Bean ordered.

"Thank you sir. Good to meet you," he said to Guilfoyle and Bennett despite the fact that introductions had not been made.

"That was Captain Jack Crawford," Bean explained after the man left the mess, "a former Indian scout and now the fort's postmaster and trader. He's also a poet."

"A poet?" asked Guilfoyle.

"You'll hear it for yourself soon enough," promised Bean, rolling his eyes. "He's what you might call a wild west character—used to be a scout for General Crook and later Buell. Claims he saw action against the Sioux and the Apache, but I never found anyone who saw him fire a shot. He dresses like his hero, Buffalo Bill Cody, and even wears his hair and handlebar mustache the same way. Lately he's been promotin' gold mines in the Black Range to rich investors from Denver."

After lunch, Guilfoyle wired Hatch a lengthy report about the pursuit of Nana, the Chihuahua situation, and the current status of Company B. He joined Bennett for a refreshing and cleansing swim in the Rio Grande, then retired to his quarters for a well-deserved nap.

He was awakened near sunset by Bennett, who told him that dinner was served—not in the mess, but on the parade ground.

"We're eating out?" asked Guilfoyle sleepily.

"It's a fuckin' picnic," Bennett said.

In all of his four years in the army, Guilfoyle had never seen anything like it. The parade ground had been transformed into an outdoor restaurant, complete with tables and chairs, a mesquite fire for grilling meat, and a large serving table covered with food. The enlisted men, both black and white, were lined up to be served by Maria and Captain Jack, while the officers stood around conversing in small groups.

The mood in the fort was downright jovial, thought Guilfoyle. This could be the Plaza in Santa Fe instead of a military post.

"Gentlemen," said Captain Bean, "you don't have to line up. Officers eat first. Step over here and Maria will serve you." Guilfoyle and Bennett followed the captain over to the serving table.

"A steak, Lieutenant?" asked Captain Jack.

"Thanks. This is right neighborly of you."

"It's practice," Captain Jack told him. "Maria and me are opening up the Scout's Hotel over there in Paraje. We're going to call it 'the soldier's home and bivouac, the miner's safe retreat.'"

"Is there that much hotel business around here?" Guilfoyle asked, sweeping his arm in a gesture that included the *Jornada del Muerto* and indicated the territory's vast emptiness.

"There will be, once you and your men wipe out the Apaches."

Don't hold your breath, thought Guilfoyle, but he said nothing except "Thanks for the food."

An hour later after everyone was fed and the parade ground was lit up with torches, Captain Jack stood on the serving table, which doubled as an impromptu stage. As the men turned to watch him, he put his finger over his lips in an attempt to quiet the crowd. When they were reasonably silent, he began his performance.

"Tonight we are assembled to honor the Indian Scouts of Company B, Ninth Cavalry, led by Lieutenant John Guilfoyle. As you know, they have spent the last two weeks chasing and fighting the deadly Apaches, who are led by that crafty old chief, Nana. Twice these soldiers of Company B have engaged the enemy and twice they have emerged victorious. But the Apaches have not given up yet, so there will be more battles to come. The first poem tonight honors those brave men who must face death on a daily basis. It's called, 'Who the Heroes Were.'"

He nodded to the drummer standing beside the table, who began a soft, yet military, tapping on his drum. Captain Jack stared at the rising moon for a few seconds, looked out over the crowd, and began reciting his poem.

"You 'never was scared in battle?' Here,
Old comrade, don't make a break like that!
The man don't live who was free from fear
When the vicious bullets began to spat;
And the cannons belched from their iron throats
The deafening notes of the song of war—
The frightful, terrible thundering notes
That caused the eternal earth to jar."

Captain Jack paused to allow the tapping to build into a cresendo, and then fade away.

"I've heard men say they were just as cool
In the heat of battle as they would be
In a quiet seat in a Sabbath school,
But they couldn't find a believer in me.
I never flinched, never shirked a call,
But several times in the war-swept South,
If I'd been shot through the heart, the ball
Would have had to hit me square in the mouth!"
He paused to allow some chuckles from the audience.
"It's the silliest sort of talk we hear—

And hear from soldiers of solid worth—
That they stood in the front and felt no fear
When the rumbling of battle convulsed the earth.
I hold that our bravest men were those
Who felt alarm at the cannons' roar,
Yet never rearward turned their toes,
But stood like men till the fight was o'er."

Captain Jack hung his head during the polite applause. It was evident to Guilfoyle that the soldiers were uncertain how to react to a poetry reading. They were probably waiting for the dancing girls to come out. The poet-scout recited a few more of his verses until it was obvious that the crowd was becoming restless.

"Now for a bit of storytellin'," said Captain Jack. "Since we're here tonight to honor the Apache fighters of Company B, let me tell you about the time I almost captured Victorio."

"Right," whispered Bennett. "And I was almost elected president."

His story, which rambled on for nearly a half-hour, had little to do with Victorio and everything to do with Captain Jack. After suffering through numerous digressions, Guilfoyle finally understood what had happened. Jack Crawford had been sent by General Buell into Mexico with a interpreter in an attempt to persuade Victorio to surrender. He had located Victorio's camp, but the interpreter refused to go near it. Then they left and returned to the United States. The entire purpose of his story was to introduce a song he had written which was inspired by a letter from his wife.

"In her letter," Captain Jack continued, "my dear wife Maria wrote the following words: 'Remember, my love, that while you are struggling for us amid dangers and hardships, you have little ones at home praying for you.' That letter and the soft, dreamy surrounds threw me into a poetic mood, and from my saddle pocket I procured a piece of paper in which some jerked meat had been wrapped, and with a short stub of pencil, by the glare of that luminous queen of light overhead, using my saddle as a table, I wrote this song."

Captain Jack picked up his guitar, strummed it a few times, and began to sing.

"There are little ones praying for me far away,
There are little ones praying for me;
With tiny hands pressed before each little breast,
Their sweet faces in dreamland I see.
'Bless papa, dear Father, where'er he may go,
And where duty may call him to roam;
Through the hills or the valleys of Old Mexico,
Watch over him and bring him safe home.'"

Maria, who was standing next to the serving table, joined her husband in the chorus.

"So to-night I am happy in Old Mexico,
While I sit in the moonlight alone;
For surely 'tis pleasant to feel and to know
There are little ones praying at home."
Captain Jack pointed to the moon as if thanking it for being a prop.
"The moon in her splendor is shining to-night,
By her beams I am writing just now,
While an angel of love seems to smile down from above
With the bright star of hope on her brow;
And whisper in language so sweet to my soul,
'I am with you wherever you roam;
And remember when weary and foot-sore at night,
You have little ones praying at home.'"

As Maria joined the poet-scout in a repeat of the chorus, Guilfoyle leaned toward Bennett. "I think we've found the perfect punishment for Chihuahua," he whispered. "Instead of hanging him, we'll tie him up and have Captain Jack sing to him for hours on end."

Bennett laughed aloud, which drew a reproving glance from Maria just as she was singing "little ones praying at home" for the last time.

"That's it for me," said Captain Jack, "all you men remember your little ones and loved ones at home!" The applause that greeted the ending of his performance indicated that the troops had endured just about all the poetry they could for one night. The poet-scout was followed by a local Mexican band that played *rancheras* as they strolled around the grounds.

Guifoyle, however, was quickly losing interest in the music. His mind was focused on the bar of gold in the saddlebag under his bunk in the officers' quarters.

"Look at this," Hatch snarled as he showed the *Daily New Mexican* to his wife. The headline read, "Hatch Reneges on Promise to End Apache Threat," and the general cursed the article as a libelous mishmash of rumor and sensationalism. However, in deference to his wife's tender ears, the word "hogwash" was the worst profanity the general used to describe the story.

"Now Edward," scolded Evelyn, who was making gravy in the kitchen, "you're getting all worked up over nothing. Just relax—dinner will be ready—"

"Over nothing?" Hatch exploded. "This man Greene is out to ruin my reputation and you say it's nothing?"

Evelyn remained calm even though her husband's face was turning beet red. "I just meant that there's nothing you can do about it. Freedom of the press and all that."

Hatch gulped the remainder of his bourbon-and-branch and poured another one. "There *is* something I can do about it," he muttered.

"You can't court-martial a civilian," Evelyn joked.

"No, but I can kill an Apache or two."

"I thought you had troops to do that."

"Well, they're not getting it done, so I'm taking the field."

Evelyn stared at her husband. In a low, calm voice, she said, "Edward, you are nearly fifty years old. You're in good shape for a man of your age, but I hardly think you're up to chasing Indians for weeks in the New Mexico sun."

Hatch relaxed for the first time that evening and smiled at his wife. "Calm down, Evelyn. The word 'field' merely indicates that I am not going to sit on my backside here in Santa Fe and take abuse from the newspapers. Today I issued Special Order 96, which directs various units of the Ninth to move to forts in the southern part of the territory. I'm moving my headquarters to Fort Craig."

"When?" asked Evelyn.

"Tomorrow."

Ever the Army wife, Evelyn merely said, "I'll pack your bags tonight."

"That way," Hatch continued, "I'll have hands-on command instead of waiting around for telegrams."

"Go sit down," she ordered. "Dinner's ready."

As they dined on Evelyn's leg of mutton with mashed potatoes, gravy, and fresh green beans from her garden, at her request the conversation turned from chasing Apaches to other matters.

"Did you walk through the Plaza today?" Hatch asked.

"No, I was trapped here all day cleaning and cooking," Evelyn answered. "Why? Was there a gun fight?"

"There was this huckster on the Plaza charging people twenty-five cents to look at Billy the Kid's trigger finger preserved in a jar of alcohol. He was doing a brisk business."

Evelyn was astonished. "My word! How on earth did he get that finger?"

Hatch pointed in the direction of the fireplace. "The same way I got Abe Lincoln's original axe."

"Now Edward Hatch, stop it. That is not Abe Lincoln's axe. I know for a fact you bought it at Seligman's store."

"Yes, I did, and Seligman told me the history of that axe. It's Abe's axe all right—it's just had three new handles and four new heads."

Despite being taken in, Evelyn had to laugh. "I see. It's Billy's finger all right—but which Billy?"

"Precisely. Oh, by the way, Governor Sheldon called me into his office again, two weeks to the day since that last meeting."

Evelyn rolled her eyes. "Not more Apache stories, I hope."

"Not this time. Oh, I told him I was moving my command to Fort Craig, but the real reason he called me in was to show me Lew's last official proclamation."

"And what was that?"

Hatch smirked. "Sheldon said he found an envelope in his desk addressed to Lew's successor as governor...."

"Are you teasing me?"

"In the envelope was a proclamation." With a flourish, Hatch pulled a piece of paper from his pocket and read from it. "Declaring that his last official act was, quote, 'to agree to the request of the Santa Fe Railroad to proclaim the name of Hatch's Station for a town between Rincon and Deming in honor of Edward Hatch's exemplary service to the people of New Mexico.'"

"Why Edward, you have your own town!"

"Maybe we should retire there," he jested. "We'll shorten the name to 'Hatch.'"

"Oh no you don't. I remember our stay at Fort Thorne. What a miserable place."

"Fort Thorne has been decommissioned permanently, darling. But the little town of Hatch nearby will someday be famous world-wide."

"Famous for what?"

"I'm not sure; I just have a feeling about it."

"Well I have another feeling," Evelyn said with a smile.

"And what's that?"

"If you don't catch Nana, Sheldon will change the name of the town of Hatch to Bonney."

They laughed for quite a while over that prediction. After a while, Evelyn served *flan* for dessert, and the couple spent the rest of the evening discussing likely locations for settling down after the general's retirement from the Army. The topic of Nana did not come up again.

The following morning, Hatch directed Captain Loud to send a report on the military operations to Secretary of War Robert Lincoln, who had sent an inquiring telegram two days before. Hatch told Loud to request additional troops from forts in Texas, Colorado, and Arizona, and funds to repair Forts Craig and Cummings.

"All of that to chase forty renegades," Hatch sighed. "Let's see if the Secretary of War is really interested in defeating the Apaches," he said to Loud.

"In my humble opinion, Washington doesn't give a rat's ass for New Mexico," Loud replied. "That telegram from Lincoln merely means citizens are complaining to him."

"At any rate," Hatch continued, "let's play by the rules. Make sure Sheldon knows about Special Order 96 and our offensive against Nana."

"Yes, sir. Good luck in the field."

"I'll need it," Hatch said ironically. "I've only got the enemy outnumbered a hundred to one."

Later that morning, a military wagon carried Hatch and his baggage to the depot at the end of Montezuma Avenue, where the general boarded the passenger car for the short ride on the spur line to Lamy. There, he waited about two hours for the southbound train, which, he later learned, had been delayed by cattle crossing the tracks near Las Vegas. There was nothing for Hatch to do at the tiny station but sit in the shade and continue the torturous task of reading *Ben-Hur*, which Evelyn had pressed into his hand just before he had kissed her goodbye.

"Remember, Edward," she had said, "Lew was good enough to name a town after you. The least you can do is finish his book."

"But I'm too busy," Hatch had protested.

"Nonsense. It's a long train ride down there and I know how boring those remote forts can be."

"Yes, dear," he had acquiesced.

Hatch was about one-fifth through the book and had been stuck for over a week at the point where Ben-Hur was arrested for dislodging a roof tile which had fallen on the head of the Roman soldier Gratus—a story line he thought was completely contrived. Hatch was having difficulty concentrating on fiction because his mind was filled with reality, but the description of Ben-Hur as a prisoner was a tempting parallel to what

Hatch wished for Nana: bareheaded, half-naked, his hands bound behind him, a thong fixed to his wrist and looped over the neck of a horse.

Now wouldn't it be satisfying, Hatch thought, *to have Nana in that condition and then drag him through the Plaza to be hanged in public.* Although he knew he was supposed to feel sympathy for Ben-Hur, Hatch identified more with the Roman soldiers than with the persecuted Jew who was the hero of the story. Despite the distractions of the real world, Hatch persevered and plowed through Wallace's tedious prose in search of some action.

By the time the train arrived at Lamy, Ben-Hur was a galley slave for life, the best oarsman aboard the *Astroea.* When they reached Albuquerque, Hatch felt better about the book because of the combat scene with the pirates—a sea battle was the only warfare he had not yet experienced. But the sea rescue and the adoption of Ben-Hur by Arrius was unconvincing, and Hatch's attention wandered again. He checked the table of contents, discovered a chapter entitled "A Roman Orgie," and skipped ahead seventy pages to read it. But he was disappointed to discover that the orgy involved drinking rather than fornication, so he finally put the book aside. For the remainder of the train ride to Socorro, Hatch studied a military map of the territory and made notes on his battle plan.

At the small depot in Socorro, Hatch was met by a contingent of cavalry led by Captain Bean and Lieutenant Guilfoyle. He was pleased to note that they brought a horse for him to ride instead of a wagon. After the usual greetings and a brief stop at a saloon to pick up a couple of bottles of bourbon at Hatch's request, they headed south at a steady trot. At the head of the troop with Bean, Hatch felt in control of things for the first time in weeks.

"Glad you're here, sir," said Bean. "The renegades are in trouble now."

Hatch, who disliked obsequious officers, merely nodded to the captain.

Once during the three-hour trip to Fort Craig, Bean dropped back to speak to one of his men and Guilfoyle rode up beside Hatch. "I need to speak to you, sir—in private."

"Indeed, Lieutenant," the general agreed. "I want a full report on your encounter with the renegades. We'll meet after dinner tonight and you can brief me for the full staff meeting in the morning."

The sun was setting as the small troop approached the fort. Bean said, "Sorry for the condition of the fort, sir. As you can see, it's in dire need of repair."

"I've asked the Secretary of War for the funds, but don't get your hopes up."

Hatch was given the commanding officer's quarters for the duration of his stay, and it was there that he met with Guilfoyle after the obligatory dinner with his field staff. They sat at the small table and Hatch poured each of them a shot of bourbon. The lieutenant, who seemed unusually subdued to Hatch, recounted the pursuit of Nana, the incident of the poisoned spring and subsequent battle, and the treachery of Chihuahua.

"You did all you could do, Lieutenant," said Hatch. "Tomorrow during the staff meeting we'll go over plans to finally trap that bastard Nana. Also, I'm going to court-martial and hang Chihuahua as quickly as possible—with Mescalero witnesses present so all the Apaches will get the message that we will not tolerate renegades or traitors."

"There's one other thing, General," Guilfoyle said, reaching into his boot. He withdrew a small, cloth-wrapped bundle and placed it on the table in front of Hatch, then slowly unwrapped it until the gold bar glistened in the light from the oil lamp.

"My god," exclaimed Hatch, picking up the bar. "Where did you get this?"

"In a cave at that peak in Hembrillo Canyon. I think it was one of Victorio's caches. There's hundreds more like it stacked like firewood. A fortune, sir." He described the location of the cave and explained how he found the gold.

"Who is 'LaRue'?" asked Hatch.

"I have no idea, but we did come across an old mine several miles from the peak and found that same name carved into some timbers."

"How big is this stack of gold, anyway?" asked Hatch.

"I paced it off. One stride out from the wall, four strides long, and chest-high."

Hatch gave Guilfoyle a wry smile. "And what do you propose we do about this treasure, Lieutenant?"

Guilfoyle finally smiled back. "I was hoping you'd have an idea about that, sir."

"Well, it's a shame we're chasing Apaches. If not, I could send a special detachment of a few trusted men—led by you, of course—to recover that gold. But we can't do it now. Imagine what the newspapers would say if they got wind of a treasure hunt when we were supposed to be catching Nana."

"Who owns the gold? The Army?"

Hatch topped off each glass with bourbon. "I'm not a lawyer, but I'd say the first person to recover it owns it. I'm not sure that the U.S. Army has anything to do with it, unless it was stolen to begin with. Does anyone else know about this gold?"

"Definitely not."

"Good. Damn, it's a shame Lew Wallace isn't still governor. He was treasure-happy, you know."

"No, sir, I didn't."

"He would have told everyone he was going to Washington, then he'd have doubled back and personally recovered the gold. He would have found a way to sell it and then split the money with us."

Guilfoyle looked distressed. "But what do we do about it *now*?"

"Nothing," said Hatch.

"Nothing, sir?"

"That's right. Until we solve this Apache problem, the treasure will stay right where it is. Tell no one—that's an order."

"Yes, sir."

Hatch picked up the gold bar. "And I'll take this for safe-keeping."

Guilfoyle resisted the urge to snatch the bar out of his commanding officer's hand. He thought that maybe he had done something really stupid by telling Hatch about the gold.

Promptly at seven the following morning, Hatch's staff assembled
in the officers' mess for a strategy session. Present were Hatch, post
commander Bean, Guilfoyle, Bennett, Lieutenant Gustavus Valois
from Fort Wingate, Lieutenant George Washington Smith from Fort
Cummings, Second Lieutenant William Taylor from Fort Bayard, and the
poet-scout Jack Crawford. They were served refried beans, mutton stew,
soft bread, and coffee by the mess sergeant, who quickly left the room
after serving the men.

Hatch gave them ten minutes to finish eating and then ordered, "Let's
begin." Bean assisted the general in unrolling a large map of New Mexico
on one of the mess tables as the rest of the men crowded around.

"We are here," said Hatch pointing to a dot with the legend reading
"Ft. Craig." He moved his finger north. "Fort Wingate is here and easily
accessible to the east-west tracks of the Santa Fe, which tie into the north-
south tracks at Belen." His finger followed the railway lines and moved
south on the map. "Down here are Forts Cummings and Bayard, both
near the east-west Southern Pacific tracks, which meet the Santa Fe tracks
at Rincon. We can easily move men and materials along the railway lines,
and that's how we will trap Nana. As you can see, wherever the renegade
is in any of these ranges, we have him three-quarters surrounded already.
Using the telegraph from here, I can, within a day or two, move men to
the closest point where Nana was last seen. Also, by moving out cavalry
from all four forts into these ranges, eventually we're going to cut his trail
and track him down. Now, the main question I have for you is: where is
Nana?"

Captain Bean pointed at the San Mateo range on the map. "The last
word we have is that he's approximately here. Three days ago, a group
of miners from the towns of Winston and Chloride, along with some
Mexican farmers, attempted to track down Nana. They rode up into Red
Canyon and were promptly attacked by the renegades. The Apaches killed
two of the vigilantes, wounded seven, and took all their horses. They were
damn lucky all of them weren't killed."

Hatch shook his head. "Amateurs and fools. Well, at least we know
where to start. Lieutenant Guilfoyle and Chief-of-Scouts Bennett will pick

up the trail at Red Canyon. By the way, arriving on the train tomorrow will be some Navajo scouts recruited at Fort Wingate and some 'tame' White Mountain Apaches from San Carlos."

"I'll take the Navajos if you don't mind," said Bennett, and the rest of the group laughed.

Hatch waved his hand for silence. "Does anyone have an idea of what Nana's up to or where he's headed?"

Guilfoyle pointed to the Black Range. "Since the area around Ojo Caliente is his band's homeland, it makes sense to me that Nana's headed there."

"Good thinking. We have a small post at Ojo Caliente. I'll send reinforcements. In two days time, Lieutenant Valois will lead his men south from Fort Wingate while Lieutenant Smith is moving his troop north from Fort Cummings. Hopefully, with Guilfoyle pursuing from the east, we'll trap the renegades in the Black Range."

"Or," said the poet-scout Crawford, "they'll move west through the Mogollon Range into Arizona."

A moment of uncomfortable silence fell over the group before Hatch glared at Crawford and retorted, "If they do that, they'll be General Willcox's problem. Our duty is to remove the renegades from the Territory of New Mexico. If they cross over to Arizona or Mexico, we have done our job. But still, I'd rather kill or capture them here. In fact, I have added incentive to accomplish that goal."

He reached into his boot, pulled out the gold bar, and set it in the middle of the map. Guilfoyle was startled—but said nothing—and he was relieved that the name of LaRue was not visible. If Bennett saw the name, he would immediately be suspicious. The other men stared silently at the gold.

"Where did you get that?" asked Bennett.

"That's classified information," said Hatch. "But I'll tell you this much: this gold bar is a bounty on Nana's head. The first one of my men to bring me that renegade, dead or alive, gets this gold bar as a bonus."

"That's hardly necessary, General," said Smith. "We all know what our duty is."

Hatch smiled broadly but avoided Guilfoyle's glance. "I know you do, Lieutenant, so just consider this bar a reward for the risks you are taking."

"Dead or alive," mused Bennett, whose tone left no doubt which status he would prefer for Nana.

"Preferably alive," added Hatch, "so I can personally see to his hanging on the Plaza at Santa Fe. Now, I need to speak with each of you individually and give you specific instructions about this military operation against the renegades."

Hatch set up private meetings with all of his officers for later that morning and pointedly ignored Crawford, who was beginning to feel out of place. Finally, the poet-scout cornered the general as he was about to leave the mess.

"What about me?" he asked.

"What about you?" countered Hatch.

"I'd like to go after that gold, sir," said Crawford. Hatch thought he looked ridiculous in his absurdly long hair and his Buffalo Bill get-up. He could imagine the pleasure Nana would get from a scalp like that.

"What is your current military status?" asked Hatch.

"Post trader and volunteer scout," replied the poet-scout.

"Request denied," said the general, dismissing him. He turned to Captain Bean and said, "I'd like to see the prisoner now."

As they walked across the parade ground, Bean said to Hatch, "Sorry about Crawford. He's a little eccentric."

"Keep that man out of my sight," ordered Hatch.

Bean was surprised at the general's vehemence and could not keep the sarcasm out of his reply. "Do you want me to remove him from the fort?"

"That won't be necessary. Does the prisoner speak English?"

"Bennett says he can understand and speak very basic words. But so far he has said nothing."

They entered the guard room and exchanged salutes with Sergeant Williams, who had been sitting in a chair directly on top of a wooden trapdoor that was built into the hard dirt floor.

"Let's see the traitor," Hatch said, and Williams moved the chair and lifted the trapdoor. A short stairway provided access to the dimly lit dungeon.

"Go ahead, sir," said Bean. "There's not room for both of us down there. Sergeant, go outside and open the shutters so the general can see what he's doing."

The dungeon was much smaller that Hatch expected, consisting of six solitary confinement cells measuring about six feet tall, three feet wide, and five feet deep. In the cell closest to the stairs, Chihuahua sat, staring silently at Hatch. An untouched plate of cold beans rested on the dirt floor just outside the iron bars.

The opening of the small shutters provided sufficient light for Hatch to see that the Apache seemed to be in good shape despite his gunshot wounds and severely swollen face.

"Can you understand me?" asked Hatch.

Chihuahua said nothing and continued his ferocious stare.

"The charges against you are mutiny, desertion, treason, and murder," Hatch continued, his voice rising. "Do you know what these words mean?"

There was no response from the prisoner.

"You will be tried, convicted, and shot," Hatch told him sternly, looking for any sign that the Apache understood what he said. Frustrated, Hatch reached down, picked up the plate of beans, and flipped it vertically through the bars. The metal plate struck Chihuahua on the forehead and the beans splattered on his face, but the Apache never moved.

"Don't forget to eat your last meal," Hatch suggested as he climbed back out of the dungeon. Bean helped pull him up the stairs. "The prisoner is uncooperative, Captain. Schedule the court-martial for the day after tomorrow."

"Yes sir," said Bean, who was beginning to wonder when Hatch would leave for Santa Fe and return command of the fort to him.

Guilfoyle was waiting when Hatch returned to his quarters. "You're early, Lieutenant. Our meeting is at 2 p.m."

"I wanted to speak to you about the gold bar," said Guilfoyle in an angry voice. "It is mine and you had no right to offer it as a reward."

Hatch shook his head. "No, son, it is *our* bar and besides, you said there were plenty more where that came from."

"But—" Guilfoyle began.

"Don't you understand? The sooner we get rid of Nana, the sooner we can recover the rest of the gold. A reward is the obvious solution."

Guilfoyle was in a quandary. He couldn't tell Hatch that Bennett knew about LaRue because then he'd have to explain about the sacks of gold nuggets they had found at the old mine. "Everyone will wonder where it came from," he protested weakly.

"Let 'em wonder," said Hatch. "The source of the gold is our secret."

Apache Scouts.

6. Ojo Caliente

As was their custom on a raid, the Tcihene and Mescalero warriors mounted up and moved out at first light with Nana in the lead. Unconsciously, the old chief recorded every detail of his environment: the cool temperature and higher moisture of the morning air, the light breezes from the west scented with wild flowers and the faintest hint of wood smoke, and the movements of the birds and animals around the war party. He noted the location of circling vultures and steered clear of them so their shadows would not fall on his band, and knew the location of every concealed rattlesnake along the trail. When spotting a coyote, he would hold up movement of the band to avoid contact and the possibility of bad luck or disease.

The old chief had planned the raid carefully by spending the previous day scouting the town with the Mexican name, Garcia. There were more horses corralled there than he had seen on the entire raid. And because the last battle with the White Eyes had cost his band eleven horses, they would take as many as they could.

The little town of twenty houses was also a perfect target because it was distant from Fort Wingate, so the war party could return to the mountains before the Blue Coats arrived. His Power told him that the Mexicans at Garcia had much-needed ammunition stored in their mud houses. It would make up for the bullets they had hurriedly cached during the fight at the spring with the White Eye lieutenant.

Istee, who was riding next to Kaytennae, realized that he was not being treated as a novice now, but rather as a warrior of equal stature. No longer was he required to bring water, build the fire, and care for all the horses. When he spoke the vague warpath language as required of a novice, the others now told him to speak clearly. Nana had even snatched the single eagle feather from his hair.

He had briefly mentioned his new status to The Dreamer, who had said, "You have killed well, son of Victorio." Istee had not enjoyed making the three kills but knew they had helped his band and hurt the White Eyes. He felt bad about shooting the defenseless trader, but his two kills of Blue Coats at the spring had been more like target practice than murder. Istee was thankful he didn't have four kills because the last one would have been the little girl if Kaytennae and The Dreamer had not intervened.

He briefly recalled the scene when Nana and the rest of the band had joined up with him and Kaytennae at the camp in the forest by the Big River. Nana had seen the little White Eye girl sitting by the fire and said to Istee, "Kill her."

"No, keep her alive as a wife for all of us," Sánchez had joked, which made everyone laugh, because they knew no one would have sex with a White Eye girl because their luck would be spoiled.

Kaytennae and The Dreamer had exchanged glances and Kaytennae picked up the girl while The Dreamer went to speak to Nana. Istee had followed Kaytennae to the group of trees where the horses were corralled and had watched him place the girl on a horse, give her some water and food, and send her away. When they had returned to the camp, Nana asked where the girl was.

"She escaped," Kaytennae had said solemnly, and Nana had laughed at his words.

But the old chief wasn't laughing now, Istee noted. They had reached the hill overlooking the town and Nana was very serious as he gave instructions to his warriors. He pointed to half of them and said simply, "Get the horses." Then he pointed out several of the mud houses and said to Kaytennae, "The ammunition is there." Kaytennae designated several warriors, including Istee, to follow him. Finally, when he was ready, Nana sang a brief song to Ussen and then gave the final instructions to his warriors: "Ride fast and kill anyone who moves." He gave the Tcihene war cry and the band thundered down the slope and into the town.

The first to die was a Mexican farmer feeding hay to his milk cow. Comescu shot him in the back as he ran for his house, then began firing into the house. The sound of the shots lured two men with rifles into the streets, but they were trampled before getting off a shot. At first, none of the citizens of Garcia interfered as their horses were released from the corrals and driven off.

But then, some of the Mexicans began shooting from their windows, and Nana's horse was shot out from under him. Despite his age and bad foot, Nana managed to land on his feet and immediately charged the house that had been the source of the shots. He made it safely through the gunfire to the side of the house, stuck his rifle around the corner and through the window, and began shooting. Screams from inside told him his ploy had worked, and he signaled two of his warriors to storm the door. Inside they found a dead man. His wife and two children were huddled in the corner. The warriors dragged them outside and shot each of them in the head while Nana searched the house and found eight large boxes of rifle bullets.

Kaytennae and Istee had similar success in two houses where they found no people but several pistols, rifles, and ammunition. Soon the shooting ended and Sánchez brought a new horse for Nana, who was passing out ammunition to his warriors.

"Ten White Eyes killed, Grandfather," he reported to Nana.

Istee was startled when Nana cried out loudly in triumph.

"We captured many, many horses and found some tobacco," Sánchez added, holding up a bottle, "and I took some *mezcal*."

"Don't drink any of that until we camp," ordered Nana, who knew of Sánchez's love for the Mexican liquor. The chief limped over to a woodpile, pulled an axe out of a *piñon* log, and carried it to the body of the only White Eye of the village, which was lying in the dust. Without uttering a word, Nana calmly chopped the head off the corpse. Guessing what the old chief was up to, Kaytennae hurled his lance, which stuck in the dirt next to Nana's left foot. He impaled the head of the Mexican on the Army bayonet that served as the point of the lance and sank the other end into the soft earth.

The warriors laughed as the head swayed in the wind but Istee was nervous because he thought he felt the eyes of the dead upon him. He wanted to ask Nana why he did such forbidden things to the bodies of the enemy, but was afraid of bringing ridicule upon himself.

"That avenges Mangas Coloradas," said Nana. As he urinated on the headless corpse, he ordered: "Burn all the houses."

Sánchez quickly made a fire and soon the warriors were carrying torches to each of the adobe houses. Istee grabbed a torch and ran into a house, intending to set it on fire. But his curiosity caused him to hesitate when he spotted some things he had never seen before: a number of thick sticks in a box, and a shiny tube that extended and then folded back into itself. Thinking the sticks might be some sort of ammunition, he took one, left the house, and called out to The Dreamer.

"Good," said the shaman. "These are big-noise sticks which can destroy things. Watch." He went back into the house and retrieved the box, then located a cap and fuse and fastened them to one of the sticks. He warned everyone to stay back at a safe distance, then lit the fuse with Istee's torch and threw the stick into the house. A few moments later, the house was blown apart by an enormous explosion.

The Tcihene and Mescalero warriors laughed and shouted with pleasure over the destroyed house. Nana was very impressed.

"Can the big-noise sticks be moved safely?" he asked.

"Only if they are carried like a baby," The Dreamer replied.

Quickly, he located some slabs of wood. With rawhide thongs, he fashioned a rough cradleboard and tied the sticks onto it. The caps and fuses fit easily into a leather pouch.

"Who will carry our baby?" asked The Dreamer.

"Victorio's son will have the honor," said Nana.

"If you drop the baby," warned The Dreamer, "you won't live long enough to hear the big noise."

After they left the destroyed town, Nana momentarily stopped his war party at the railroad tracks nearby. He pointed at the wires that were strung atop the poles that were planted along the tracks. "I don't know how the Blue Coats do it," he said, "but Victorio told me they send messages along those metal ropes up there." At his order, Sánchez quickly climbed one of the poles and cut the wires with his knife. From then on, they cut the message ropes every time they encountered them.

That night they camped near the Enchanted Mesa on Acoma land, but took care not to disturb the Acomas because they had no quarrel with them. Nana realized the Acomas knew they were there, but would not risk a fight with his band. Kaytennae slaughtered a horse and they grilled and ate the fresh meat for hours. Sánchez drank an entire bottle of *mezcal* and entertained the band by dancing in the Mexican style, which he had learned while living with them.

Istee sat next to The Dreamer, who was smoking tobacco in a small clay pipe. "Look what I found," he said to the shaman, and passed the metal tube to him. "I call it a 'far-sight' because when you look through it, distant things appear to be close."

"This will be useful," said The Dreamer. "The White Eyes call it a 'telescope.' We can use it to count the number of Blue Coats chasing us."

Istee laughed a little at the joke and then asked the question that had been bothering him all day. "Why does grandfather cut up the bodies of the dead Mexicans and White Eyes? I was taught to avoid the blood and scalp of an enemy, and never to cut up a dead person because he would have to wander through the underworld in that condition."

The Dreamer was silent for a moment and passed the pipe to Istee, who glanced in Nana's direction. "As a novice, I am not allowed to smoke."

The Dreamer laughed. "You are no longer a boy, no longer a novice. You have become a warrior and now can smoke, marry, and have children." He waited until Istee had taken a few puffs of tobacco smoke before proceeding.

"In the early days, before the Mexicans and White Eyes invaded our lands, scalping and cutting up of enemy bodies was never done for the very reason you said. But many years ago the Mexican army paid money for every Chiricahua scalp that was brought in. That is why some—but not all—of our chiefs and warriors began scalping the enemy."

"But grandfather chopped off the head—"

"If you will listen patiently, I will tell you the story," insisted the Dreamer, and Istee fell silent. "You know of one of your greatest leaders, Mangas Coloradas. After he was captured by the Blue Coats, they tortured him by burning his feet with red-hot bayonets before they shot him. Then they scalped him and buried his body. Two days later, the Blue Coats dug up his body and cut off his head, which was very large. They boiled the head in a big black pot until just the skull was left. His skull was sent as a gift to the White Eye chief in Washington."

Istee's eyes went wide at the tale and he didn't know what to say. The very thought of cooking the skull of Mangas Coloradas made him sick to his stomach. "I don't think I could cut up a dead body," he said finally.

"You could if you had enough hatred," said The Dreamer.

"Is hating part of becoming a warrior?" asked Istee, who had never hated anything, even the two Blue Coats he had killed.

"No, hating is the result of having our land stolen from us and being made slaves. Besides, you know that the White Eyes and the Mexicans are not human beings as are all of our people."

Nana suddenly appeared beside them. If he noticed Istee smoking, he made no mention of it. "Get some rest," he suggested. "We have a very long ride tomorrow."

"Another raid, Grandfather?" asked Istee.

"No. We have food and ammunition. Tomorrow, we go home to the Warm Springs."

The woman warrior Lozen watched the strange Blue Coat camp from her concealed position on a nearby bluff. She had been there for two days studying the daily routine of the camp so she could sneak inside it and free Chihuahua. At first she thought that the best plan was to make the attempt during darkness, but the Blue Coats closed the gate at sundown and the log walls of the camp would be difficult to climb, especially with Chihuahua wounded and sentries on the top of the wall.

The previous evening, after praying to Ussen as his spirit disappeared in the western sky, the strategy had been given to her. When the Blue Coats opened the gate, there was a steady stream of White Eyes and Mexicans between the fort and the small town across the river. Lozen was particularly interested in the Mexican women who worked in the camp. They all dressed alike, and their clothes were familiar to her because on occasion she had dressed like a Mexican when she and Sánchez had gone to Mexican towns to trade for supplies. Ussen gave her the idea to dress like a Mexican woman to get inside the camp; once there, she knew her Power would help her find Chihuahua. The first step was to get the necessary clothing.

Lozen moved quickly from her position, leaped upon her horse, and rode south and waded across a shallow spot in the Big River. She tied her mount to a tree in the forest and followed a well-worn trail to the small town on foot. A short distance from the town, she hid behind a cottonwood tree and waited. Hours passed, but Lozen never moved. She knew the rescue would be tricky, but reminded herself that it was neither the most dangerous nor the most difficult task she had ever undertaken. She remembered the time she had helped a young Mescalero girl find her way back home and they were very hungry. The only thing to eat had been a longhorn steer, and she had stalked the huge animal and killed it with only a knife.

A noise on the trail alerted Lozen that someone was coming. She stole a glance and realized that Ussen was helping her that day. A Mexican woman carrying a basket was taking the trail to the river to wash clothes. Lozen waited until the woman passed her, then silently followed. When the woman reached the river, she dumped the clothes out of the basket and onto the ground, then began to wash a shirt in the river.

Lozen sprang from concealment, and ran to the river bank, knife in hand. The Mexican woman heard her and turned around, but before she could scream, Lozen was on top of her and quickly slit her throat. She dragged the dying woman into the brush and stripped off her clothes. Then she fetched the basket and rummaged through it for anything else of use. She found a small blanket and tied it over her head in the Mexican style, and hid her knife under the waistband of a long skirt. In a few minutes, a disguised Lozen was atop her horse and wading back across the river. She tied up the horse again and walked the rest of the way to the Blue Coat camp.

As expected, the gate to the camp was wide open. Moving in a purposeful manner with head down to avoid eye contact with anyone, Lozen shuffled into the camp and immediately turned to her left to avoid some mounted Blue Coats who were leaving. Several dozen more Blue Coats were marching back and forth in the center of the camp to the orders of another. The only two Mexican women she saw were sweeping dirt from doorways, so she found a broom leaning against a wall, took it, and imitated them while she observed the movements of the enemy and tried to locate Chihuahua. Since she obviously could not stand in the middle of the camp with palms outstretched to call on her Power to find him, she would have to rely on more earthly methods.

Her disguise was working well; no one was paying any attention to her at all. She decided to risk a soft quail call, but got no response, probably because the camp was noisy with the sound of stamping feet and yelling Blue Coats. Still sweeping, she slowly worked her way around the inside perimeter of the camp, giving the quail call when no one was near her.

Some of the buildings were made of mud, some were stone, but every one she passed was full of Blue Coats, and Lozen wondered if they would soon be chasing her band. Many of the activities she saw were unfamiliar, but of course she recognized the corral instantly and noted that it had its own rear gate as well as a gate into the camp. There were more than twenty horses standing around inside it.

After she passed the corral gate, she tried the quail call again and was surprised to hear an echo of it coming from beneath the ground. At the base of the building she was sweeping in front of were two small openings. Lozen realized Chihuahua was being held in a hole beneath the building in front of her. Without hesitating, she walked up to the door, fumbled with the latch until it released, and entered the building.

A buffalo soldier who was sleeping in a chair woke up and said something to her that she could not understand. Lozen began to sweep and said the only two words she knew in Mexican, "*Buenas días.*" The guard made no reply and closed his eyes. Lozen turned her back to the guard and, sweeping with one hand, she reached under her skirt with the other to free her knife. With both hands holding the knife and broom together, she swept her way behind the guard. Using a technique her brother Victorio had taught her, Lozen slashed the buffalo soldier's throat twice so his voice would not work and then stabbed him twice in the heart to kill him. He made quite a bit of noise as he fell off his chair and thrashed about on the floor, but could not scream.

Lozen moved behind the door and waited in case anyone had heard the noise. But no one opened the door, so after a short time Lozen dragged the body of the buffalo soldier into a corner and used her knife to pry open the door in the floor. She climbed down the steps and saw Chihuahua hunched over in a small cage made of metal bars. He reminded her of the caged eagle her brother had kept at their stronghold in the Blue Mountains.

"Where have you been?" he asked softly.

Lozen ignored the traditional greeting. "Can you walk?"

"I can walk and ride, but I cannot climb," he replied.

"How do I get you out of here?"

"Around the guard's neck is a metal ring," said Chihuahua. "On the ring is a piece of metal that will open this door."

Lozen scrambled up the steps and returned in a few seconds with the ring. "How does it work?" she asked.

"See the hole in the door? You put each metal thing into it just as a man would put his thing into a woman. Soon you will find the right one and learn how it is done."

Lozen was embarrassed but pleased that Chihuahua was healthy enough to tease her about her virginity. One after another, she tried to fit the metal sticks in the hole. The fourth stick worked, and after she turned it to the right, the door with bars creaked open. Chihuahua climbed out of the cage and from above Lozen helped push him up the steps. Once out of the hole, he limped over to the body of the dead buffalo soldier and began to search it.

"Now you walk like grandfather," Lozen joked.

He straightened up and passed her a box of matches. "We can start a fire."

Lozen understood his strategy, but there was nothing to burn in the stone guard house. "I will find a place," she said.

"I will wait here until the fire starts and then run to the corral."

"Choose a good horse for me," she said as she picked up the broom and walked out the door.

She moved across the grounds as quickly as possible without attracting attention to herself, and opened the door to the building that was like the stores she had seen in Mexico. There was no one inside so Lozen immediately rummaged around to find anything that would burn. She found many large pieces of paper with White Eye writing on them, cut them into shreds with her knife, and scattered them about the room. She found an oil lamp and dumped its contents onto the papers, and then piled several chairs on top. Then Lozen lit a match, and threw it down, where it immediately caught the oil on fire.

The door burst open and a White Eye with hair longer than hers saw Lozen and the fire at the same time, screamed something unintelligible, and lunged toward her. She dodged aside, brought her knife up into his stomach and barely had time to pull it out before the man fell face-forward onto the floor. Lozen quickly concealed her knife and calmly walked out the door and toward the corral. She was about halfway across the grounds when some of the marching Blue Coats began to yell and point at the smoke coming out the door that Lozen had passed through. She forced herself to be calm and not run as the soldiers rushed past her.

No one was paying any attention to her as she opened the gate to the corral. Chihuahua was not there, but the back gate was open so she assumed he had escaped. A large roan mare with a bridle was tied to a post, and Lozen approved of Chihuahua's choice of horses for her. In no time she was on the mare's back and riding out the gate.

To her surprise, Chihuahua was waiting for her just outside the gate and they rode off at a fast gallop. She led him south to the place where her other horse was tethered, and after recovering it, she turned west.

"Where are we going?" he yelled to her.

"Grandfather said to meet him at Juh's stronghold," she yelled back. "On the way we will stop at San Carlos so you can see your wife." She heard happiness in his answering chuckle.

That night they camped in the foothills of the San Mateos. By the light of a small fire, Lozen cleaned Chihuahua's wounds with water and herbs and then bound them some of the clothing she had taken from the Mexican woman.

"You will live," she told him, and gave him half of the dried deer meat in her parfleche. Later, they slept together side by side, but neither one touched the other.

Nana had led his band halfway to the Warm Springs homeland of the Tcihene when his advance scout Sánchez reported back that there were Blue Coats poised to intercept them. It was not a large force, but Nana decided to take no chances. He divided his war party into two groups; Kaytennae would lead nine warriors and take most of the horses on a route between the San Mateos and the Black Range, while Nana would lead Comescu and the others in a fight to divert the Blue Coats. The two groups would meet as soon as possible at the Warm Springs.

"Be careful of the baby," Nana told Istee with mock seriousness.

After Kaytennae's group moved out, Nana chose his position carefully—a steep-walled, narrow canyon where he could rain down bullets on the enemy. Allowing the Blue Coats to come to him would provide enough time for Kaytennae and the rest to move on to the Warm Springs without interference.

Because he had spotted one of the Navajo scouts, Nana knew that the Blue Coats had discovered his position high up the canyon walls. He snorted in disgust at the thought of sheepherders tracking him down. Sánchez had carefully counted the enemy and Nana knew that the Tcihene outnumbered the Blue Coats. Since they had the higher ground, Nana decided to let the enemy attack his position. It made no sense to him that a weaker force would attack a stronger, well-positioned one; but then who could understand how the White Eyes reasoned?

During the first advance of the soldiers up into the canyon, Tcihene sharpshooters easily picked off five of the Blue Coats, but that fact did not prevent the soldiers from continuing to fire at them. They kept up a steady fire but were unable to hit any of well-hidden Tcihene and Mescaleros. Nana allowed the soldiers to use up ammunition for a while, and then waved his hand and directed Sánchez to start a flanking movement. Soon a hail of bullets from the east forced the Blue Coats to retreat.

Nana ordered his force to abandon their positions and pursue the slowly retreating Blue Coats on foot. After they were routed from the canyon, he planned to chase them on horseback and wipe them out. But the Blue Coats had left a buffalo soldier behind to cover their retreat. He was well-positioned between the Tcihene and the soldiers, hiding among the large boulders on a slight rise near the mouth of the canyon. Because of the low angle of the slope behind the soldier, there was no way for anyone to get above him and throw rocks down on him. He obviously had plenty of ammunition and was a good shot—he wounded two Mescalero warriors when they tried a frontal assault on his position. Soon, nearly twenty of Nana's men closed in on the buffalo soldier's position, but because of the black man's accuracy, they could not dislodge him from that position, or pass by him. After a while, Nana knew that the rest of the Blue Coats were probably mounted and riding like the wind.

Nana realized that his warriors were wasting valuable ammunition on a single Blue Coat, and besides, he admired the enemy soldier's courage so much he decided to let him live. After all, he had no quarrel with the black buffalo soldiers—they were simply paid warriors who were not stealing Tcihene land. With hand signs he ordered his men to fall back and then led them out of the canyon by way of a hidden trail.

Since it would not be good strategy for him to follow the route of Kaytennae and the others, Nana decided to take the long way to the Warm Springs, around the eastern side of the mountains. When his war party arrived at the southern end of the range, they could cross to the west and their homeland through mountain passes, or stay in the foothills and ride up the wide canyon.

The following day they rode hard in case a larger group of Blue Coats had found their trail and were following. In the late afternoon, with the sky dark and threatening rain, they arrived at a small ranch beside a stream. Because there were two dozen horses in the corrals, Nana gave the Tcihene war cry and his war party attacked. There was no resistance because the only people at the ranch were a Mexican mother and her three children.

Nana himself rode his horse through the front door of the house and shot all four of them. He emerged moments later carrying a young boy by the ankles, then rode over to the corrals. He spotted a meat hook hanging from a post and impaled the boy head-first upon it. Comescu laughed, and soon the rest of the warriors joined him.

They ransacked the house and small barn but found little of value. They took only a revolver with bullets, a couple of knives, and some blankets. Nana ordered the horses to be rounded up and told Sánchez to burn the buildings. In a few minutes the warriors were headed up the valley, driving the herd of horses in front of them.

Nana intended to take the horses to Warm Springs, but changed his mind when he saw the tell-tale dust to their rear which meant that the Blue Coats were chasing them. Since it made no sense to lead the enemy to the homeland, Nana abruptly changed direction and headed toward the Black Mountains to the west. He assigned Comescu and two of his Mescalero warriors the responsibility of running the horses on ahead while he and the others took a stand on the first hill they came to, concealing themselves behind the junipers. When the Blue Coats came within range, Nana and his men opened fire, pinning them down with little cover.

The old chief held his position until he could see that the Blue Coats were trying to flank him, then called for a retreat. On horseback once again, the Tcihene and Mescalero warriors rode toward the Black Mountains and took a position at the next hill offering good cover. The Blue Coats followed, and the battle began all over again. Meanwhile, the horses were drawing closer to the foothills.

The Blue Coats had divided their force into three groups in an attempt to surround Nana's men at each hill, but because of the accurate fire from the warriors, they were forced to keep their distance. When Nana moved his men to the third hill, he looked up and the dark clouds and smiled because he knew he was going to get help from the Thunder People. The wind picked up, and when the first sound of thunder reached their ears, Nana's warriors began to make the sound "*pis, pis,*" in imitation of the nighthawk, who flew so fast that lightning could not hit him.

The thunderstorm struck with such violence that the rifles of both sides seemed puny by comparison to the lightning bolts that crashed about them. Nana hoped that none of his men caught the lightning sickness and screamed at them to remove anything red they were wearing so they would not attract the lightning.

All shooting stopped when the hill was enveloped by the dark clouds that poured out so much rain that Nana could barely see his fellow warriors. Nana had a healthy respect for the Thunder People and would have said a prayer asking them not to frighten his people, but he had no time for it. Instead, he used the confusion of the storm as a cover for yet another retreat that was hampered by poor visibility and skittish horses. This time he did not stop at the next hill but made a run for the steeper foothills through the sheets of rain, realizing that he knew the territory far better than his pursuers and that they would not travel during the worst of the storm. He laughed as he imagined the Blue Coat's reaction when the rain stopped and the enemy was nowhere to be seen, as if the Thunder People had snatched them and sewn them up in the clouds when they repaired the split in the sky.

Twilight coincided with the storm's ending, and as the rain turned into mist, Nana's band was threading its way through the twisting tangle of canyons and arroyos on the mountain high above the foothills. Nana knew that the Blue Coats would not risk moving at night in such rough territory, so all pursuit would wait until morning. Soon they encountered Comescu and the horses, made camp, and turned their efforts to setting a trap for the Blue Coats.

Nana realized that the rain had washed away all sign of his band and their herd of horses, and that his warriors could easily escape and move on to Warm Springs. But the opportunity to trick the enemy was too tempting. At first light Nana was up, sang his morning song to Ussen, and gave orders. The horses were moved to a nearby box canyon, where his warriors built a crude corral of rope and brush to contain them near a spring.

Mangus was given instructions by Nana—he was to ride a horse out of the canyon and abandon it near the Blue Coat forces. Nana knew that the horses would try to return to the herd, and told his warriors that the Navajo scouts would follow either the horse or the trail of the horse back to the canyon. They would then tell the Blue Coat leader, who would naturally attempt to recover the stolen horses.

Nana positioned his men behind the first ridge of the canyon walls, completely out of sight of anyone on the canyon floor. One lookout, Sánchez, was stationed among the tall trees at the highest point of the canyon. Then they waited, but the Navajos did not arrive until the sun was high in the sky. As Nana expected, the two of them carefully scouted the canyon, located the horses but not the warriors, and rode off down the mountain.

A short time later, Sánchez flashed a sun signal to Nana that the Blue Coats were on their way. He stood up so his men could see him, and raised his right hand in a signal for them to hold fire until he began shooting. Then he disappeared behind the rocks.

A small Blue Coat force of fifteen mounted troopers led by the two Navajos slowly entered the canyon. Nana waited until they were about halfway to the horse corral before he stood up and fired at the White Eye leader of the buffalo soldiers. But the great distance caused his aim to be too low, and he missed the White Eye but shot his horse out from under him. Nana's men immediately directed heavy fire on the enemy from three sides, hitting both men and horses. Once the surviving Blue Coats found cover, they returned fire; but Nana's band was well hidden among the rocks and trees and no bullets found their mark.

Shortly after the fire fight began, Nana was startled to see a buffalo soldier leap upon a horse and ride fast for the mouth of the canyon. All of the Tcihene and Mescalero warriors shot at him, but the soldier escaped. Nana guessed that the man was not a deserter, but rather a messenger to another Blue Coat force. His theory was confirmed by a frantic series of flashes from Sánchez, which meant that his position was threatened. If the Blue Coats gained the high point of the canyon, Nana's men would be trapped between the two enemy forces, and they would lose both warriors and horses.

Nana directed most of his men to move to Sánchez' position. Because of his bad foot, he could not move fast enough to help them, so he and two Mescaleros attempted to pin down the Blue Coats in the canyon. But their fire was considerably less than before, which gave the buffalo soldiers and their White Eye leader the opportunity to mount up— sometimes two to a horse—and escape from the trap.

Meanwhile, at Sánchez's post among the tall pines, the warriors arrived just in time to prevent the Blue Coats from taking the highest position of the battle. A furious volley from Nana's men killed or wounded ten of the thirty Blue Coats advancing on them, and the rest quickly dismounted and took cover. They were joined by the soldiers who had been trapped in the canyon, but the entire enemy force was unable to dislodge Sánchez and those who had joined him. In fact, the Blue Coats began to fall back in order to rescue their wounded men, and Sánchez pressed the attack down the slope.

Nana, with no one left to shoot at, led his two warriors down into the canyon, where they mounted horses and drove the herd out of the corral. Once they passed the mouth of the canyon, they moved the horses north to another, much smaller canyon, where Nana stationed the two Mescaleros to guard the herd. Then he rode off in the direction of the gunfire.

By the time he arrived at the battle scene, his warriors were well on their way to routing the Blue Coats. The buffalo soldiers were in retreat and Sánchez was steadily pushing his men toward them. Nana could not tell if any of his men were hit; if they were, they were still fighting. There was only one problem that Nana could see: the retreating Blue Coats had taken a fairly strong position among some trees on top of a ridge, and they were able to provide cover for soldiers who were recovering their horses.

Nana rode up to Sánchez and gave him instructions about where to meet, then rode off to retrieve the horses. Sánchez and the warriors kept the Blue Coats pinned among the trees until the shadow of a tall pine touched the rock Nana had indicated. Then Sánchez gave a piercing wolf call and they stopped shooting. The Tcihene and Mescalero warriors abruptly disappeared into the landscape and quickly moved north on foot. It was important for them to vanish before the Blue Coats regrouped; otherwise, they might be chased down by a mounted enemy.

They ran as fast as the terrain would allow and soon located Nana and the horses. They mounted and were driving the herd of horses ahead of them when Nana did a quick count and discovered one of his men was missing. He asked Sánchez about it.

"The Mescalero warrior they call One Who Chews was shot in the heart," explained Sánchez. "We piled big rocks on his body so the Blue Coats will never find it."

"Good," said Nana, who was saddened by the loss of a warrior but believed the Blue Coats would become discouraged by their inability to recover any Tcihene or Mescalero bodies.

While Nana and most of the war party were having an easy time with the Blue Coats, Kaytennae and his small contingent were wondering how to handle the soldiers they had found. Their journey from Acoma country had been uneventful until they had neared their ancestral homeland. Kaytennae had sent out advance scouts, and their report was not encouraging. The Blue Coats had constructed a camp of mud buildings near the sacred warm springs of the Tcihene and had manned it with a small force of soldiers, perhaps twenty of them.

Kaytennae was faced with two choices. He could wait for Nana and the main war party to arrive or he could attack a force twice as large as his own. Fortunately, The Dreamer had an alternative solution.

"We can attack tonight," he said as they sat around a small fire and smoked tobacco.

"But we never fight in darkness," Kaytennae protested.

"All the more reason to surprise them," countered The Dreamer. "These are not normal times," he added.

Istee, who overheard the debate, could not suppress a giggle at the understatement. In his entire life of sixteen summers he had never known such a thing as normal times. They were always at war with either the Mexicans or the White Eyes, always fighting.

"We should wait for Nana," insisted Kaytennae. "He will know what to do."

"And who will you wait for when he is gone?" asked The Dreamer.

Kaytennae frowned and realized that the shaman had made a good point. They could not depend upon Nana forever. "Do you have a plan?"

The Dreamer gazed up at the darkening skies. "Later tonight the moon will be nearly full, so we will be able to see the enemy."

"Even the black-faced buffalo soldiers?" asked Istee, and his innocent question made them all laugh.

"Aim for the teeth," suggested Kaytennae, his jest an indication that he now agreed with The Dreamer.

The Dreamer, usually very serious, smiled as he told them his plan for recapturing Warm Springs. "As much as we can, we will use our old weapons, arrows and knives. We don't want to wake up the enemy with gunfire."

Later, when the moon was high in the night sky, the small band of warriors advanced on foot to the Blue Coat camp. First they located the two sentries posted at either end of the meadow where the enemy had built their mud houses. One was asleep, and Kaytennae quickly took him out with a knife to the throat. The other sentry was sitting on a rock, his rifle cradled in his arms like a child. Blanco, the most accurate of the Tcihene with bow and arrow, crept as close as he dared to the sentry and then in one fluid motion drew his bow and released an arrow. The steel point of the arrow struck the buffalo soldier in the throat and he fell off the rock onto his back. What would have been a scream of pain came out as a low gurgling sound that quickly ended when Blanco repeatedly stabbed the soldier with his black-handled knife.

There were three mud buildings with soldiers in them, so Kaytennae divided up his force. He would take three men and enter the largest building, while The Dreamer and Sánchez would each lead two men into the smaller ones. The Dreamer selected Istee and a Mescalero named Round Nose, and together they crept toward the building. Istee drew his knife as the shaman slowly opened the wooden door. The faint light of the moon passing through a single small window illuminated five vague shapes asleep on the floor. By pointing, The Dreamer indicated who Istee and Round Nose should attack, then moved silently into position over his victim.

But before they could strike, gun shots and screams rang out from next building and startled them. "Now!" shouted The Dreamer, who then plunged his knife directly into the heart of the waking soldier below him. Round Nose did the same but did not strike a vital organ and was forced to leap upon the struggling soldier and stab him repeatedly.

Istee was striking down at his man when the buffalo soldier suddenly sat up. The knife grazed the soldier's shoulder, producing not only a cry of pain and rage from the black man, but also a powerful blow which caught Istee on the side of the head and momentarily stunned him and caused him to drop the knife. The soldier, who was much larger and heavier, leaped to his feet, grabbed Istee's throat, and began to strangle him. As much as he struggled, Istee could not free himself from the huge hands that were crushing his windpipe.

Meanwhile, The Dreamer realized that they no longer had the advantage of silence and surprise, so he pulled a revolver from his belt and calmly executed the other two soldiers with single shots to the head. Then he turned and saw Istee slump to the floor and a huge buffalo soldier pivot and face him. For a moment no one moved—they were frozen in position. Then the soldier suddenly reached for his rifle, and The Dreamer shot him twice in the stomach. The dying soldier then fell over Istee's body.

"Go help Kaytennae," The Dreamer ordered Round Nose, who quickly left the building. The shaman then pulled the body off of Istee and quickly checked the young warrior. He was unconscious but still breathing, so The Dreamer left him lying there and rushed outside. He saw that Kaytennae and the others had the large building surrounded and were firing shots through the two windows. The buffalo soldiers returned the fire sporadically but could not see what they were shooting at.

"What happened?" The Dreamer asked Kaytennae when he found him.

"They were not all asleep," Kaytennae explained. "One of them saw us when we went inside and started shooting. Two of our people are wounded."

"How many soldiers are inside?"

"I don't know. Maybe ten, twelve."

"Build a fire," suggested The Dreamer. "We'll smoke them out."

The trapped buffalo soldiers never had a chance. Once a roaring bonfire was built, the Tcihene and Mescalero warriors took turns lighting pitch-filled branches and hurling them through the windows. When the building filled with smoke, the buffalo soldiers could not breathe and decided to break out. They ran out the door and tried to reach their horses, but were methodically cut down by rifle fire. When it was all over, The Dreamer counted fourteen bodies from the large building and five each from the smaller ones. Nana would be quite pleased; it was the biggest victory of their war of vengeance.

Istee slowly gained consciouness and found himself covered with blood. But except for a sore neck, he was not hurt. He staggered to his feet and stumbled out the door to find his fellow warriors engaged in a victory dance around the fire. Kaytennae was beating the rhythm on a drum while each of the warriors danced aroung the fire. A chorus sang of the feats of each man as he danced. The only ones not dancing were two wounded men and The Dreamer, who was treating their injuries with herbs.

"Where have you been?" joked The Dreamer as Istee walked up to him.

The standard, rhetorical greeting brought blood to Istee's face because he felt that he had failed during the fight. Instead of answering, he asked: "What happened?"

The Dreamer laughed and pointed to the row of enemy bodies laid out in front of the large building. "Go look at the third buffalo soldier from the left."

Istee obeyed and returned with his eyes wide in amazement. "He is as big as a bear," he told The Dreamer.

"Yes, my young warrior, you chose the biggest buffalo soldier we have ever seen—a buffalo-bear easily twice your weight. You have nothing to be ashamed of." He nodded in the direction of the fire. "You'd better go dance now."

Istee heard his name being called by the singers and had no choice but to move toward the fire. As he took his turn dancing, they sang of the novice who killed three of the enemy on his first raid and then embellished the story a bit as they told of his defeat of the bear-man. He was relieved when the singers called the name of Round Nose and he could return to The Dreamer.

"How can I get the enemy blood off me?" he asked.

"Wait until tomorrow," suggested The Dreamer. "We'll all bathe in the Warm Springs. Go sleep now."

Istee retrieved his blanket from his horse and curled up behind one of the smaller buildings. He hated the feel and smell of the buffalo soldier's blood but was too tired to even remove his clothes before he fell into a deep sleep.

In the morning, The Dreamer took charge of the removal of the bodies. "Let's get rid of them before *nantan* gets here," he ordered. He would not allow any mutilation, though he did permit the warriors to take anything of value from the corpses. One by one the bodies were thrown across the backs of horses and carried to the end of a deep ravine a short distance from the Blue Coat camp. The corpses were pitched over the edge and many large rocks were rolled down on top of them.

"There will be a bad smell around here for many moons," Kaytennae said.

"Let's move on to the Warm Springs," suggested The Dreamer, and the warriors mounted, rounded up the extra horses, and rode up the slope to their sacred springs. There they made camp and waited.

Nana and the rest of their war party arrived when the sun was high in the sky. The old chief called an immediate council and everyone shared information about the battles that had been fought. His warriors were elated about their victories over the Blue Coats, but Nana was a realist.

"There are Blue Coats everywhere," he said. "If we stay around here, eventually they will trap us."

"Where shall we go next?" asked Kaytennae.

"I know where I must go," interjected The Dreamer. "It's time for me to return to San Carlos and show the bar of gold to the Blue Coat *nantan*."

Saddened by the thought of their shaman leaving, no one said a word for a few moments. Then Nana broke the silence. "He is right. It is time to go south."

"Then it is over?" asked Comsecu. "No more raids?"

"We will raid as we move south because the Blue Coats will still be chasing us and we will need horses and ammunition. You and your people may ride with us to Juh's stronghold or return to Mescalero."

Comescu grinned. He knew that the Blue Coats would be waiting for him at Mescalero and would either shoot him or put him in jail, a fate far worse than death. "It will be nice to visit our brothers to the south," he said. "The White Mountain of the Mescaleros will still be there when we return."

"When do we leave?" asked Sánchez.

"We will stay here for only two or three days," said Nana. "I want to enjoy our return to our homeland. Too bad our women aren't here with us. We will have a feast, soak in the Warm Springs, rest for a while."

Istee was amazed to hear Nana say those things. It was so unlike Grandfather to take a rest that he wondered if old age was finally catching up to him. But Istee, like the others, was certainly not going to object to taking a few day's rest.

"Of course," said Nana, "some of you will take turns scouting so the Blue Coats won't surprise us here."

"I think we killed all the Blue Coats," said Istee.

Nana frowned. "We can never kill all the Blue Coats," he said sadly. "That's a job for Ussen."

Istee was puzzled by that idea. "Then why doesn't He do it?"

"Ask him," Nana suggested, nodding at The Dreamer. "The Dreamer always know the answers to questions like that. Enough of this. Let's begin the feast."

Along with the horses, they had also captured two steers from the White Eye ranch. Kaytennae quickly shot each one through the heart and then butchered the two animals and set their heads aside. Some of the meat he cut into thin strips to be dried for the long trip to Juh's stronghold. He saved the choicest cuts from the ribs to be roasted over the fire, and then gave directions to Istee.

Using the point of a lance and his hands, Istee dug a pit in the ground as deep as his knees when he stood in it and as wide as his two legs spread open. Although he did not protest, he was irritated that now he had dirt as well as blood covering his clothes. When he had completed the pit, he covered the bottom of it with rocks; and then Kaytennae placed the two cow heads on the rocks so their long horns stuck out of the hole. Istee and Sánchez placed more rocks on top of the head and then gathered wood and built a large fire over the hole.

Nana inspected the dinner preparations and nodded his approval. "We have time for a bath before we eat," he announced.

The entire war party assembled beside the pool of warm water fed by an underground spring that bubbled up in the middle of it. Nana raised his arms as if to embrace the landscape as far as the eye could see, then he sang a song.

Ussen gave us this land.
Through our forefathers
It has come to us.
It was our land
Before the White Eyes came;
It is still our land.
The Warm Springs soothe us
And protect us from harm.
Thank you Ussen for this warm water
And the land around it.

The Tcihene and Mescalero warriors began to undress and The Dreamer moved over beside Istee and whispered, "Don't foul the Warm Springs with enemy blood. Wash the blood off downstream and leave your clothes in the stream so they will be clean. Then you may enter the pool."

Istee walked a considerable distance from the pool and followed the shaman's instructions. He returned to the pool naked, found a spot in the crowded pool, and sank beneath the soothing water. It was the most wonderful sensation he had ever experienced.

"Enjoy it while you can," advised Nana. "It may be a long time before we can come back here."

"But what do the White Eyes want with our mountains?" asked Istee. It was a question he had never been able to answer because the White Eyes always built their towns in the lowlands, never in the mountains—except for the miners, of course.

Nana sighed. "It is hard to answer that question, son of Victorio. The White Eyes have always wanted to conquer and destroy us. Ussen only knows why, and He is not telling. For a while it looked like we might be able to live side-by-side with them. Victorio was promised by the White Eye *nantan* in Washington that we would could stay on our land around Warm Springs for as long as the mountains stood and the rivers ran. The White Eyes said they would give us food and blankets if we would stop raiding their towns and ranches. Victorio agreed and was given a piece of paper, but I cannot remember the White Eye words for it."

"'Executive Order,'" said The Dreamer in English, "'The highest law of the White Eye land,'" he added sarcastically.

"But they lied!" sneered Nana. "They gave us no food, no blankets, but they did give us diseases and many of our people died from them and from the freezing cold. Then the White Eyes gave Victorio another piece of paper that said we had to leave Warm Springs and move to San Carlos and live with The Dreamer's people who were imprisoned there. At gunpoint, we were forced to march from the mountains and live in the desert, where only scorpions and rattlesnakes can survive. That summer even more of our people died. Babies were eaten by insects. Pregnant women died of the weakening disease. Finally, Victorio rebelled and we left San Carlos and returned here. The Blue Coats attacked us, and that is when Victorio vowed he would never be imprisoned on a White Eye reservation again. Once he told me that the White Eyes did not want our land so much as they wanted to kill every single—what is the White Eye word?"

"'Indian,'" said The Dreamer.

"Every single 'Indian' who lived, whether he be Tcihene, Mescalero, Navajo, or Acoma."

"But why?" asked Istee.

"Because we are not like them," Nana answered, "and the White Eyes kill anyone they don't like, even Mexicans."

Silence descended over the warriors relaxing in the warm water. The sun had fallen behind the peaks and twilight was descending on their camp. A short distance away, the cooking fire glowed a bright red and the delicious aroma of cooking meat reached them. Istee suddenly realized how hungry he was.

"Whenever I sit in this warm water," Nana said, "I am reminded of Child of the Water and how he overcame his enemies as we must overcome ours." When he heard that, Istee knew Grandfather was in the mood to tell more tales. His growling stomach would have to wait.

"Even though he was only a child, he had killed the enemies of our people known as Giant Deer, Giant Owl, Giant Buffalo, and Giant Bear," Nana announced dramatically. "But there was still one enemy creature whose name we dare not say—Nameless Monster—who looked like a man but was not human. He had great Power in his eyes and if he looked at someone, it would kill him. Child of Water did not know how to kill the Nameless Monster, but he received help from a friend called Giant Lizard.

"'Nameless Monster is not alone,' warned Giant Lizard." Nana used a high, hissing voice and everyone laughed at his imitation of the imagined sound of a lizard's speech. "'High atop that mountain, in a crater filled with fire, is a horrible family of Nameless Monsters.'

"Since it was his mission to protect our people, Child of the Water knew that he must destroy the entire family of monsters. So he asked Giant Lizard for advice.

"'The monsters up there can see me but do not fear me,' said Giant Lizard. Crawl under my belly and hold on and I will carry you up to the crater. Take this bag of powder with you and when we get to the top, throw it on the fire.'

"Child of the Water did as the Giant Lizard said, and the Nameless Monsters paid no attention to him. When they reached the top of the mountain, The Child looked into the crater and saw the horrible family of monsters crawling around in the fire. He threw the bag of powder into the fire and it made evil-smelling fumes that blinded the Nameless Monsters. Then Child of the Water killed all the monsters with his arrows and made the land safe for our people."

Nana paused for effect, then concluded his tale. "Every struggle, whether it is won or lost, strengthens us for the next one to come. We do not have an easy life, but that is good because easy living makes people weak and then they cease to struggle. Sometimes, as we have seen from

Victorio's death, we need to be defeated so that we may gain the strength and courage necessary to be victorious again. Our war of vengeance has proven that to be true."

Nana continued his storytelling until long after it was completely dark. He told of how Ussen gave corn to Killer of Enemies, and how White Painted Woman gave the Tcihene the coming-of-age ceremony. At the request of Sánchez, he made them laugh with more tales of Coyote. He recounted how Gopher helped Coyote have sex with a girl prairie dog by tunneling under her, and how even Coyote the trickster could be tricked himself. Istee howled until tears came to his eyes when Grandfather described how Woodpecker tricked Coyote by giving him a boy dressed as a girl for a wife.

Finally, Kaytennae said, "Grandfather, we are starving to death."

Nana laughed. "The heads are cooked. It is time to eat the brains. See, my tales lasted just long enough."

They climbed out of the pool and dressed. Istee was forced to wear sopping-wet clothes, but by then was so hungry he ignored the discomfort. Kaytennae looped a rope around the horns of the cow heads and pulled them out of the glowing coals. With a war club he cracked open the heads to reveal the steaming brains. While they cooled so they could be eaten, Comescu and Blanco cut tender strips of meat from the ribs of the steers, threaded them onto sharpened branches, and grilled them over the coals.

In a few minutes, the feast was ready. The warriors squatted around the fire while Nana plucked the eyes out of the cow skulls and ate them, as was his due as leader. He then cut out the tongues and passed them around so everyone could have a taste. Then the warriors helped themselves to the brains by dipping their fingers into the skulls and pulling out a portion of the delicious food. After these appetizers, they ate as much of the grilled rib meat as their stomachs would hold.

After he had stuffed himself, Istee joined The Dreamer, who was lying on his back staring at the stars. "I want to know why Ussen does not kill all the White Eyes for us," he said.

"Maybe He thinks that's our job," replied the shaman. "Maybe He has more important things to do. Or just maybe…the White Eye god is more powerful than Ussen."

Istee was shocked by the concept. "The White Eyes have a god?"

"Yes. He is called 'Jesus.' He was killed by his enemies but came back to life three days later—that is how powerful he is."

"How do you know these things?"

"For a while I stayed in the White Eye town they call 'Santa Fe.' Some of the White Eyes wanted to teach my people their ways, so I was sent to what they call a 'school.' There I learned enough of the White Eye language to talk to them. They had many pieces of paper with writing on them fastened together—"

"I saw those things," interrupted Istee. "In the trader's wagon."

"They are called 'books,' and the White Eyes' most important book is a 'Bible.' It tells of Jesus and how he came back to life—a good story."

Istee was puzzled. "Is Jesus as strong as Ussen? Do they ever fight?"

"No one knows. Some people believe that a people are only as powerful as their god. Right now the White Eyes are more powerful than we are, so maybe Jesus has fought Ussen and won an important battle. But remember, as Nana said, that a struggle only makes us stronger."

"Do you think that someday Ussen will defeat Jesus and then we can kill all the White Eyes?"

The Dreamer laughed. "You ask good questions, young son of Victorio. When you get to Juh's stronghold you should ask the Mountain Spirits for your Power. Maybe they will give you all the answers to the questions you ask."

Again Istee was shocked. The Dreamer said things he had never heard before. "But I thought we could not ask for Power, that it just came to us when we least expected it."

"There are no hard and fast rules about acquiring Power. You have already proven you can endure fear and pain; prove to the Mountain Sprits that you can endure hunger and they will grant you your Power."

"For how many days must I go hungry?"

"Until the Power comes to you."

"But how will it come?"

"It will speak to you through a bird, a plant, or even a rock."

"And what will my Power be?"

The Dreamer laughed again. "Now you ask foolish questions. No one knows what his Power will be until he receives it." He reached for Istee's hand, put something in it, and closed his fingers over it. "Here, take this and eat it before you ask the Mountain Spirits to grant you Power. It will help you fight the hunger. Now, let's go back and sit in the Warm Springs. Maybe we can convince Nana to tell us about how Coyote married his own daughter."

The Dreamer rose and left Istee sitting on the ground. Istee opened his fingers to see what the shaman had given him. It was a piece of the cactus The Dreamer called *peyotl*.

As the sun rose on the third day of their stay at the Warm Springs, Nana sang the Morning Song and then urged his warriors to pack up their food and weapons. This time he did not need Lozen to tell him that the enemy was near, because he knew that the Blue Coats would be searching for their brothers who had camped in the mud buildings.

"Don't forget to carry the baby," he told Istee.

Istee did not reply as he struggled with the cradleboard that held the big-noise sticks.

Nana chuckled. "Don't worry, you won't have to carry it as far as Juh's stronghold. We'll leave the baby at our cache in the Flower Mountains."

After the warriors were mounted, they all rode off to the south except for The Dreamer, who turned east in the direction of San Carlos. Istee pulled up his horse and waved farewell to the shaman, but The Dreamer was lost in his own thoughts and did not see him.

Buffalo Soldier Camp.

7. Fort Cummings

To Colonel Edward T. Hatch, commander of the Military District of New Mexico, it seemed like the nightmare of the Victorio campaign was happening all over again. Now, as then, his problems were equally divided between the Apache renegades, the politicians, his superior officers, and the press. The obvious solution to all of his problems was to capture or kill the Apache leader—which again was proving to be far easier said than done.

On the morning of August 25, 1881, he left his uncomfortable bed at Fort Craig at 6 a.m. after a nearly sleepless night. He breakfasted on eggs and beans in the officers' mess and then went directly to the post commander's office, which he had appropriated from Captain Bean. He stared at the maps and reports for an hour, but accomplished nothing. He hated to admit it, but his strategy was breaking down. Heavy rains had washed out the railroad tracks near Raton and had prevented infantry Companies B and D from moving from Fort Lewis, Colorado, to Fort Craig. Telegraphs were periodically malfunctioning and messages that should have taken minutes now took days to arrive. He suspected sabotage by the renegades but knew he could do little about it.

Frustrated and discouraged, Hatch left the office and walked over to the stables. He ordered the post saddler to saddle a horse for him, then returned to his quarters, picked up a towel and his leather toiletries kit, and strapped on his Smith and Wesson "Shofield" model .45 caliber revolver. Back at the corral, he mounted the large roan gelding selected for him and rode out of the corral and onto the parade ground.

"Leavin' us, General?" Captain Bean called to him.

Hatch suppressed a curse. There was absolutely no privacy at all in the fort. "I'm going for a morning ride. I'll be back in a while."

"Do you need an escort, sir?"

"No, Captain."

Two privates opened the log gate for him and Hatch urged his mount to a trot. The sun had cleared the Sierra Oscura range to the east and Hatch could tell that it was going to be another day in the mid-nineties. He rode down the slope toward the Rio Grande and made a noble attempt to relax. He fervently wished that Evelyn were with him—he missed her cheerful personality that always seemed to put things in their proper perspective. In a few minutes he reached the forest of giant cottonwoods along the river that the Mexicans called the *bosque*, found a trail, and slowed his horse to a walk.

As he rode slowly through the trees, he could not help but contrast the peacefulness of his surroundings with the recent violence. The escape of Chihuahua, the death of Private Brown, and the stabbing of Jack Crawford had shaken him up, and he was trying to piece together exactly what had happened. During the fire that had gutted the post store, Chihuahua had broken out of the dungeon. Since it was highly unlikely that any Army personnel had been involved, the Apache woman who had stabbed Crawford had probably infiltrated the fort, perhaps during the night. During Chihuahua's escape on horseback, the traitor had scattered most of the fort's spare horses, and it had taken Bean's men two days to round them all up.

It could have been worse, he supposed. What if the woman had set fire to the post magazine rather than the store? The only good news about the situation was that Crawford was recovering quickly under the care of Surgeon Collins, and had even written a poem about his experience which he had entitled "The Poet-Scout Meets the Indian Maiden." Fortunately, Hatch thought, Crawford had not yet recovered sufficiently to perform the poem in public.

Hatch found a spot out of view of both the fort and the town and tethered his horse to a tree. He pulled a bar of homemade soap out of his leather case, stripped off all his clothes, and waded into the river, which was surprisingly cold. As quickly as he could, he lathered soap all over his body, submerged himself in the water until it was up to his neck, and quickly moved out of the river and onto the bank. After drying himself, he took out a mirror and began to shave.

As hard as he tried to relax, his mind would not allow it. Many of his best officers were going down to defeat. Captain Charles Parker and his men of Company K from Fort Wingate and his men had been routed at Carrizo Canyon near the Gallinas Mountains; and Lieutenants Valois and Burnett of Company I had both been severely wounded during a series of futile engagements near Alamosa, which was less than fifty miles from Fort Craig.

But those losses paled to insignificance when compared to the disaster at Ojo Caliente. When no word had come for days from cavalry Companies B and H from Fort Bayard, which had been stationed at the small post at Ojo Caliente, he had sent a unit of fifty troopers and scouts to investigate. They had found a ghastly sight—a mass grave of twenty-four bodies nearly buried in rocks. The entire contingent had been wiped out—something that had never happened before, even during the Victorio campaign.

Hatch had deliberately delayed reporting the incident, fearing that the newspapers would crucify him. His official report to Department

Headquarters at Fort Leavenworth had been sent by regular mail; he hoped that by the time his superiors realized the enormity of the slaughter, Nana would be captured or driven out of the territory. He had sent his two best men on Nana's trail, Guilfoyle and Smith, and he could only hope that they would trap the damned renegade.

He finished shaving, and the first inkling of an idea came to him. It involved plotting Nana's movements so far through the territory and making a guess about where he might go next. During the entire campaign so far, all they had done was pick up his trail and follow him. Nana's strikes had appeared to be random; but what if there were a logical pattern to them after all? He cursed the fact he had left his map back at the post office, but was encouraged that his little ride and bath had accomplished something. Hurriedly, he dressed, mounted, and rode back to the fort at a gallop.

He rode through the gate and dismounted in front of the commander's office, then turned his horse over to a private and ordered him to take it to the corral. When he entered his office to check the map, Hatch discovered a sealed packet with his name on it. A note on top read: "This came for you by courier this morning from the depot at Socorro. Cap't. J. Bean."

Inside the packet was more bad news that delayed his tracing of Nana's movements. A memorandum from Captain Loud detailed the trouble brewing in both Santa Fe and Washington. "Gov. Sheldon," wrote Loud, "apparently thinks *he* is commander of the Military District of New Mexico. He has convinced the legislature in emergency session to authorize a paid volunteer force of one thousand men to fight the 'Apache menace.'"

"Goddamn it," shouted Hatch, who hated any civilian interference in military matters. But the worst news was still to come.

"Sheldon," wrote Loud, "is now in Washington attempting to have you removed as commander. According to my sources, he told Congressman Luna that he was 'getting no cooperation whatsoever from the military or the bureaucrats at the Department of War.' He took the train to Washington five days ago and supposedly Luna has arranged an appointment with acting president Arthur. I have a feeling you might need the enclosed information should Gen. Pope contact you." Inside the packet were telegrams, letters, clippings, and reports pertaining to what Loud had labeled as the "Nana File."

Despite the distressing news, Hatch knew that Pope was on his side. During the Victorio campaign, the general had always supported him and had sent reinforcements whenever Hatch had needed them. However, he knew that a governor of a territory would have more influence in Washington than a commander of a military district.

The following day, as Loud had predicted, Hatch received a long telegram from General John Pope, commander of the Division of the Missouri. It had been routed from Washington through department headquarters at Fort Leavenworth, and the only thing good about it was the date at the top: it was dated the same day, which meant the telegraph system was working again. In the telegram, Pope wrote that he had met with Sheldon, acting president Arthur, and the Secretary of War, Robert T. Lincoln.

"Governor Sheldon is extremely distressed and is calling for your replacement," wrote Pope. "I told him that everybody knows that the Apaches are a miserable, brutal race—cruel, deceitful, and wholly irreclaimable. I also said that the Army had every confidence in your ability to resolve this matter of the renegades. But this time I have no Joint Resolution of the New Mexico legislature praising you, so I must have some support from you personally. I want you to come to Washington as soon as possible and speak with Sec. Lincoln so he can hear your side of this matter."

Hatch was furious by the time he finished reading the telegram. The idea of traveling to Washington right now was preposterous. In fact, during the Victorio campaign, Pope had come to New Mexico because he knew Hatch was too busy to leave his command. But he knew better than to let his anger show. He would simply use his knowledge of Pope to protect his own interests; the general in Washington despised civilian interference as much as he did.

"I have never heard of a commander in the final stages of a military operation being recalled to Washington," Hatch wired back. "I am concerned not about defending myself, but rather about defending the citizens of the Territory of New Mexico. Replace me if you think it is politically expedient, but first hear my side of the debate. I have been grossly misrepresented in the press and am the victim of systematically prepared falsehoods. Gov. Sheldon has no military experience with Apaches but is easily swayed by the false intelligence of stampeded citizens. You should be aware that the local press is also calling for your replacement by Gen. Miles. As you know from personal experience, dealing with renegades is an intricate and difficult problem. However, we have made good progress and have the enemy on the run. There have been six engagements in the past two weeks and my scouts tell me that chief Nana is heading toward Mexico. I have a plan to trap him before he gets there. I hereby request that you grant me a two-week delay for this meeting in Washington. Such a delay will give me time to oversee the final stages of our campaign against the renegades."

Hatch felt much better after sending the telegram. Pope would not dare interfere in the final stages of the campaign for fear that he would be blamed if it failed. However, Hatch's improved mood lasted less than a day. The following morning, he received Pope's reply. Although the general granted permission for a two-week delay for the trip to Washington, he was not letting Hatch off easily.

"I must show Sec. Lincoln that some definite progress is being made," Pope wired. "I want you to prepare a complete report about everything that has happened so far, plus your recommended action, and forward it to me within one week."

"Shit," said Hatch when he finished reading the telegram. He thought Pope must have been infected by the bureaucratic bug from living in Washington so long. In the middle of a war, what do we do? Sit down and write a report about it.

Hatch retired to his quarters, opened a bottle of bourbon, and began reviewing the material in the packet Loud had sent from Santa Fe. Loud had been his usual efficient self: the Nana file was very complete—and very depressing.

A recent editorial in the *Silver City Daily Southwest* said: "We are dreaming of a golden age—a future empire—and filthy, dirty, lousy Indians have us in a state of siege." The editorial went on to suggest that Hatch be removed as commander of the military district of New Mexico and be replaced by General Eugene Carr, who commanded the Sixth Cavalry in Arizona.

"That insufferable bastard," Hatch said aloud to no one. He still remembered Carr's very vocal criticism of him during the Victorio campaign. Carr had complained to Pope that Hatch was "uncooperative" and "arrogant" when in fact those adjectives fit Carr perfectly. He poured himself a stiff shot of bourbon.

Even his supposed friend Greene at the *Daily New Mexican* had turned against him. His editorial read: "Every day's dispatches add to the fearful list of those killed and captured by the sneaking, murderous redskins. Make every Apache in New Mexico a *good Indian*, and then only can we enjoy a lasting peace." By "good" Indian, Greene of course meant a dead one. His editorial concluded: "The people of New Mexico demand of the United States government either the removal of General Hatch or that they be permitted to deal with the Indians as they may find necessary, even to extermination."

Despite the fact that he hated certain Apaches, namely Nana and Chihuahua, Hatch was opposed to wholesale extermination of any people. And he believed that anyone who suggested such evilness had a blacker heart than the proposed victims. He cursed spineless newspaper reporters who not only thought themselves to be judge and jury, but also gods who could, with the stroke of a pen, impose the death penalty on anyone they disliked.

In another clipping, the editor of the *Albuquerque Journal* suggested that Hatch would not be safe from mob action, without a bodyguard, on the street of any town in southern New Mexico—even the one that had recently been named for him! Hatch found that comment to be hilarious, and laughed until tears came to his eyes.

Yet another article, this one from a bleeding-heart writer for the *New York Sun*, actually took the side of the Apaches. The story claimed that

Hatch's troopers had burned alive two members of Nana's band and used "torturous practices" to extract information from Apache women and children. *Hell,* thought Hatch, *we have yet to find a single Apache body, much less a living victim.*

As he sorted through the rest of the clippings, Hatch came across one newspaper article that finally made sense. It was in the *Rio Grande Republican* and was headlined: *IS NANA AVENGING VICTORIO?* The writer speculated that the old chief was raiding to revenge the killing of Victorio, a fact he blamed on whites in New Mexico—particularly General Hatch—who had driven Victorio from his homeland and into Mexico. The author of the article, Antonio Salas, apparently knew quite a bit about Apache customs, because he pointed out that Nana's raid coincided with the band's usual seasonal trip into New Mexico.

If that was true, thought Hatch, then Nana was making a limited strike and would soon be returning to his base of operations in the Sierra Madre range in Mexico. He remembered Pope's advice from the Victorio campaign: establish a barrier of troops across southern New Mexico and send scouting parties both north and south of the line. That, in effect, was the very strategy he was using now.

Hatch soon realized that he could not write the report that Pope had ordered. What could he possibly say? That no one really knew where Nana was or where he would strike next? Could he really remind Pope about the slaughter at Ojo Caliente? What good would it do to recount all the damaging—and mostly inaccurate—newspaper reports?

He decided he would rather resign from the Army than write such a humiliating report. He cursed Sheldon for interfering in his business and fantasized briefly about having the governor and the newspaperman Greene imprisoned in the dungeon nearby. He thought about the bars of gold less than a hundred miles away; and gradually a plan came to him. What if he had not been here when Pope's second telegram had arrived? Then he would never have received the order to write a report. And, if he could catch Nana or drive him out of the territory, there would be no need to write such a report. With the campaign against Nana concluded, he and Guilfoyle could devise a way to recover the gold. But first he would have to find a way to stall Pope.

It was nearly 9 p.m. before Hatch had perfected his plan. He left his quarters and walked over to the telegraph office, which was adjacent to the post commander's office. He sat down in front of the telegraph and tapped out a brief message to Washington. "Gen. John Pope, Commander, Division of the Missouri, Washington, D.C. Hostiles moving south toward Mexican border. Col. Hatch left early today for Ft. Cummings to intercept them. Will forward your telegram to him there." Hatch grinned as he tapped out the name of the sender: "Cap't. John Bean, Commander, Ft. Craig."

The following morning, Hatch was up early and packing for the trip to Fort Cummings. He told Bean that he was moving his base of operations for the duration of the campaign against Nana, and ordered that a detail of five troopers accompany him down the *Jornada del Muerto* to Engle.

"It doesn't make sense to go north to Socorro to catch a train heading south," he explained to Bean as they breakfasted in the officers' mess.

"What's the big hurry?" asked Bean.

"I stayed up late plotting Nana's movements," replied Hatch. "I think I know where he's heading and how to trap him. But since our troopers don't carry portable telegraphs, I'm going to have to go into the field and tell them what the plan is."

Bean stared across the table at Hatch, who seemed extremely nervous to him. He knew Hatch had received a telegram from Washington and wondered if that was what was bothering the general. "Didn't Nana attack some town up near Albuquerque? What makes you so sure he's not heading north?"

"Patterns, Captain, patterns of movement. The attack on Garcia, which is actually closer to Laguna Pueblo than to Albuquerque, was just a feint. I think the old-timer was trying to get us to concentrate our forces around Fort Wingate, while he was off thumbing his nose at us as he rode south to Ojo Caliente. After I leave, I want you to send a wire to Captain Hunt at Fort Cummings and tell him to be on the lookout for hostiles in the area."

"Well," said Bean, "he's got both Guilfoyle and Smith on patrol down there. Plus another unit under Taylor's command from Fort Bayard. Also, remember that Companies B and D of the infantry should be in the area soon. The tracks up by Raton have been repaired. In fact, you may be riding on the same train with them."

"Excellent. Tell Hunt to send out a fourth unit under the command of Captain Dawson to patrol the border. Dawson will be supported by B and D companies as soon as they arrive."

"Yes, sir. Anything else?"

Hatch thought for a moment. "Just forward all telegrams from Washington to me. Oh, and send a wire to the depot at Engle and have them hold that train for me."

Hatch left immediately after breakfast with his contingent of five troopers. They carried extra canteens because there would be no water for the horses along the forty-mile trip to Engle.

The trip down the *Jornada del Muerto* was hot and uneventful. They arrived just before dark, found the train waiting for them, and discovered that—because of a problem with the boiler—they could not leave for Fort Cummings until the morning. Companies B and D were not aboard, adding further to the general's frustration. Hatch spent an uncomfortable night sleeping on the floor of a freight car while engineers repaired the boiler by the light of torches.

At daybreak, the train pulled out of the small depot at Engle; and Hatch—who had hardly slept at all—was relieved to finally be on the way. He opened his leather dispatch case and retrieved the only good thing Loud had forwarded to him from Santa Fe, a letter from Lew Wallace that had traveled halfway around the world. Hatch felt slightly guilty reading it because he still had not finished *Ben-Hur*. He had reached the part about the chariot race, which he thought was fairly exciting, but had not read any further.

Wallace's letter was short and to the point. He had received a letter from a friend, described only as a "influential Congressman" with close connections to the Army, who had assured him that the situation regarding Hatch was "being taken care of." "Everything now seems to be in place," Wallace wrote. "Assuming everything is under control militarily in New Mexico, you will gradually be transferred further east and receive another command at a post in a more civilized region."

Hatch laughed when he read the phrase "under control militarily." Undoubtedly, news of raiding Apaches had never reached Constantinople. But he appreciated his friend's efforts to extract him from New Mexico and vowed that he would finish *Ben-Hur*.

The train stopped at Rincon to pick up passengers and then crossed the wooden bridge over the Rio Grande. Hatch realized that they were nearing the town that Wallace had named after him, and closely watched the landscape. The tiny town of Hatch's Station consisted of a railroad siding and three adobe houses set in the midst of irrigated farmland. There was not even a sign, Hatch noted with disappointment. He guessed that the five people he spotted in the fields were the entire population of his town, and wondered what crop they were picking.

About an hour later, the train slowed and finally stopped at the siding at Cooke's Spring that was used by Fort Cummings. Hatch jumped down from the train and was greeted by Captain Hunt, who had a horse for him to ride.

"Any good news?" asked Hatch.

"Not much," replied Hunt, a thin, clean-shaven man in his late thirties. "I got the telegram from Bean and deployed my forces as instructed. Where are Companies B and D?"

"Your guess is as good as mine," replied Hatch.

The fort was located a few miles from the siding at the east end of Cooke's Canyon, which had been a notorious Apache ambush site prior to the fort's construction. The first thing Hatch noticed was a tent city outside the walls of the fort. He was about to question Hunt about it, but did not want to show his ignorance. Hunt casually suggested an inspection tour, and they rode through the unattended sally port.

In a few minutes, the reason for the tents was obvious—the fort was falling apart. Guilfoyle had told him that it was in "disrepair," an enormous understatement. The fort was mostly uninhabitable, a near-ruin with crumbling adobe walls. The officers and men lived in tents both inside and outside the walls, and the officers' quarters and enlisted men's barracks were in such bad condition they could only be used as storage rooms.

"Why didn't you tell me the fort was in such bad shape?" he asked Hunt after his inspection tour.

"General, I reported this several times to Captain Loud. He wired back that there was no money to repair a fort that would just be abandoned after the Apache threat was contained."

Hatch cursed under his breath. Now he would have to sleep in a tent for the remainder of the campaign.

When the Navajo scout known as Buffalo Grass reported to Bennett that he had lost the renegades' trail, Guilfoyle just shrugged. He had been expecting such a development ever since they left Ojo Caliente, because Nana had led them on a nearly impassible route through the western slopes of the Black Range. The country was so rough that they had been forced to shoot two of their horses that had broken their legs, and two troopers had been injured in falls. Not once had they gotten close enough to Nana to fire a shot.

"Now what?" asked Bennett as the unit rested in the shade of some junipers.

Guilfoyle unfolded his worn map and studied it in silence for a few minutes. Finally, he looked up. "We need a rest. Lake Valley is the closest town, so let's head there."

A few scattered cheers broke out from the troopers and Guilfoyle smiled ruefully as he ordered his unit to mount up. *What a change*, he thought. After they had found the bodies of the men slaughtered at Ojo Caliente, his men had been so angry that they couldn't wait to hit the trail and get revenge against the hostiles. But after eight days of futility, their anger had been replaced with discouragement. He didn't blame them, since he felt the same way. If they couldn't engage the Apaches, maybe a couple of days' rest would improve everyone's attitude.

"So what's in Lake Valley?" he asked Bennett.

"Only the richest silver mine in the West," the chief scout replied. "It's called the Bridal Chamber. There, they don't have to blast the silver out of the ground. The vein's so rich that they saw out the horn silver in big blocks. You can light a match, hold it up to the vein, and the silver just melts right off. It's so pure it's worth a dollar an ounce."

The thought of such pure silver reminded Guilfoyle of the gold bars in the cavern at Victorio's peak, and he silently cursed both Apache renegades and the U.S. Army for preventing him from claiming it. *Patience*, he told himself, *have patience.* The gold had been there for years and would still be there after the Apaches were beaten and he had resigned his commission. He suddenly realized that Bennett was staring at him, expecting a response. "That's a lot of money," he said.

Bennett grinned. "They've already recovered over a million ounces with no end in sight."

"If we have time, I'd like to see that mine," Guilfoyle told him.

However, Guilfoyle's proposed tour of the Bridal Chamber was not to be. As they rode into the dusty, ramshackle mining town, a miner ran up to them, screaming about the murdering Apaches. He was nearly incoherent, and it took Guilfoyle a minute to calm him down to the point where he could be understood. The Apaches—he didn't know which ones—had attacked two nearby ranches, the Ousley and Irwin places. Perry Ousley had been killed and his ranch house burned to the ground; Sally Irwin had barely escaped with her child as the Apaches also torched her house. The miners were organizing a posse to run the renegades to ground and kill them all.

"Where are they now?" asked Guilfoyle.

The miner had a blank look on his bearded face. "The 'Paches? Damned if I know."

Guilfoyle rolled his eyes. "No, the miners," he snapped. "Where are they?"

"Over at Cotton's Saloon. I was headin' that way myself."

Guilfoyle gave orders to Sergeant Williams to dismount the men and water the horses, and then he and Bennett followed the miner down the street. He noted that Lake Valley was much larger than he expected—there must be at least a thousand people living there.

They walked through the swinging doors of the saloon and into a near-riot. Perhaps thirty noisy miners were crowded into the room, and they were all angry and near-drunk. When they spotted Guilfoyle's uniform, the din increased.

A burly man wearing a vest separated himself from the crowd and walked aggressively toward Guilfoyle and Bennett. "You army bastards are supposed to protect us and look what's happened," he snarled. "Instead of fightin', you come drinkin'!"

Guilfoyle looked him over as if he were inspecting a dead rat. "And who the hell are you?"

"Name's Daly. I'm the super of the Lake Valley Mining Company—and commander of our volunteer forces." The crowd gave him a cheer.

"Well, Mr. Daly, you can hardly hold us responsible for what the Apaches do."

Daly tried to stare the lieutenant down. "If you'd do your job and kill those sons a bitches, they wouldn't be raidin' our town."

"Well, my men have been chasing and fighting the renegades for two months now—"

"Your niggers can't fight," interrupted Daly. "They can hardly even put their pants on." The crowd hooted in delight.

"Permission to kill this asshole, sir?" asked Bennett, who suddenly had his cocked revolver pointed squarely between Daly's eyes. The miner wisely fell silent.

Guilfoyle paused as if considering the request and then said, "Nah, then I'd have to file a damn report about it." He gestured for Bennett to put his gun away, and the chief scout reluctantly obeyed. "Now, Daly, tell me what your 'volunteer forces' are up to."

Before he could reply, an Indian walked into the saloon and thirty men reached for reached for their guns.

"At ease!" ordered Bennett. "Can't you see he's Navajo?"

"How can you tell?" sneered one of the miners.

Bennett ignored him and walked up to the Navajo scout. They conferred in a confusing mixture of Navajo, Spanish, and English for a few moments and then the scout left the bar.

"One of Smith's scouts," Bennett explained to Guilfoyle. The saloon was now quiet. "He located Nana's trail heading into Gavilan Canyon."

"Let's go!" shouted Daly.

"Wait a minute," countered Guilfoyle. "This is a job for the Army, not civilians."

"You've had your chance, Lieutenant. Now it's our turn and there's not a damn thing you can do about it."

Guilfoyle knew Daly was right. He also knew that he was duty-bound to protect these amateurs. "Okay, okay, we'll team up."

"Yeah," said Daly, "we'll take the lead and you can take our rear."

Guilfoyle followed the miners out of the saloon and quickly gave orders. He sent the Navajo back to Smith's troop with instructions for them to proceed to Gavilan Canyon as quickly as possible as support. Then he briefed Sergeant Williams about the miners, but omitted their racial slurs. He did not want any of the miners shot in the back with Army bullets. In a few minutes, his men were mounted and following the miners, now a disorganized mob riding as fast as they could for the mountains.

A half-hour later, they reached the mouth of Gavilan Canyon. Guilfoyle called a halt and rode up to Daly. He didn't like the looks of things at all. The canyon was extremely narrow and the walls were very steep, which meant the troops must travel in single file. He could imagine the old chief sitting up there behind a rock with a big grin on his face.

"It smells like an ambush to me," he told Daly. "Let me send some scouts in there first."

Daly was incredulous. "And let them get away? No wonder you chicken-shit soldiers never get anything done."

Guilfoyle tried to press his point, but the miners would have none of it. Daly led them single file into the canyon, and there was nothing Guilfoyle could do except order his men to follow them. Soon, a long line of miners and soldiers stretched from the middle of the canyon to its mouth.

Then all hell broke loose. Intense rifle fire rained down upon them seemingly from all directions. Daly and five other miners were shot off their horses and killed instantly, while at least that many were wounded.

"Take cover, take cover!" Guilfoyle screamed, but his orders came too late to save some of his troopers. Three were killed in the first volley and four more were wounded. The rest of his managed to scramble to the immediate safety of rocks and brush and watched in shock while the Apaches picked off milling horses. The remaining miners ran as fast as they could toward the mouth of the canyon, but found their way blocked by the carcasses of the soldiers' horses and the stampeding pack train mules.

Guilfoyle shouted orders not to return fire unless the target was in view, but the noise from the Apache rifles was so deafening that no one heard him. His men began firing in panic at the well-secured enemy positions above them, but the bullets glanced harmlessly off the rocks. He knew that his first duty was to try to rescue his wounded men.

"Sergeant!" he yelled during a momentary break in the din of rifle fire. Sergeant Moses Williams managed to scramble over next to him.

"Yes, sah?"

"We've got to save those men. Identify the Apache positions as best you can and have your men direct fire at them. Then, you, me, and one other man will attempt to pull those men to cover."

Their momentary panic over, the troopers passed the word about Guilfoyle's orders and waited for the signal from Williams. When it came, they returned fire and kept the enemy pinned down as best they could. Guilfoyle, Williams, and Private Augustus Walley scrambled from cover, ran to the wounded men, and began to drag them from the defile. Williams and Walley were immediately successful, but Guilfoyle's man was pinned beneath his dead horse.

As Guilfoyle struggled to free the man, Williams glanced back and in horror watched as a young Apache boy rose from behind a rock and calmly shot the lieutenant three times. Guilfoyle died instantly.

Williams knew that now he was in command of Company B and there was nothing to do but retreat. He and Walley used the same technique to rescue three wounded miners and four troopers, then Williams gave the order for retreat. Walley and himself would provide the covering fire while Sergeant Brent Woods, who had managed to control five horses, would lead the retreat. Williams figured that the Apaches would seize the rest of the horses and the ammunition in the packs before following the troopers, and he was right.

The gunfire from Williams and Walley forced the enemy to hold their positions while Woods led the rest toward the mouth of the canyon. But soon, several of the Apaches figured out what was happening and began a flanking movement left. Williams knew he could not hold his position any longer, and the two men slowly fell back. When they reached the mouth of the canyon, they found Woods and the other survivors entrenched behind a barricade of rocks. Their position insured that no Apaches could leave the canyon without getting killed.

An eerie silence descended upon them. Williams' ears were ringing as he gave orders for the wounded to be moved to the nearest ranch, about four miles away. He and Walley kept watch over the mouth of the canyon, but no Apaches appeared. Williams figured they were probably plundering the pack train.

Twenty minutes later, a patrol of about fifty men under the command of Lieutenant George Washington Smith arrived at Williams' position. Williams quickly explained what had happened.

Smith promptly took command and asked for volunteers to go back into the canyon. "The renegades are probably gone," he said. "I'm sure they must have seen us coming."

Bennett, Williams, Woods, and Walley volunteered to accompany Smith back into the canyon. They moved carefully from rock to rock, but no shots rang out. When they reached the site of the ambush, as Williams had expected, the packs and the horses were gone. The Apaches had left behind only the bodies of the miners and the troopers.

Williams found Guilfoyle's body and pointed it out to Smith. The Apaches had castrated him, gutted his body as if it were a deer, and removed his eyeballs and tongue. Nearby lay the body of Saddler Tom Goulding, whose nose and mustached upper lip had been sliced off and hung on a nearby cholla cactus.

Hatch felt miserable. He was experiencing the lowest point in his career and was having great difficulty dealing with it. Nothing had gone according to plan during this campaign, and he was constantly being humiliated by a senile savage who thwarted him at every step. And now he had lost his best lieutenant. He shuddered at the thought of Bennett's description of Guilfoyle's body.

It was enough to drive a man to drink, which was precisely what the general was doing on a Saturday night in early September. He was sitting alone in his large tent, which was pitched on the parade ground in crumbling Fort Cummings, alone with a bottle of bourbon. A single oil lamp cast flickering shadows on the canvas, and except for an occasional howl of a coyote, the camp was silent. He was responsible for the quiet because his mourning order for Lieutenant Guilfoyle and the others, issued that very day, had specifically directed that there would be no singing or carousing in the camp for one week.

He poured himself another shot of bourbon and picked up *Ben-Hur*, which was marked at Chapter II of Book Sixth, "The Lepers." He read for a few moments but quickly decided that Lew's words read like a comedy compared to what he had been through recently, and he put the book aside. He was quite aware of the fact that he was feeling sorry for himself, but did not know how to shake the feeling. The only people he could really talk to—namely Evelyn and John Loud—were far to the north in Santa Fe while he sat alone in a tent in a God-forsaken desert.

That morning, right after Smith had told him of Guilfoyle's cruel fate, the telegram he had been dreading arrived. It was, of course, from General Pope in Washington and it was quite direct: "Where is your report?"

Unfortunately, the telegraph system was working perfectly, so stalling was difficult. Hatch had wired back: "What report?" Pope had countered by sending a copy of his original telegram, so there was nothing for Hatch to do but lie. His final telegram of the day to Pope had apologized for the confusion and the primitive telegraph system in the territory. He said he had never received the original telegram and would promptly start on a complete report about the situation with the renegades.

But before starting such a report, he spent several hours preparing a recommendation for Sergeant Moses Williams and Private Augustus Walley to receive the Congressional Medal of Honor. It was the first time he had ever written such a recommendation for black troopers, but no matter—they certainly deserved it. If they had not taken charge, Company B would have been wiped out and dozens more troopers and civilians would have been killed. He had interviewed all the witnesses as to their valor and had included their statements in his long report, which he would forward by courier to the Department of War in Washington. Hopefully, it would be read along with his report and give the bureaucrats a complete picture of the horrors of the Apache conflict.

Tomorrow, he thought, *tomorrow he would begin writing the report that would end his Army career.* He wondered how he would begin the report. Certainly not in the usual, dry Army manner; but rather in some way that would get their attention. *Fighting the Apaches is not like fighting the Mexicans or the Confederates,* he would write, *it's more like fighting ghosts. They are an enemy you cannot see, cannot find, cannot kill. Yet they can strike at you when you least expect it and then disappear into the landscape. The Apaches don't obey the rules of war; but rather operate by their own evil methods: murder, torture, and mutilation.*

Hatch laughed, knowing he would never dare to write those words. He poured himself another shot of bourbon and realized he was getting drunk. After downing the bourbon in one swallow, he felt trapped in his tent and decided to get some fresh air. He pulled his boots on and parted the flap of the tent, stumbling slightly as he left it.

The parade ground was illuminated by various small campfires and the light from the half-full moon. Hatch decided to climb up to the guard tower and survey his domain, the falling-down fort that had become a tent city. He took a deep breath in a futile attempt to clear his head and slowly climbed the ladder made of tree limbs tied together. When he was about halfway up, a black face peered over the top ledge.

"Who goes there?" came the challenge. Hatch immediately conjured up an image of a Roman soldier issuing an identical challenge in *Ben-Hur*.

"Colonel Hatch," he panted. "Just out to look at the stars."

"Well, sah, they shore is out tonight," the soldier said as he helped Hatch climb over the ledge.

"You're temporarily relieved, Private," said Hatch. "Wait for me down below."

The tent city sprawled to the west looked better at night than it did during the day, Hatch decided. Some of the tents were illuminated by the campfires and others with lamps glowed from the inside out, resembling giant *farolitos*. The image of *farolitos* made him think of Santa Fe Plaza and then Evelyn. He wondered how she was getting along, and then knew the answer to the question as soon as he asked it to himself. She was fine, operating perfectly within her daily routine, patiently waiting for his return like a good army wife. God, he hated being in the field. He despised tents, primitive conditions, and the ever-present dirt and dust.

Hatch turned away from the tents and stared south into the desert. He knew he was very close to having everything he wanted: retirement, with all the money he would ever need. He hated himself for constantly thinking of it, but the fact remained that with Guilfoyle dead, he was the only person who knew of the gold in Victorio's peak. If he could just get rid of Nana, he could recover the gold, retire on schedule, and live the life of a wealthy man.

Suddenly he spotted some movement near the spring, which was about a quarter-mile southeast of the fort. He wondered if the liquor was getting to him because he was witnessing mounted men watering their horses—it could only be Apaches—in the very shadow of the fort! He strained to see them more clearly, but clouds kept passing over the moon and obscuring his already limited vision. When the clouds momentarily cleared the moon, he clearly saw one of the Apaches raise a lance in a mocking salute.

Then the group, that numbered perhaps thirty or forty, rode off fast to the southwest.

Was it Nana's band? he wondered, and again answered his question as soon as he asked it. Of course it was—and they were heading southwest, toward the Sierra Madre range.

"Soldier!" he yelled over the ledge.

"Yes, sah?"

"Fetch Lieutenant Smith as fast as you can."

A few minutes later, Smith joined Hatch on the guard tower, and the general described what he had seen. Smith was skeptical.

"It's unlikely they would risk coming so close to the fort," he said.

"Nana would," insisted Hatch. "Anyway, go after them."

"Sir?"

"You'll need two Navajo scouts. Take Bennett and Williams with you and no more than ten other men. No wagon. Take the best horses and light and fast, just like the Apaches. Follow them, but since they'll outnumber you, don't engage them unless they attack you or civilians. Ascertain that they've entered Mexico, then ride back here as fast as you can."

"Yes sir, we'll leave at first light."

"No, Lieutenant, you'll leave right now."

Hatch returned to his tent and slept fitfully until first light. Then he dressed, left the fort through the sally port, and walked to the spring. He could easily see the prints of dozens of horses and a trail leading off to the southwest. He knew that the end of his problems could be just a few hours away--unless, of course, Nana decided to double back. But Hatch had a hunch that Nana would not be this close to the border unless he intended to cross it. Along the southern boundary of New Mexico, the mountain ranges affording good cover were more widely spaced than those in the center of the territory.

He was about to return to the fort when a strange-looking object on a rise just east of the spring caught his eye. He moved closer and determined it to be a scarecrow of sorts, made of yucca stalks. The crude figure was propped up against a cholla cactus and was wearing a woman's calico dress. On the crude head was an officer's cap, and a gunbelt and holster was strapped over the dress. Hatch couldn't help but wonder if the cap and holster had belonged to Guilfoyle.

Angry at the insult, Hatch tore the scarecrow down and kicked it apart. He retrieved the cap, dress, and holster and returned to the fort. Inside, he threw the dress into a campfire and gave the cap and holster to the quartermaster without explanation. He checked with the corporal who was operating the telegraph in what used to be the commanding officer's quarters, but there were no messages for him. Bored, he returned to his tent, retrieved his copy of *Ben-Hur*, and began to read about lepers.

At about noon the following day, Smith's scouting party returned and the lieutenant reported to Hatch in his tent.

"We trailed the renegades past the Florida mountains and stopped once we reached the west side of the Tres Hermanos range," he said. "The Apaches were still riding south, so they obviously entered Mexico."

Hatch smiled for the first time in days. "That, Lieutenant Smith, is the best news I've heard in months. You are dismissed. You and your men are on leave for a week."

The general left his tent and hurried over to the telegraph office. "I want to send the same telegram to three different places," he told the corporal. "To Washington, Fort Leavenworth, and Santa Fe."

"All lines seem to be up and working, sir," the corporal replied.

Hatch found a pen and a piece of paper and composed his message. "Forces of the Ninth Cavalry and the Thirteenth and Fifteenth Infantry have defeated the renegade Nana," he wrote, "and have driven him and his men out of the Territory of New Mexico. This Apache is no longer a threat to the citizens of the United States. Complete report follows."

"Send it first to General Pope in Washington," Hatch directed, "then to Leavenworth and finally to Governor Sheldon in Santa Fe, care of Captain Loud." He imagined that John would thoroughly enjoy delivering the telegram personally.

Now that the problem of Nana was solved, he could begin to make some plans. The first step would be to seal off the border so that Nana would either be forced to stay in Mexico or Arizona; in either case, he was someone else's problem. For the sake of appearance, he would have to stay at Fort Cummings for a few weeks and continue living in a tent, but that was a minor inconvenience when compared to the ultimate reward of retrieving the gold hidden in Victorio's peak.

By midnight, Hatch and consumed half a bottle of bourbon and had devised a rough plan for the recovery and sale of the gold.

Late in the afternoon on the last day of September, Captain John Loud knocked on the door of the Hatch house on Washington Avenue in Santa Fe. Evelyn, who was in the kitchen at the time, put aside her pie crust, wiped her hands on her apron, and opened the door.

"Why hello, John," she said. "Please come in." She was pleased to have a visitor; company was enjoyable when Ed was in the field.

"I can't stay long," he told her. "Things are happening fast and furious."

"I've heard rumors."

He handed her an envelope. "Here's a letter for you from the general. He sent it up from Fort Cummings on the train. Knowing him, he probably explains everything in it."

"We're moving, aren't we?" Evelyn asked.

"Looks like it, ma'am."

After Loud left, Evelyn opened the letter. "Dearest Evelyn," he wrote, "As you know, we chased Nana out of the territory and then President Garfield died shortly afterwards. Those two events caused a lot of changes. After President Arthur took over, he ordered a reorganization of the Division of the Missouri. The most significant change was that the headquarters of the Ninth is being moved to Fort Riley in Kansas. In his letter informing me of this change, General Pope congratulated me on the removal of the Apache threat, and said that he thought the Ninth 'needed a well-deserved rest.'

"I confess I am both pleased and disappointed by the orders. I am pleased that we are moving east—at least that is the right direction.

However, Kansas is little better than New Mexico and I would have preferred a posting closer to Washington. Also, I know you have come to love our home in Santa Fe.

"So, I am to move the command to Fort Riley by 31 October, which doesn't give us much time. I am stuck down here sealing off the border to make sure the renegades don't return, but that operation will only last a week or so. Then I must move to Fort Selden for a while to preside over some courts-martial. (Damned deserters!)

"I guess you'd better start packing up our things. You can write or cable me at Fort Selden, and I should be home by 25 October at the very latest. If everything goes well, I may have a big surprise for you. Also, I have been thinking seriously about retirement. I miss you. All my love, Edward."

Evelyn had mixed feelings about her husband's letter. She was disappointed about moving to Kansas, curious about his "big surprise," and slightly shocked at his reference to retirement. He rarely mentioned retirement in a serious way—it was mostly a joke about a far-distant future. She wondered if it might be possible to convince him to retire before they were transferred to Kansas. Even if that were possible, she didn't think he would want to live in Santa Fe because New Mexico had too many bad memories for him. He would prefer somewhere back east, like Boston or maybe even his hometown of Bangor.

She wondered what he would do without the Army, for the military life was the only life he knew. He had no other training except for two years of college and a short time as a lumberman before the war between the states. He could be a civil servant, she decided, take some government job. So maybe they would move to Washington.

Evelyn finished making her pie, placed it in the small oven of her wood stove, and then went into the back yard to check her chile drying project. She had roasted and peeled the green chile pods from her garden and was now drying them in the sun. *Chile pasado*, the Mexicans called it, chile of the past. She knew she wouldn't be able to find chile of any kind in Kansas, Boston or Washington, so knowing that seeds from the green chile were immature, she carefully removed the seeds from the some of the dried red pods hanging in her kitchen..

That evening she wrote her husband a letter and told him that whatever he decided about retirement was all right with her. She also said that she preferred Santa Fe to Kansas but would not mind living back east again. "Things are boring around here without you," she wrote. "I get together with some of the officer's wives for tea every Wednesday and Friday afternoons. We meet at the bandstand in the Plaza and usually go to the Palace, which has been so nicely remodeled.

"The garden's just about gone, but there are still plenty of tomatoes and chiles. John Loud went hunting and shot a deer, so there's been venison lately. I'll bet you're eating beans and salt pork, poor dear.

"Mr. Greene of the newspaper called at the house and said to pass on his congratulations. What a hypocrite, after all the bad things he wrote about you. I felt like pouring a bucket of water over his head but I was a good girl. He did say that Santa Fe has more than 6,000 people living here now.

"Have you finished *Ben-Hur* yet? Maybe if you retire we could take a trip to Europe and drop in on Lew and Susan in Constantinople."

Since there was no door to knock on, Private Walley stood outside Hatch's tent and announced, "Colonel Parks to see you, sah." Hatch immediately opened the flap and greeted his friend.

"Dick, good to see you. Come in."

Parks shook hands with Hatch and followed him inside. "Your fort is falling down, Ed. And I thought Fort Selden was bad."

Hatch smiled. "This posting is temporary, as you well know. Old Fort Cummings will be decommissioned soon. Have a seat. I know it's hot."

Parks sat on the offered chair and removed his hat and jacket. Hatch peeked out the tent flap to make certain no one was hanging around, then spread out a map of southern New Mexico Territory on the small table which served as his field desk.

"I'm thinking about retirement," he told Parks.

"Shit," said Parks. "What other kind of work do you know besides soldiering?"

"None, and that's the point," Hatch answered mysteriously. "I wouldn't even be thinking about it unless I thought I was going to become very wealthy."

Parks considered that statement for a moment. "Is that why you asked me here?"

"Yes. I need help. You're the only Army man in New Mexico I completely trust. I have found an easy way for both of us to become suddenly rich. Are you interested?"

"Is it legal?" asked Parks.

"I believe so."

"Then I'm very interested."

Hatch reached into his boot, retrieved the gold bar, and placed it in the middle of the map. Parks responded with a low whistle.

"I know where lots of those bars are," Hatch explained. "I need your help to retrieve them and move them to a safe place."

"How many bars?" asked Parks.

"Tons of them," Hatch replied, and then told his friend about Guilfoyle's discovery and description of the cache.

"How large was the stack of bars?" insisted Parks after he had heard the whole story.

"Guilfoyle told me one pace out from the wall, four paces long, and chest-high."

Parks began to calculate figures on a corner of the map with a pen. "About three by twelve by five feet," he said, "that's a hundred and eighty cubic feet." He then turned the map over and drew a square measuring one foot on each side.

"What are you doing?" asked Hatch.

"I'm figuring out what all that gold weighs. How else do I know how many wagons we need?"

"I knew there was a reason I brought you into this," Hatch told him.

Parks set the gold bar on end inside the drawn square foot and proceeded to trace around the end until he had filled the square with smaller rectangles. Forty-eight retangles filled the square foot. "Since the bar is roughly six inches long, we'll double that number to ninety-six, the total fitting inside a cubic foot, and multiply that by one-eighty, the total number of cubic feet. Let's see, that's seventeen thousand, two hundred and eighty total bars. How much does this bar weigh?"

Hatch took the bar and hefted it. "Two pounds? Three?"

"Does your sutler's store have a scale?" asked Parks.

"I'll be right back," Hatch promised. In a few minutes he returned and said, "Two and a half pounds."

Parks began multiplying again. "The seventeen thousand-odd bars weigh forty-three thousand two hundred pounds, nearly twenty-two tons. So we'll need at least thirty wagons."

"Or ten wagons making three trips each," Hatch pointed out. "Look, multiply those forty-three thousand pounds by sixteen."

Parks concentrated for a minute, then announced, "Six hundred ninety one thousand, two hundred. Ounces, I presume."

"Yes. Now multiply that number by a conservative twenty-two dollars."

"The total value of the gold," said Parks dramatically, "is fifteen million, two hundred and six thousand, four hundred dollars. Give or take a couple of million."

"Excellent," said Hatch. "Now, how do we get it?"

"First, I'll ask again, is what we're doing against the law?"

Hatch shrugged. "What law way out here? The gold is a very old treasure on public land. We'll place ourselves officially on leave, so what we do with our own private time is our own business. We'll be ordinary citizens."

"But we need help, Ed. We can't load out all that gold ourselves, it would take weeks. We're going to have to use the troops at our disposal to move all that weight."

Hatch thought for a moment. "Okay, so we may be technically breaking the law by using Army troops. It's a risk we'll have to take. I have a plan, Dick. Guilfoyle told me that those bars are so dirty you can't tell they're gold until you clean them up. Let's invent a military mission to recover lead for bullets. We'll send wagons from here and Selden up to Hembrillo Canyon, put the bars in burlap sacks, load the 'lead' and carry it to Rincon, which is only thirty miles away. We can store it there under guard and send wagons back and forth to Victorio's peak. I'll commandeer a couple of freight cars and transport the 'lead' to Santa Fe, where I'll store it in a secure warehouse."

"Then you take retirement in protest of moving headquarters to Kansas while there's still an Apache threat here," suggested Parks. "I'll resign in support of you. Then what?"

"I've thought quite a bit about the next step. Obviously we can't dump all that gold on the market at once because it would cause the price to fall. The gold will be stored in a warehouse in Santa Fe or Albuquerque. I'll make sure that during the move of Ninth headquarters to Fort Riley, the report of the 'lead' shipment will be lost. After we retire from the Army, we'll open our own mining company. We'll spread the rumor we're backed by Lew Wallace—everyone knows what an interest he had in gold mines."

"What do we do for mines?" asked Parks.

"We'll buy up depleted mines for next to nothing and tell everyone we have new techniques for gold recovery. Since the name LaRue is already on the bars, we'd better call our company 'LaRue Mining.' We'll be wealthy miners, take our wives on European vacations, meet up with Lew Wallace in Turkey."

Parks laughed. "We'll be the cream of Santa Fe society."

"Eveyln will love it," said Hatch. "Her wish come true." He checked his pocket watch. Three-thirty. He took a bottle of bourbon out of the trunk next to the cot and poured them each a drink. He lifted his tin cup in a salute. "To a successful operation."

Parks briefly touched his cup to Hatch's, downed the bourbon in one swallow, and wanted to get back to business. "We've got the long-range plan. Now, let's work on the immediate one."

Hatch nodded. "We need to decide where the wagons and men are coming from. Since Nana's crossed the border, we're over-staffed and over-supplied here."

Parks shook is head negatively. "Well, I don't trust Hunt or his men. The fewer officers involved in this, the better. In fact, let's run the operation from Fort Selden and forget about soldiers or wagons from here. That way we can use just my men, who never question my orders. If I tell them we're moving lead, they'll believe me."

"Agreed," said Hatch. "We'll wait here for a few days until I've deployed most of the men to other forts. We can perfect our plan during that time. Then we'll take the train to Fort Selden. You can wire ahead for them to have the wagons ready."

"This is going to be fun, General," said Parks, holding out his cup for another drink.

"And profitable, Colonel, highly profitable."

Apache Camp.

8. Stronghold

Deep in the Blue Mountains, Nana led his war party to a small canyon with an opening so narrow it could barely admit a horse. Beyond the entrance was a thick jungle with a stream running through it, and a well-used camp with soot-blackened stones already in place for a fire. Nana stationed Sánchez on watch just outside the canyon and gave instructions to Kaytennae.

"A zigzag trail runs up the side of the mountain there," he said, pointing to the high mountain with the flattened top. "Juh's lookouts will have already seen us and will come down to greet us, but I want you to climb the trail and meet them. Follow this stream until you find the trail that leads to the land of the Nednhi."

Kaytennae left immediately and Istee, without being told, began to gather wood for the fire. It was already too late in the afternoon to attempt to climb the trail, so they would stay overnight in the small canyon. Istee marveled at the bright, beautifully-colored birds and flowers and decided that he liked the Blue Mountains better than anywhere else that the Tcihene had roamed. During his collection of fallen branches, he heard a buzzing sound and quickly located a beehive attached to a ledge high up on the canyon wall. He ran back to the camp and told Nana, who beamed with pleasure.

The old chief took a bow and arrows from Kaytennae's horse and followed Istee back to the beehive. Then he began shooting arrows into the hive until it broke apart and the pieces fell on the ground. Some bees rose from the chunks and flew back to the ledge, so Nana gestured for Istee to run and gather up what had fallen. Then he showed Istee how to squeeze the pieces until the thick liquid ran onto his tongue. Istee thought it was the most delicious food he had ever tasted, better even than roasted *mescal* or cactus fruit.

Just after the sun set, Kaytennae rode into camp accompanied by Naiche, the son of Cochise. They dismounted and Naiche embraced Nana with the *abrazo* of the people.

"Welcome to our land," he said. "You are safe because no Mexicans dare come here."

"Where is Juh?" asked Nana.

"He and Geronimo have gone to San Carlos to talk to the Blue Coats about better conditions for our people still imprisoned there. They should return soon. In the meantime, your wife and people await you at the stronghold. There is also a surprise for you there."

Istee was very curious about the surprise and was disappointed when Grandfather didn't ask Naiche about it. But perhaps Nana already knew what the surprise was.

"We will leave at first light," said Nana. "Join us for the evening meal."

Later, while feasting on the meat of a deer shot by Sánchez, Naiche told Nana and the rest of the warriors about the disease and starvation that tormented his people at San Carlos. Conditions were so bad on the reservation that he predicted a war to the death with the White Eyes. Nana merely nodded; he had been through it all before.

The next morning Naiche led Nana's men on the long climb up the zigzag trail, a journey that lasted until the sun was high in the sky. Istee thought they would never get to the top, and knew he had never been up so high in his life. He imagined leaping from the trail and soaring out over the trees like an eagle.

Waiting for them at the top of the trail were Chihuahua and Lozen— Naiche's surprise! With them were the rest of the Tcihene band that had survived the massacre at Tres Castillos, including Nana's wife, Nah-des-te, and Kaytennae's wife, Guyan. There were many embraces and much laughter as family and friends greeted each other. Nana seemed particularly happy. "There is much to tell," he said.

Nah-des-te looked at her husband adoringly. "Can we now live in peace?" she asked quietly.

Before Nana could answer, Lozen interrupted. "For now, yes, Grandmother," she said. "None of our enemies are near."

"Thank Ussen for that," murmured Nah-des-te, glancing up at the sky.

Nana called for an evening feast and Naiche agreed. Nah-des-te had obviously been anticipating their arrival, because she and the other women had made a large batch of *tizwin*. Nah-des-te quickly organized the women to begin preparing the food for the feast.

Kaywaykla offered to show Istee around the stronghold, and the young warrior agreed, even though he had to endure a barrage of questions. As Kaywaykla guided him through the camp, Istee realized how perfectly the stronghold was situated. A wide, flat ledge, it jutted out from even taller mountains rising behind it. On every side of the ledge were sheer cliffs that were impossible to climb. The zigzag trail was the only way up or down, and it was easily guarded. A stream ran from the mountains through the camp, and over the cliff in a spectacular waterfall. Because of the fact that three different bands occupied the stronghold, there was an odd mixture of wickiups and teepees in the camp. Istee could not begin to count all the people there; it was the largest gathering of his people he had ever seen.

"You have to see this," said Kaywaykla with excitement in his voice. He led Istee over to a cage woven out of thin branches. Inside was a green bird with a red and yellow head and a large beak. The bird dropped the pine cone it was eating, cocked its head, looked at Istee, and said clearly, "Where have you been?"

Startled, Istee jumped back. Kaywakla laughed. The bird said, "Where have you been?" again, then whistled and said, "Call me Pretty Boy, Pretty Boy."

"Go ahead," urged Kaywaykla.

Istee, feeling a little foolish, said, "Hello, Pretty Boy."

As if on cue, the parrot uttered the Tcihene curse, "Your shit!" Istee howled with delight.

"I taught him to say that," Kaywaykla said proudly. "But Grandmother hates this bird. Because it talks, she says there must be a witch inside it. I don't believe that."

Later, they sat together on a rocky ledge that overlooked lush green canyons, and Istee told his friend about his long raid with Grandfather, how the warriors had accepted him as one of their own despite the fact he was a novice, and the excitement he felt at shooting the Blue Coat leader. He also told Kaywaykla about Nana cutting up the bodies of both the buffalo soldiers and the White Eyes.

"I could never do that," said Kaywaykla.

"I never touched a dead enemy," agreed Istee.

"Do you think Grandfather will continue the war against the White Eyes?"

"Yes, but there are too many of them."

"But our people are fast and clever."

Istee shook his head sadly. "Everywhere we went there were White Eyes and Mexicans. Kaytennae told me there are more White Eyes and Mexicans in just one village than all of our people everywhere."

"I just hope I get a chance to kill some of them," said Kaywaykla.

"I think that you will," Istee replied.

That night the Tcihene and the Nednhi feasted on freshly roasted horse meat while Lozen told of the rescue and escape of Chihuahua from the Blue Coat fort. What amazed Istee the most about the story was the fact that Chihuahua had been kept in a hole in the ground.

"You were buried alive!" he said.

Chihuahua grunted his agreement. "It was far worse than living in a cave. Not only did I have to smell the White Eyes and buffalo soldiers, they treated me like a caged animal. I'll never forget the Blue Coat chief they call Hatch screaming at me. Someday, I hope I get the chance to kill him."

"It may come sooner than you think," said Nana.

Three days after Nana's war party arrived at the stronghold, Juh returned, accompanied by his closest friend, Geronimo. From high above, Istee and Kaywaykla watched them enter the canyon below with many horses. They left the horses and some warriors there and began the slow climb on the zigzag trail.

"Go tell Grandfather," Istee said to Kaywaykla, who obeyed.

By the time they reached the top of the trail, there was quite a crowd waiting for them. Juh was the largest Chiricahua man Istee had ever seen. Grandfather was tall, but Juh towered over him and his body was twice as thick. His heavy hair was braided and fell almost to his knees. Geronimo was smaller than Juh, but solid and muscular. Nah-des-te ran up to Geronimo, who leaped down from his horse and embraced the sister he had not seen for twenty moons.

Juh, whose face was smeared with red clay, rode between the lines of outstretched arms until he reached the place where his young son, Daklugie, stood. Then he dismounted and placed the reins in his son's hands. When the boy smiled with pleasure, Juh lifted him onto the back of the horse and then turned to greet his wife, Ishton.

Although the two bands were very happy to see the Nednhi leaders, the news they brought was not good.

"The Dreamer is dead," said Juh without emotion. "The Blue Coats killed him."

Istee expected Nana to be shocked by the news, but all the old chief said was, "How did it happen?"

"Bring us *tizwin* and we will tell you," Geronimo replied.

After the women brought the drinks, Juh and Geronimo sat around the fire. Juh began the story but became so excited that his stuttering made it very difficult to understand him. After only a few minutes, he turned to

Geronimo and shrugged. Geronimo picked up the story.

"The Dreamer arrived at San Carlos with the bar of gold and showed it to the Blue Coat leader known as Colonel Carr. He told Carr that Nana had much more gold he wanted to trade to the Blue Coats in return for the land at Warm Springs. Carr told him he would have to ask the Great White Eye Chief in Washington. He took the bar of gold from The Dreamer and it was never seen again."

"Our plan did not work," interrupted Nana.

"No," said Geronimo, "but The Dreamer had another one. He wanted to give our people their pride back, so they would rise up and fight the White Eyes who made them slaves. So he asked for permission from Carr to hold dances. We were surprised when Carr said yes."

"But The D-D-Dreamer's dances were new," Juh reminded him.

"Yes. The Dreamer moved from San Carlos to the river known as Cibecue and hundreds of followers went with him. Before the dances, he would give the dancers the plant known as *peyotl*, and they would see many strange sights—even our chiefs who came back from the dead."

"We know of that," Nana said simply and Istee shuddered as he remembered the visions of his father and Mangas Coloradas.

Geronimo finished his *tizwin*, called for another, and continued. "The dances were new, not like the old ones. The dancers were arranged like the spokes of a wagon wheel, with The Dreamer in the center. As they circled around him, he would sprinkle them with the sacred pollen. Many people saw the dead chiefs he brought back to life, but some did not and became angry with The Dreamer. When they threatened to kill him, he told them that the dead chiefs would remain invisible to them until all the White Eyes were driven out of our land. The Dreamer said, 'I have been guided my entire life by dreams; I receive special knowledge and wisdom through dreams because the Power of the dream shows me the truth.'"

Nana nodded solemnly in agreement, and Geronimo continued the story. "Carr sent Blue Coats to Cibecue and warned The Dreamer not to spread such tales, but The Dreamer asked Carr's men what had happened to the gold bar. They said Carr had sent it to Washington with Nana's proposal, but The Dreamer did not believe them. The Dreamer held more dances, but again warned that the dead could not be seen until the White Eyes were gone. He was paid very well for his dances, and soon had over a hundred horses, which he gave to us to take back here."

Istee was spellbound by the story and could imagine the scene at Cibecue. The Dreamer was very powerful and persuasive, and with all the White Mountain people starving and being treated as slaves, he must have appeared to be a very great shaman. He would have given them the hope they needed.

"The Blue Coats became suspicious of the dances," continued Geronimo, "and soon came with a very large force and arrested The Dreamer. The White Mountain people demanded his release, but Carr refused. The big man and I led an attack against the Blue Coats, but they shot The Dreamer before we could save him. Then we killed most of the Blue Coat force in a great battle. But we knew that they would soon be back with ten times as many soldiers, so we took what horses we could and rode back here."

A few moments of silence followed the telling of The Dreamer's sad fate, and Nah-des-te took the opportunity to bring everyone more *tizwin*. Even Istee, who was sitting on the outer edge of the group gathered around the fire, was given a gourd filled with the mild beer.

"We need a plan," said Juh after a while, and some men grunted in agreement. "Tell us, Grandfather, what happened on your raid."

All eyes turned to the old chief as he recounted the story of their long campaign against the Blue Coats. Compared to the tale of The Dreamer, Nana's narrative roused his audience, and he was frequently interrupted by war cries from the enthusiastic audience. Then he asked Lozen to retell her story of the rescue of Chihuahua, and even though most had already heard the tale, more triumphant shouts were forthcoming.

After Lozen finished, Geronimo waved everyone to silence. "Last night," he began, "the big man and I were camped by a stream in a beautiful canyon not far from here. The big man was able to sleep at once, but I was thinking about The Dreamer's plan to deal with the White Eyes by trading gold for the return of our lands. As smart as The Dreamer was, his plan did not work, and I wondered why. Then I fell asleep and dreamed that I was trapped by the largest rattlesnake I had ever seen. I wished that I had Grandfather with me so he could use his Power over the snake, but I was all alone. I tried to run away from the snake, but he used his four legs and I could not outrun him. You know that the rattlesnake has four legs, but no one can see them except people like Grandfather, who know the snake. The legs are made of turquoise and are shaped like balls, and that is how the snake rolls along with such speed. I could not escape from the snake, so I had to stand and fight. All I had with me was my knife, and I knew that I only had one chance to save my life from the snake's poisonous mouth. When the snake struck at me, I pretended I was a snake too and whipped the blade of my knife in a little circle, cutting off the snake's head. The body of the snake still tried to attack me, but it could not hurt me without the head."

A collective sigh of relief swept the group, which made Geronimo smile. "I did not need The Dreamer to tell me what that dream meant," he said. "The snake represented the White Eye army, and its head was the Blue Coat leaders. If we cut off the head of the Blue Coat snake, the body will be unable to hurt us."

"It is a snake with many heads," said Nana.

"We have many knives," replied Geronimo.

"Which heads should we chop off?" asked Juh.

Together, they made list of the Blue Coat leaders they hated the most: Crook, Carr, Willcox, and Hatch.

Chihuahua, who had remained silent, suddenly stood up. "I ask the council to allow me to kill the snake called Hatch."

"How will you do that?" asked Lozen.

"I will think of a way," Chihuahua replied.

"You won't have to," said Nana. "I have a plan."

The following day, Juh declared that in celebration of Nana's victories there would be a social dance followed by the Dance of the Mountain Spirits. It would be a one-day, shortened version of the usual four-day Maidenhood Ceremony. Istee was excited because a social dance meant he might get to speak to—or even dance with—a certain girl who had caught his eye. Although he had never even said one word to her, he could tell by her glances that she was interested in him. She was Jacali, daughter of Juh, and Istee thought she was the prettiest girl he had ever seen. Her features were more delicate than some of the other Nednhi girls, and her hair was particularly long and luxuriant. Now that he was a warrior, it was only natural to think of taking a wife. He knew by her dress that Jacali had been through her Maidenhood Ceremony, but one thing he did not know was if Juh had already selected a husband for her. Under normal circumstances, Istee would simply go to his father and tell him of his interest in Jacali. Victorio then would have spoken with Juh about the situation and perhaps a marriage would have been arranged. But now that he had no father, Istee didn't know what to do except place himself as close to Jacali as possible and see if she really liked him.

By late morning, the meat was roasting and the *tizwin* flowing as the celebration got underway. A large area around the main campfire had been meticulously cleaned of rocks and twigs to assure that the dancing would be perfect. Four small juniper trees had been planted around the edge of the dance ground, one tree at each of the four directions. To start the celebration, Istee thought that Juh or Geronimo might make speeches, but when the drumming started he knew that the feelings of the Nednhi and Tcihene would be acted out, not spoken.

First came the fierce dance, which was the same one they had danced before Nana's war party had left the Blue Mountains. Each warrior was called upon by name to dance around the fire and show in action what he did during the raid. When Istee's name was called, he overcame his nervousness and mimed his shooting of the Blue Coat leader.

Next came the round dance, where the Tcihene and Nednhi warriors demonstrated how much they hated the White Eyes and Mexicans. The men, all beating on drums, danced closely together and circled the fire while singing songs that asked Ussen once again to drive their enemies from the land. Some of the warriors took turns inventing songs, and Chihuahua brought cheers and laughter when he sang:

I've been wandering around,
Wandering around;
When I got home,
Everyone had moved!

The women then made a circle around the men, facing them, and sang songs that requested that the men share whatever spoils of war they had seized. With Nah-des-te leading them, they repeated the refrain:

Whatever you have brought back with you,
Give me some of it.

That song was the cue for the partner dance. Istee and the other men who had been watching the round dance moved toward the fire and joined the men who had been dancing. Istee knew there were strict rules for the partner dance. Married people could not dance together, nor could those men and women who were blood relatives. Thus the dance of the Tcihene and Nednhi would work well because not too many of either band were closely related to each other. Another important rule was that the women chose their partners and the men were obligated to pay them for the dance out of the booty they had recovered. Just in case Jacali asked him to dance, Istee was prepared. Earlier in the day, he had rummaged through the things he had taken from the trader's wagon and had found a thin leather belt with delicate silver shells sewed on it. He thought it had probably been made by the Navajos.

The women moved toward the group of men and chose their partners by poking them or pulling at their clothes. The partners then formed a long line with the men and women facing in opposite directions. For a while Istee thought he was not going to be chosen, but his wishes were granted when Jacali ran over to him, smiled and pulled at his sleeve. Together they joined the line of dancers, moving four steps out and four steps back, over and over to the rhythm of the drumming. Istee was thrilled when Jacali linked her arm with his when they met in the line.

"You have been staring at me for days," she said softly.

"I thought you were staring at me," he countered.

"Maybe I was," she giggled. "Do you have anything to pay me for this dance?"

Istee was enormously flattered by her attention but tried not to let it show. "I do," he answered, "but you will have to wait until the dance is over."

They moved apart again but continued to gaze into each other's eyes. When they next came together, Jacali said, "Well, if you won't pay me until later, at least you could sing me a song."

Istee laughed at that and remembered a love song that he had heard years before. He sang to her:

Maiden from a distant land,
Why do you talk to me?
Why do you talk to me?
Maiden, you talk kindly to me,
And I will surely remember you.
Your words are so kind,
And I will surely remember you.

Jacali smiled with pleasure at the song as the line of dancers separated into two lines, the men facing the women. Each line moved four steps toward the other, then four steps back, over and over. Jacali and Istee touched hands when they were close.

After a long time, the rhythm of the drumming changed, a signal that the Dance of the Mountain Spirits was about to begin. Abruptly the drumming stopped, the lines broke up, and Istee and Jacali moved away from the fire and found a good spot to watch the most exciting dance of the night.

"Here is your payment for the dance," he said, giving her the belt. Jacali's eyes went wide with delight.

"It's very beautiful," she said. "I will wear it every day."

Soon the dancers entered the clearing from the east and a collective sigh arose from the audience as they circled the fire. Four of the dancers were dressed like the Mountain Spirits, in yellow buckskin skirts, knee-high moccasins, and dark leather masks. Their chests, shoulders, and arms had been brightly painted by different shamans in black, white, and yellow. The dancers wore carved and painted wooden headdresses that rose like horns from their skulls, were painted with snake designs, and were decorated with downy eagle feathers. They carried flat sticks painted with zigzag lines that represented lightning. The fifth dancer had a white mask and costume, wore no skirt, and had a much smaller headdress.

Despite their costumes, Istee recognized the dancers. Gaunchine of the east was Delzinne of the Nednhi, and Gauncho of the south was Martine, also of the same band. The Tcihene dancers were Kaytennae, who was Gaun of the west; and Sánchez, who was Gaunchi of the north. The fifth dancer, Gauneskide the fun-maker, was played by the Nednhi who was called Fun because of his constant clowning.

After circling the fire four times, the Gaunchine spread his arms wide, which was the signal for the singers to begin their songs for the masked dancers. Geronimo, more shaman than *nantan*, led the singers in the prayer-song:

> At the place called Home in the Sky,
> Inside is the home's holiness.
> The door to the home is of white clouds.
> There all the Blue Mountain Spirits
> Rejoice over us.
> Kneel in the four directions with me.

The four Mountain Spirit dancers did the free-step dance, bending over as if to pick something up and then blowing it away with their breath to expel any evil spirits from the gathering. While they performed the free step, Gauneskide the fun-maker pretended to stumble, and acted drunk to amuse the audience. The singers then switched to the short-step song so the dancers would not get tired, and finally sang the high-step song. When the dancers did the high-step dance, the crowd yelled in delight, for it by far was the most difficult. When the songs were finished, the dancers filed out of the clearing in an easterly direction.

After a brief pause, the drumming resumed and the singers began the next phase of the dance by praying the pollen song:

When first my Power was created
Pollen's body, speaking my words,
Brought my Power into being.
So I have come here for pollen again.

The drummers began and the Gaun dancers filed back into the clearing and stopped before the easternmost juniper tree. Some of the Nednhi threw pollen on them and repeated the pollen song. Then each dancer stood in front of his own tree, with fun-maker standing directly behind Gaunchi of the north. Each dancer in turn danced to the fire and back to his tree four times. While this was happening, selected members of the audience formed two lines: women on the north side of the fire and men on the south side. The dancing continued for a long time as the singers sang twelve different songs.

Istee and Jacali were sitting together, holding hands and watching the Gaun dancers, when Juh and Nana came up to them. They quickly pulled their hands apart, but Nana had noticed and smiled at them.

"Since your father is gone, I decided to act in his place," Nana explained. "Everyone here at the stronghold has seen the way you two look at each other. Now you dance together and hold hands. I have asked our *nantan* here if he thinks a marriage between you would be a good thing."

"And I said I thought it was," Juh said. He looked directly at Istee and asked, "Do you wish to marry my daughter?"

Things were happening so fast that Istee's mind was racing. He wanted some time to think about it, to discuss it with Grandfather, but was afraid of insulting Jacali and Juh by postponing his decision. So he simply said, "Yes."

Juh turned to his daughter and asked her the same question. Embarrassed, she stared at the ground, a sign of assent.

"In times like these," Juh said to Nana, "we cannot indulge in lengthy courtships or games of flirtation."

"That is right," Nana agreed. "We need our young people to produce more warriors and maidens. The son of Victorio has proved himself to be a good warrior. Let's hope he's as good as a husband."

"When will be the ceremony?" asked Istee.

"When do you want it to be?" countered Juh.

"After I have spent four days alone with the Mountain Spirits," Istee blurted out. "I want to see what Power I am granted."

"If any," Nana said dryly. Then he prompted Istee by saying, "Tell Juh what presents you have to give."

Istee caught on quickly. "I have two good horses I captured on our raid," he said. "They are for you and your wife."

"Good," said Juh. "It is all arranged, then." He and Nana walked away from them.

"I am very happy," Jacali confessed.

Istee took her hand. "I am too," he told her. "I came only to dance but found a wife."

Jacali was laughing as the Gaun dancers left the clearing for the last time.

At first light the next morning, Chihuahua, Lozen, and Kaytennae were ready to leave the stronghold. Seeing them off were Juh, Geronimo, Nana, and Istee.

"Grandfather's plan is a good one, so ride fast," said Geronimo.

"Yes," promised Chihuahua. "Soon we will cut off the snake's head."

Istee approached Chihuahua and gave him the telescope he had found. "You may need this far-sight to make sure you find the right snake."

Chihuahua laughed and held it up in triumph. "We will use the White Eyes' tools against them."

"Let's go," urged Lozen, who was carrying a long-bladed war lance.

The three Tcihene warriors scrambled down the zigzag trail in much less time than it took them to climb it. In the canyon at the bottom they carefully selected six of the best horses they could find, loaded their scant supplies on three of them, mounted the others, and began their journey north.

It took them quite a while to work their way through the steep canyons of the Blue Mountains, but once they reached the foothills they rode hard, switching to the fresh horses at regular intervals. Kaytennae was reluctant to raid for horses because raiding would draw attention to them, and then time would be wasted by running and hiding from the Mexicans. So they took care to feed and water their mounts, instead of running them into the ground as they usually would. And because they were such a small war party, they easily avoided the occasional force of soldiers they spotted along the way. Even when the soldiers were not in sight, Lozen would call a halt so she could locate them with her Power, and then they would ride in a different direction.

Kaytennae wondered if the snake they sought would still be at the same fort with the nearby spring where they had watered the horses. If not, Chihuahua knew the location of the other forts and spoke enough of the White Eye language to find the Blue Coat leader named Hatch.

At night they made no fire and thus did not cook game for fear of drawing attention to their camp. They survived by eating dried meat that had acorns, *piñon* nuts, and berries pounded into it. To keep their desire for revenge keen, Chihuahua told them again and again about being imprisoned in a hole in the ground, Lozen recounted the death of her brother Victorio, and Kaytennae repeated the story of the murder of The Dreamer.

Three days after they left Juh's stronghold, they reached the cache in the Flower Mountains. There they recovered food, some ammunition, and the cradleboard with the big-noise sticks. They decided to corral the extra horses near a spring and return for them later. Now they were less than a half-day's ride from the fort, but they had to proceed even more carefully because of the big-noise sticks and the fact that many Blue Coats patrolled the nearby railroad tracks and stagecoach trail. Also a difficulty was the lack of cover; the Flower Mountains were the last range between them and the fort. Lozen solved the problem for them.

"We will stay here today and travel tonight," she said. "We know this land very well and the moon is big. No one will see the dust we make and the Blue Coats will be asleep."

They waited until long after the sun had set to make their move. Leaving the protection of the foothills of the Flower Mountains, the three warriors rode north across the wide plain at a steady pace. Lozen was in the lead, followed by Chihuahua, who had endured some good-natured joking because he was wearing the cradleboard. Kaytennae brought up the rear, his rifle out as he rode, just in case they stumbled upon a Blue Coat camp.

But the ride was without incident and soon they were in the foothills above the enemy fort and the many tents that surrounded it. The first faint light was beginning to show in the east. They held a brief council and divided up the duties. Since he was the only one who knew what Hatch looked like, Chihuahua would stay in the foothills and watch the fort with the far-sight to find out if the Blue Coat leader was still there. Lozen and Kaytennae would take the big-noise sticks and scout for a location for the ambush. They would cache the cradleboard and return to Chihuahua's position after dark.

Lozen and Kaytennae mounted their horses and rode out of the foothills until they reached the railroad tracks. There was no sign of a train, so they followed the tracks to the northeast.

"It is too flat here," said Lozen, "and there is no cover."

"There are hills ahead," replied Kaytennae.

It was midmorning before they located an ideal spot to trap a train. The tracks curved to the east and then cut through a small group of hills. Beyond the hills the tracks ran straight on level ground for as far as the eye could see.

"Let's build a train-stopper," suggested Kaytennae, but Lozen disagreed.

"It is too soon. If we block these tracks now, maybe another train will come and hit the train-stopper. Then the White Eyes will know we are around. It is better to wait until we know which train our enemy is riding on."

Lozen pointed to a wooden trestle that carried the tracks over an arroyo. "We have nothing that will cut through those posts. But if we could burn that bridge, the train would fall through and crash and we wouldn't need to build a train-stopper."

"But we can't burn it without raising smoke," Kaytennae answered. "And if the Blue Coats see smoke, they will send soldiers to find out what is burning."

"We could start the fire when we get a signal that the train is leaving from the siding near the fort," Lozen suggested.

"But the smoke would warn the White Eyes driving the train. And we don't know how long the fire would have to burn to destroy that bridge."

"You are right. We will have to build a train-stopper quickly after we know that the enemy is on the train."

"Well, at least we can gather the rocks," Kaytennae said. Together they scoured the area and rolled the largest rocks they could find to a place near the tracks. When they had collected enough rocks, they cached the big-noise sticks and rode away from the tracks. After riding north toward the largest peak in the area, they found shade in the foothills beneath some juniper trees and waited until dusk.

Later that evening, Lozen and Kaytennae returned to the lookout site where Chihuahua was waiting. "The enemy called Hatch is there," he told them. "This morning I watched him leave his tent and walk around some buffalo soldiers all standing in line. Then he went back to his tent and stayed there for most of the time. Other Blue Coats came to visit and food was brought to his tent. The far-sight makes me think I could shoot him from here."

Kaytennae laughed at the joke. The distance was obviously too far for an accurate rifle shot. "We should have brought Grandfather so he could send a rattlesnake into the enemy's tent."

"I could sneak into their camp tonight and kill him with my knife," offered Lozen.

"No," said Chihuahua, who realized that Lozen was serious. "There are too many guards. I watched them today and they patrol the camp very well. We have a plan to kill that snake, so let's stay with it."

"But the plan depends on Hatch leaving here by train," protested

Lozen. "And where is the train?"

Chihuahua, who had far more knowledge of Blue Coat ways than either Lozen or Kaytennae, urged them to be patient. "He came here by train—we saw that many days ago when we were camped in these very mountains. So he will leave by train. We will wait."

Their vigil lasted two more days. On the afternoon of their third day of watching the fort, they heard the sound of a train approaching from the southwest. From their vantage point, they could see that it stopped at the siding closest to the fort, but what they did not know was when it might leave. Quickly, they made preparations. Lozen would remain behind and keep watch while Chihuahua and Kaytennae would ride on ahead and build the train-stopper. When Hatch boarded the train, Lozen would signal them. The number of flashes would indicate which car he was riding in. Then she would ride as fast as she could and get ahead of the train.

"Here," Lozen said, giving the war lance to Chihuahua, "you will need this."

Chihuahua and Kaytennae skirted the fort to the north and then rode hard to the east. When they reached the low hills, Kaytennae flashed a signal to Lozen and she responded with a single answering flash. Then the two men rolled the biggest rocks onto the tracks. Some of the boulders were so large it took all the strength of both of them to move them. They placed other rocks on top of the large boulders until the pile was as tall as a man and twice as long.

Kaytennae kept watch to the west and finally spotted the signal from Lozen—five flashes, which meant that Hatch was in the last car on the train. He recovered the big-noise sticks from the nearby cache and followed Nana's instructions. The four sticks were lashed together with rawhide strips, and Kaytennae took them apart. He made certain that the top of each stick was on tight, then used the same rawhide strips to tie the four sticks onto the blade end of the war lance. He twisted together the four short strings coming out of the tops of the sticks to make a single string.

They rode away from the barricade and positioned themselves behind the last hill before the tracks became straight again as they crossed the flat plain. Using his fire drill, Kaytennae built a small, smokeless fire with some brush he gathered. He found a thick branch of a mesquite tree and removed the thorns with his knife, then took a handful of pitch out of his pouch and smeared it over the end of the branch. Then he carefully spread pitch on the strings coming out of the big noise sticks.

Chihuahua knelt down and put his ear to the hot metal track.

"It is coming," he said to Kaytennae.

They rehearsed their roles with pantomime as they waited for the train. There was no need for them to watch what would happen—their ears would tell them all.

Lozen, meanwhile, had ridden hard to the south of the tracks and had outdistanced the train, which had taken a lot of time to get up to speed. She was hidden in the low hills by the time the train rounded the curve and approached the train-stopper.

She heard the unholy scream the train made as it tried to stop. It slowed, but there was not enough room to stop completely. Lozen watched with elation as it crashed into the rocks. But unlike the other train wrecks Lozen had witnessed while raiding with Nana, all of the cars of this train remained on the tracks. The wide-eyed faces of buffalo soldiers appeared at the windows of the first four cars and Lozen laughed because she knew they expected immediate attack.

It took some time before the Blue Coats realized that they were not under attack. Lozen heard someone yell orders from the last car and then saw the buffalo soldiers slowly leaving the other cars, rifles ready. The drivers of the train got out and looked at the train-stopper and then were joined by the buffalo soldiers, who dropped their rifles and began to remove the rocks from the tracks. When the track was cleared and the rocks were pried out from beneath the train, the buffalo soldiers returned to their cars and the train started forward. Lozen mounted her horse and followed at a walk and then a trot as the train picked up speed.

Chihuahua and Kaytennae heard the train start up and, after lighting the mesquite branch, mounted their horses. They stood ready behind the hill as the train came into view, spewing smoke behind it. When the fifth car passed them, they rode out from their cover and quickly caught up with it. Chihuahua, who was nearest the car, saw the White Eye faces in the window and picked out his target, Hatch. He passed the blade-end of his lance to Kaytennae, who lit the strings with his torch.

Chihuahua, riding harder to keep up with the train, waited until the strings had burned down close to the sticks before he hurled the lance through the window of the car. The two warriors urged their horses away from the train as quickly as possible, but the force of the explosion caught them and knocked them off their horses.

A short distance behind the action, Lozen saw the railroad car disappear before her eyes, felt the concussion of the blast, and ducked as a piece of wood flew by her head. She rode toward Chihuahua, who was already on his feet and running toward Kaytennae. The train had moved on ahead for quite a distance before it stopped and the buffalo soldiers poured out of it.

Lozen rounded up the two mounts long before the enemy could close. Soon the three of them were riding at full gallop away from the train. They laughed as the buffalo soldiers fired futilely at them.

At Juh's stronghold, Nana was talking to Istee about receiving Power when the feeling came over him that a snake had been killed. Although his Snake Power did not speak to him with words, his mind clearly received a daydream image of a lance point cutting off the head of a rattlesnake.

"Go find Geronimo and Juh," he ordered Istee, who quickly ran off. A short time later he returned with the two *nantans*, who looked quizzically at Nana.

"It is done," he told them. "Victorio is avenged."

Juh said nothing and looked at Geronimo, who closed his eyes. His lips moved but no words were spoken. In a few moments he opened his eyes and said, "Grandfather is right. Hatch is dead. My Power allowed me to see the train blowing up."

Juh gave a whoop of joy and walked quickly away to tell the rest of the Nednhi people.

"Now all we have to do is kill the other Blue Coat snakes," Geronimo said. He gave Nana the *abrazo* of his people and then left.

Istee and Nana sat silently for a few minutes before Istee resumed their conversation. "Is it time for me to gain my Power?" asked Istee.

"Why not?" Nana answered. "The age you receive Power depends on your desire for it, and the willingness of the Mountain Spirits to give it to you."

"Will you teach me the ceremony, Grandfather?"

"You have just seen the Powers of two men. Which do you prefer?"

"I don't understand," Istee answered.

Nana explained. "I saw the snake being killed and Geronimo saw the train. So I have the Power over snakes and the Power to find ammunition trains. But Geronimo has many different Powers too. He has the Power to see things that are far away and to predict what will happen. He has the Power over bullets so that no bullet can ever kill him, and he also has the Power to cure the coyote sickness."

"How do I know what Powers are good for me until I get them?"

Nana laughed. "Sometimes the Power selects you when you least expect it, and sometimes you can ask the Mountain Spirits for a certain Power by learning the prayers and songs from a shaman who already has that Power. Geronimo is more of a shaman than I. He will teach you if you ask him."

Istee sought out Geronimo and asked to speak with him, a request that was granted with a nod. He explained that he had spoken with Nana about receiving Power but Nana had directed him to Geronimo.

"He doesn't think you need his kinds of Power," Geronimo explained. "He thinks my Powers would suit you better."

"Can you teach me your Powers?" Istee asked.

Geronimo accompanied his answer with arm gestures. "Wind said to lightning, 'See that tree over there? I can split it in two if I want.' Lightning answered the wind by saying, 'I can also split that tree in half.' They both had Power to do the same thing, yet the Power of the wind is not the

Power of lightning. In the same way, the Power of one man is not the Power of the other. I can only be a guide for you. I can teach you the basic things you need to know—what songs to sing, what you should carry with you, and what you must do. Then you must go alone to the Holy Home of the Power you seek and see if the Power will accept you."

"Where is this Holy Home?" Istee asked.

Geronimo pointed to the summit of the mountain that towered above the stronghold. "Up there," he said. "If you do the right things and the Power accepts you, it will teach its particular ceremony so you can call it at will. If the Power likes and wants you, you will be able to learn the ceremony very fast. If the Power does not want you, you will never be able to learn the ceremony. There are many rules for the ceremony and if you violate them, the Power will turn upon you. It's like taking an oath. If you violate your oath to the Power, it will strike back at you. If you get confused and mix up the words of the songs, or if your voice is feeble, your Power will not respect you.

"But I don't know what the Power will be," Istee protested.

"No, you don't. The Mountain Spirits will select the Power that is best for you. The basic ceremony I will teach you enables you to only speak with the Mountain Spirits. We will start tomorrow. Meet me a first light at the sweat lodge."

Istee was apprehensive but determined to do what was necessary to obtain his Power. He knew it was time—he was a warrior and soon would be Jacali's husband. He had moved through the world of the White Eyes and knew that in order to survive he needed help from the Mountain Spirits. The following morning, he joined Geronimo in the sweat lodge for his first series of instructions, which concerned only his attitude toward the Power he might receive. Geronimo told him stories of how other men had received their Power, and how they had honored it. He was told to be respectful, but not be a slave to the Power.

"You might even refuse to accept the Power," Geronimo told him, "especially if it is a Power you feel you cannot use or one whose rules you cannot obey. It is better to refuse a Power than risk the dangers of accepting one that you do not completely understand."

"But how will I know?" asked Istee.

"You will know when the time comes," Geronimo promised.

Next, Istee learned the ritual gestures and songs used to let the Mountain Spirits know that he was ready to accept the Power. Geronimo gave him special amulets to help him remember the rituals: a piece of turquoise with a hole in it, a short string of shell beads, a small eagle's tail feather, a pad from a badger's right front paw, and a piece of buckskin painted with lightning designs. By the end of the day, Geronimo was satisfied that Istee was ready to make the journey, and gave him directions to the top of the Holy Home.

"You may leave tomorrow if you believe you are ready," Geronimo said.

"I think I am," replied Istee, trying to ignore the sinking feeling in his stomach.

Word had spread around the stronghold that Geronimo was giving Istee instruction about obtaining Power, and that Istee was climbing up to the Holy Home. Nana invited him to a farewell meal prepared by Nah-des-te, and that night he sat in their wickiup dining on pit-baked venison with mesquite beans.

"Eat well," Nana advised. "It will the last food you taste for four days."

"I know," Istee replied. "Geronimo said I couldn't even take any dried meat up there."

"The Mountain Spirits will provide everything you need," Nah-des-te said confidently.

Near the end of the meal, Kaytennae's wife Guyan arrived with Jacali. "Have some food," Nah-des-te offered as the guests sat down.

"We have already eaten," Guyan replied. She looked pointedly at Jacali, who smiled shyly at Istee.

"I wanted to wish you well on your quest," she told him.

Embarrassed, Istee could only reply, "Thank you."

"When do you leave?"

"At first light tomorrow."

"I will be waiting for you," Jacali said lightly.

"I will be starving," Istee joked, and everyone laughed.

"Come along now," Guyan said impatiently. It was obvious to Istee that Jacali had persuaded Guyan to escort her on the visit. Being alone with her husband-to-be was considered improper, and Istee knew that Jacali was carefully watched by her parents. He also realized that now that marriage between them was arranged, he could no longer speak to or gaze upon Juh or Ishton—he must avoid them at all costs.

"My father says he received the horses you sent," Jacali said as she rose to leave.

"Good," Istee replied. "I will see you later."

"Goodbye," Jacali whispered as she left with Guyan.

When they were gone, Nana grinned hugely. "She loves you and she will make a good wife." Nah-des-te nodded her agreement. Istee was so flustered he could say nothing.

The following morning, rain was falling lightly when Istee began his climb to the Holy Home. Following Geronimo's instructions, he wore only a loincloth and took nothing with him except a buckskin pouch containing his personal amulets and a small bag of *tule* pollen. The rain was cold and he started to shiver, but he knew that climbing the mountain would soon warm him up.

He left the camp and trotted along the well-used trail to the spring. Geronimo had said there was a much smaller trail leading up the steep slope, so Istee searched for it in the dim light. The trail was not marked, but his trained eyes finally located its beginning by spotting some loose stones. He began the climb through the tall trees, looking for landmarks as he went. Geronimo had told him the way to the top of the Holy Home was marked by certain things, such as a large, moss-covered rock in the shape of a turtle's shell.

The rain increased as he struggled up the slope, and sometimes his moccasins slipped on the wet leaves and he had to grab onto a branch to keep from sliding back down the slope. After considerable searching, he located the rock near a ledge that overlooked the stronghold. He looked down but all he could see was mist.

Geronimo had told him not to climb at the rock but to move left until he found a lightning-struck tree that had survived. That would be the place to climb again. Istee did as instructed, working his way through the rocks and brush. Suddenly, the feeling came over him that he was being stalked. A chill ran down his spine and he looked around for a place to hide. But all he could find was a large, rotting trunk of a pine tree that had fallen, so he crouched down behind it and waited.

He heard the sound of something moving through the leaves downslope and he watched carefully, hoping to see it before it saw him. Through the rain and mist, he could see a large form moving toward him. At first he thought it was a mountain lion, but then he saw that this cat was much larger. It was yellow—almost orange—in color and had black spots all over its coat. He had never seen anything like it before. Istee's heart was pounding wildly as the cat moved closer, but then stopped a short distance from him, sat on its haunches, and stared in his direction.

Istee wondered, *was it time? Was it going to kill him and eat him, or was the Power going to speak to him through this huge cat?* As if to answer that neither would happen, the cat yawned, looked away, and then slowly rose and moved off up the slope. Only then did he see the three half-grown cubs that followed their mother. Istee let out a long breath, and then he got up from behind the log and quickly resumed his search for the lightning-struck tree.

He had told Geronimo that there were probably many such trees on the mountain, but the shaman had said he would know it when he saw it. Sure enough, he found a living tree with a long, black lightning slash on one side of the trunk. Carved into the dark scar was a zigzag lightning symbol—Geronimo's way of guiding people to the summit. He began climbing again, on the lookout for a small cave near a spring. When he located it after a difficult climb up loose, flat stones, his confidence surged. The cave looked interesting, but Geronimo had told him not to go in it. Now Istee knew why—it was probably the home of the mother cat.

The rain stopped and the clouds opened a bit to brighten up the day. Istee climbed to his right now, watching for a dead tree with a hawk's nest, which would mean that he was near the top of the Holy Home. This time, however, he had difficulty finding it. No matter how hard he struggled up the mountain, there was always a steep slope in front of him. He began to wonder if it would be dark before he reached the top. Discouraged now, he found a convenient rock and sat down to catch his breath.

His invasion of the mountain had alerted the animals. Squirrels ran up the trunks of trees and chattered at him. A blue bird with a long tail perched on a branch above him and called out a shrill alarm. Istee laughed and said, "I am not here to hurt you, little ones." A quick movement caught his eye and he watched as a hawk with a red tail swooped down from nowhere and plucked a squirrel off a branch. Istee stood up and watched the hawk soar above the trees, circle twice, and glide to a landing in a tall, dead tree with a nest near the top of it.

Excited, Istee scrambled up the slope as fast as he could. When he reached the dead tree, he thought he could see the top of the mountain. But to reach it, he had to scale a steep cliff of sheer rock that was still wet from the rain. He was halfway up when his right foot slipped, and for a moment he thought he was going to fall and split his head open. But he managed to wedge his left hand in a crack, and he dangled there by his wrist until he could find a foothold. When he finally reached the top of the cliff, he fell on his back, exhausted. He finally caught his breath and examined his wrist, which was scraped and bloody. Then he turned around and gasped at what he saw.

It seemed like he was on top of the world. The mountains spread out as far as the eye could see and there were clouds actually below him! He was on the edge of a small meadow with a single, small pine tree in the middle, which he immediately identified with. It is all alone, he thought, just like I am. Tired, hungry, and thirsty, he walked over to the tree and sat down, resting his back against the thin trunk. "It's my new home," he said aloud. After a while, Istee fell asleep and did not awaken until dawn.

During his second day on the mountain, Istee tried to ignore his hunger while repeating the prayers Geronimo had taught him. But the Mountain Spirits did not call to him.

He awoke at first light on the third day shivering with cold but excited by memories of a dream about making love to Jacali. Wondering if the Mountain Spirits could read his mind, Istee concentrated on the Power ritual until the sun was high in the sky. His thirst is so great that he wandered over the other side of the mountain until he found a spring. Water was permissible; food was not. His thirst was quenched but he felt weak. He slowly walked back to his tree and began the prayers again.

On the fourth day, he put pollen in his mouth as instructed by Geronimo, but nothing happened. He searched through his pouch to make certain he had used all the amulets and found, to his surprise, the piece of *peyotl* that The Dreamer had given him. It was not food, so he supposed it was all right to swallow it. After all, The Dreamer had used it during his ceremonies. Istee slowly chewed the *peyotl* and ignored its bitterness.

He resumed his prayers and a little later felt the first signs of the power of the cactus. Waves of warmth washed over his body and he found himself staring up at the sky. He watched a tiny speck that he assumed was a bird get larger and larger as it glided in ever-tightening circles, then closed his eyes and saw flashes of lightning and patterns like the Gaun dancers painted on their bodies.

"Istee!"

He opened his eyes and leaped to his feet in an attempt to locate whatever had called his name. At first he could not find anything, but then looked up and saw a buzzard perched in the tree above his head. The buzzard looked directly into Istee's eyes, cocked its head, and said clearly, "Istee! Istee! Istee!"

"It is alive!" Istee exclaimed. "It speaks to me!" It was exactly as Geronimo had predicted—something calling his name four times.

"Don't be afraid," the buzzard said. "The other animals sometimes say bad things about me because I eat dead animals. But Ussen has forbidden me to kill anything, so I must eat only what others have killed. But in His wisdom Ussen has allowed me to fly very high and has given me the Power to see very far and to find things."

Istee could not think of a reply. What could you say to a buzzard that talked?

"What do you desire?" the buzzard asked.

"Something good for my family," Istee replied.

"Well, you will be a shaman and have Power from dreams. Dreams will show you what to do and will tell you what will happen in the future. You will also be able to find things that are lost. But once you have this knowledge, you must share it and not keep it for yourself. You must help your family and your band, not just use it for personal gain. And remember, although you will have the Power to foresee the future, no one will believe you at first. Only after a few things you have predicted come true will they finally listen to you."

Excited, Istee said, "I accept the Power offered to me. How do I call for it?"

The buzzard then revealed the secret ceremony that would conjure him up whenever Istee needed him. Istee repeated the prayers and sacred gestures on the first try.

"You are ready," said the buzzard. "Now close your eyes and sleep."

Later, Istee was not certain whether he had slept or not. But he certainly had dreamed, and his dream was very strange. The war was over and the Tcihene were surrendering to the Blue Coats and then riding on a train. Everyone was there—Nana, Kaytennae, Geronimo, Chihuahua, Lozen, Kaywaykla, Jacali, and even himself. The train took them to a warm, flat place with odd-looking trees that he realized was a camp from which they could never escape. They lived in wooden houses like the White Eyes, and ate their terrible food.

Then his people were moved again to another camp with high fences all around it, where they were treated like slaves. Only Geronimo was allowed to leave, and then he was paraded around and treated like a prized horse. They stayed at this place for a long time, and then were taken by train to a place farther west and imprisoned until his young children were almost grown.

Somehow, the dream jumped ahead in time and Istee could see his children now as adults with children of their own. He recognized the place where they were living as Mescalero. But it was a Mescalero that looked more like a White Eye town, and the Mescaleros and Tcihene wore White Eye clothing and spoke the White Eye language. They rode around in metal wagons that moved without horses to pull them. But despite all the changes, everyone seemed happy and at least they were no longer imprisoned.

Then the grandchildren had grown up again and Mescalero was a large town with some White Eyes living in one large building in the middle of it. Snow was coming down and he saw the White Eyes being carried by metal ropes to the top of the sacred White Mountain and sliding down on the snow with pieces of wood attached to their feet. At one point in his dream, he saw Mescaleros and Tcihene, dressed as White Eyes, holding a council during which they planned how to get more money from the White Eyes. They were laughing and having a good time, as if they had won the war after all. Then he saw a large building, owned by his people, but visited by the White Eyes. He knew that there was gambling going on, but it was not the moccasin game; but rather games played with wheels and pieces of the White Eyes' paper. And the Mescaleros and Tcihene were counting the "money" they had won from the White Eyes and were laughing about it.

When the dream was over, Istee opened his eyes and saw that the buzzard was gone. On the ground beside him was some dried meat with berries in it and a basket full of *tizwin*. Without thinking about how the food and drink got there, he eagerly devoured it all. Then he decided it was time to return to the stronghold, so he walked over to the edge and carefully climbed down the steep cliff.

On his way down the mountain, Istee wondered how he could tell Grandfather and Geronimo about the future of their people. Would they believe him when he told them it was useless to fight any more, that the White Eyes were certain to win the war? If they did believe him, they would say that the Tcihene were *indeh*, a dead people. And he would have to tell them that they were not *indeh*, just changed forever.

Photograph Credits

Page x: Nana, photo by Ben Wittick, courtesy Palace of the Governors (MNM/
           DCA) 16321.

Page xi: Geronimo, photo by C.S. Fly, courtesy Palace of the Governors (MNM/
           DCA) 002155.

Page xii: Victorio, courtesy of the Arizona Historical Society/Tucson. AHS 19705.

Page xiii: Kaytennae (Gait-en-eh), photo by Ben Wittick, courtesy Palace of the
           Governors (MNM/DCA) 15902.

Page xiv: Col. Edward T. Hatch, courtesy U.S. Army Military History Institute,
           Carlisle, PA.

Page xv: Governor Lew Wallace, courtesy Palace of the Governors (MNM/DCA)
           015295.

Page xvi: Buffalo Soldier, Smithsonian Institute, Washington, DC.

Page 1:   Buzzards, courtesy Dave DeWitt.

Page 5:   Military camp in front of the Palace of the Governors Santa Fe, New
           Mexico, 1890-1900. Courtesy Palace of the Governors (MNM/DCA)
           047821.

Page 35:   Blue Mountains, courtesy Dave DeWitt.

Page 63:   White Sands National Monument, courtesy New Mexico State University
           Library, Archives and Special Collections, Ms02230135.

Page 93:   Victorio's Peak, courtesy of White Sands Missile Range.

Page 121: Fort Craig, New Mexico, courtesy New Mexico State University Library,
           Archives and Special Collections. Ms03630378.

Page 153: Apache Scouts by Edward Curtis, courtesy Dave DeWitt.

Page 183: 10th Cavalry in camp near Chloride, New Mexico, 1892, photo by Henry
           A. Schmidt. Courtesy Palace of the Governors (MNM/DCA) 058556.

Page 213: Chiricahua Apache camp on the San Carlos River, Arizona, photo by Ben
           Wittick. Courtesy Palace of the Governors (MNM/DCA) 015874.

About the Author

Dave DeWitt is one of the foremost authorities in the world on chile peppers and spicy foods. Dave researched and wrote numerous magazine and newspaper articles on chile peppers in the late 1970s. In 1984, St. Martin's Press published his first cookbook, *The Fiery Cuisines*, co-authored with Nancy Gerlach. In 1987, Dave and Nancy approached a local publisher, and the three launched *Chile Pepper* magazine with a mere 212 subscribers. By 1995, with Dave as the editor-in-chief, the magazine had surpassed 50,000 subscribers with a total circulation exceeding 80,000. The magazine was sold in 1996 and Dave launched *Fiery Foods Magazine*, a trade publication.

The earlier *Chile Pepper* magazine project led to numerous books, including *The Whole Chile Pepper Book* (Little, Brown, 1990), which now has nearly 100,000 copies in print through ten printings. Dave has 31 published books to his credit and continues to write books at the rate of one or two a year. He is also producer of the National Fiery Foods & Barbecue Show, the trade show for the multi-billion dollar Fiery Foods and Barbecue industries, now in its 20th year. His book *The Chile Pepper Encyclopedia* (William Morrow, 1999) won the award "Best Spice Book in English" at the 1999 World Cookbook Awards at Versailles. Other notable books by Dave and his co-authors include: *The Pepper Garden, Peppers of the World, Hot & Spicy & Meatless, The Healing Powers of Peppers, The Hot Sauce Bible*, and *The Spicy Food Lover's Bible*. In 1995, his book, *A World of Curries*, was nominated for a James Beard Award. Dave is coproducer, writer, and host of *Heat Up Your Life!*, a three-part video documentary series on chile peppers and spicy foods. He is also publisher of the *Fiery Foods & Barbecue Super Site*, at www. fiery-foods.com.

National TV appearances for Dave include *"American Journal,"* Cable News Network, *"The Today Show," "Home with Gary Collins," "Scientific American Frontiers," "Smart Solutions,"* and *"CBS Sunday Morning."* He has also been featured in *The New Yorker, The New York Times, Los Angeles Times, USA Today, American Way, Smithsonian*, and approximately 200 newspapers across the country.